Banderidge
Evie Series, Book 1

A novel by
Anne Calvert

Jackson, Tennessee

Copyright © 2022 by Anne Calvert

Cover and internal design © 2022 by Zoe Grace Publishing, LLC

All rights reserved.

Biblical References from:
Holy Bible, New Living Translation

The characters and events in this book are fictitious. Apart from well-known historical figures, any similarity to any real person, living or dead, is purely coincidental and not intended by the author.

Published in the United States by
Zoe Grace Publishing, LLC
Jackson, Tennessee
www.zoegracepublishing.com

ISBN: 978-1-7364079-3-6

Printed in the United States of America.

To Ted and Nancy Lorup.
Without you, I would not be.
Neither would this story.
You inspired me.

My Sincerest Thank You

To Father God who deserves all glory for this book. I am humbled that when He wanted to write this story, He chose me to be the vessel.

Ted and Nancy Lorup, my parents, for not only supporting me but because writing is in their blood too. To see the enjoyment and efforts of their writing, whether it was magazine articles, the P.A. Zoo News family magazine, a children's book, or letters of encouragement to those who needed hope, inspired me.

Shayne Plunk, Adult Services Librarian at the Jackson Madison County Library, introduced me to NaNoWriMo, where Book one was birthed, a month after I started this new journey. His encouragement and friendship have helped me be a better writer.

Stacey Pirtle for reading my roughest first draft and not telling me to keep my day job, her encouragement, thoughts, and for Tuesday afternoons spent in her kitchen.

To my beta readers: Hannah Horch, for sharing your thoughts which helped better me and my story. Jennifer Lorup, for all your encouragement, input, and suggestions. Christine Cochran, for your kind words and encouragement. Kim Wahl, for your in-depth read and suggestions, being available to answer endless questions, encouragement, and double-checking that everything lined up with the Word of God.

The members of the Jackson Writer's Club for the education, friendships, and encouragement. I am blessed that we were brought together.

To Shelley Mascia at Shelley's Editing Service for helping me look better. You are amazing!

Tammy Yosich at Zoe Grace Publishing, LLC for taking a chance with me and your care in making my dream a beautiful reality. Your support of local authors and other creatives is undeniable.

To all my friends and family who have supported, encouraged, prayed for me, and not given up on me through this long first book journey. You will not have to wait as long for Book two.

Last but definitely not least, my husband, Wesley Calvert. He suggested I work only three days a week outside the home and use the other two to focus on writing. He believed in me and my abilities long before I did and set me on my way. I will be forever grateful for the "push."

One

Evie, are you ready for your next assignment?

I am, Father God.

My sweet daughter, I am proud of you. Because you did so well with your previous assignments, it's time to move you from your place of comfort and watch you grow. You handled the two-person assignments with such ease that We decided to assign you four hurting, lost, people.

I can do it, Father.

Evie, humble and gentle in spirit, is confident. She knows where her strength is found. She shudders thinking back on the last few assignments and how some could have ended badly without the guidance and strength of her Father God.

Like the day she met Joey. Horrified, she watched as fists and teeth flew when she first found him in a vicious fight in the middle of Dirty Dave's bar. Smoke from too many cigarettes clung to her skin as she waded through pockets of indifferent people. Not wanting to watch anymore, she went outside and prayed. Pacing, she waited for her answer. Thrust out the door, arms and legs flailing, Joey landed on the ground with a groan, and with his head almost resting on her feet. Not exactly what she was expecting, but not missing the opportunity, she helped him up. Once he was on his feet, she looked up at him, quietly assessing the size of his muscles.

Joey was a tough one. In time, she learned that under all the hurt and hate, he had a compassionate heart. Hearing his story, Evie realized he learned at a young age to protect his heart. Hate on top of hurt formed an impenetrable safeguard to keep him from being hurt again. With a little care, and much of God's love and grace, Joey realized he had a purpose.

When Evie last checked, he was back in his old neighborhood loving and guiding the young kids that played on the same playgrounds he did. Experience taught him what poverty and growing up in a single-parent home were like. His passion became helping the young people in his town break the cycle and beat the odds. Evie was encouraged by Joey's fervor and prayed a special blessing for him and his ministry.

Folding her favorite purple shirt, she wonders who she will be blessed to meet this time. As she places her blue jeans in the suitcase, she realizes she has yet been assigned an elderly person. Of course, it would take helping many people for many years to cover every type of person. She tosses her short black boots and a pair of running shoes in her bag and zips it up.

Looking out the front window of the taxi at the last of the colorful leaves holding tight to the branches, Evie catches a glimpse of her shimmering blue eyes and soft smile looking back at her in the mirror.

For as long as Evie can remember, people have been attracted to her. She often heard people say that "She has such a sweet spirit." She was not any prettier than the next girl, but other children liked to be around her.

Raised in a church where her family attended every time the doors were open, Evie did not show sincere interest until her early teens. It was as if a switch had been flipped. She immersed herself in studying the Bible. After studying prayer and understanding the importance of it, she began to pray for direction and for God to show her His intention for her life.

The summer she turned fifteen, while friends her age went to camp looking for a fun time, she chose an intense, two-week discipleship camp. When asked about her experience, her response was always the same, "It was life-changing and I know wherever He sends me, I'll go."

Not wanting to miss anything, she continued to study the Word and her relationship with Father God grew.

Although she has been told she is attractive, all Evie sees looking back at her is a woman in her late twenties, slender, with short, brown, easy to manage hair, blue eyes with naturally long, dark eyelashes, and an average nose and mouth. Even her height is just over the average at five foot five inches. Physically, she sees nothing out of the ordinary.

The long journey in the taxi flies by as she thinks of how her Father knows the desires of her heart and blesses her with gifts like autumn in the mountains. As the taxi slows to make the turn, Evie sees soft gray smoke swirls coming from the chimney as lonely rocking chairs and motionless wind chimes adorn the spacious wraparound porch. Turning onto the long driveway, she gasps at the beauty and serenity of the scene before her. The rustic home nestled against the backdrop of the mountain reminds her of the cover of a magazine.

Beautiful and You created it all. Thank You, Father! I'm going to like it here.

Taking two steps at a time she crosses the porch. She knocks and admires the Autumn Blessings doormat while she waits.

"Hello! Evie, right? Come in. We are honored you are here. I am Martha." Her sweet smile matches her gentle voice.

Evie slightly taken aback by Martha's youth, grins back at her. "Yes! Thank you so much for allowing me to stay in your home."

"It is our pleasure. We would do anything to help our mutual Friend. Come, let me show you to your room. Then I will show you around while we look for Stan."

Making small talk, Martha asks about the ride to Banderidge as she leads Evie to her room. When she enters the room, Evie is transported back twenty-some years to her grandma's house in the country. Without fail, every Thursday, she could count on the smell of fresh, warm linens filling the air as she played.

Leaving the bedroom, Martha begins the tour in the kitchen. Evie gazes in wonderment from the floor to high ceiling, following the natural rock foundation of a grand fireplace.

"That is beautiful," Evie says as her eyes finally rest on the fire. As she ducks ever so slightly, she sees the arm of a chair through the fireplace. As Evie admires the see-through fireplace, Martha waits by an oversized, dark wood table set with an orange runner, sprinkled with pinecones, and a golden centerpiece spilling out a floral touch of autumn. Evie follows Martha to the next room, but not before she counts the ten chairs set around the table.

Entering the living room Martha explains, "We went with a simple floor plan in which the kitchen and living room are equal in size. The doors off both rooms lead to small sleeping rooms and one is a laundry room with a pantry. We figured we will spend more time in the kitchen and living room than in the bedrooms."

The large windows match the fireplace in magnificence. Brown furniture compliments the natural rock fireplace and makes the light brown carpet pop.

Martha ends the tour in the office thinking it is where Stan will be. The empty office has its own smaller fireplace and a great view of the side yard and part of the mountain.

"A fireplace and books, I'm not sure I would ever leave the office." Evie jokes. "It's all so lovely, not only because of the beauty but the peace here."

Martha smiles as she pulls on her coat and hands Evie hers, "Thank you. Your words are very kind. Perhaps Stan is in his other favorite place."

As Evie steps out the door, she pauses, struck by the beauty. Looking at the mountain is like looking into a box of crayons. Some trees wear the dull brown leaves which are trying to finish the good fight, while others are bright yellow of a midsummer flower. The crisp, red-leaved limbs sprinkle the mountainside chanting *Look at me.*

Martha sighs. "It never gets old."

Evie nods. "I believe it."

Of the three buildings behind the house, Martha goes toward the rehabbed vintage log cabin.

"Surely, if he is not in his office, he is in his workshop. He comes out here to tinker and spend time with the Lord. He made the table in the kitchen. You may have noticed it."

Evie replies, "Wow! That's some kind of tinkering."

Martha laughs softly. "I figured you noticed."

Entering the shop, Evie's eyes dart everywhere, trying to take it all in. It is like nothing she has ever seen. The shell of the building resembles a log cabin from a hundred years ago, but the inside is anything but a century old. Tools and tables with stationary saws, take up most of the room while a small, wooden desk with chair, rocking chair, bookcase, and an old record player fill the rest of the room. Everything but Stan.

As they walk back to the house, Martha says, "If you would like to unpack and settle in, I will fix us some warm apple cider. Maybe by then, Stan will join us."

"Sounds lovely," Evie responds gratefully.

Once in her room, she looks around.

All the perks of home and maybe more. She even has her own bathroom. Oh, the favor. *Thank You, Father.* She places some of her clothing on hangers in the small walk-in closet and the rest in the dresser drawers. She wonders if Stan made the dresser as well. After placing her shoes on the rack in the closet, she sits on the bed and admires the view from her window. Enjoying the quiet, she looks at the harvested field which is now resting.

The harvest is plentiful. Gracious Father, thank You for a safe trip. Thank You for Your favor and for choosing this host home for me. Bless this family for being so gracious and obedient in allowing me to stay here. I know You do everything for a reason and with a purpose. I know Martha and Stan fit into this assignment somehow. I pray Your perfect will be done. I trust You and know You go before me to prepare Your people. I serve as Your humble servant. Your love, grace, and strength are all I need. I love You.

Lost in thought, she is brought back by Martha tapping at the door.

"The cider is ready." Evie follows her to the kitchen. There, she finds not only two mugs of steaming hot cider but a pumpkin roll, stuffed with white cream and extra powdered sugar on top. Pumpkin, apple, cinnamon, and clove fill the room with the festive smell of autumn.

"Wow," Evie teases. "All for me?"

Martha laughs. "If you can finish it before Stan shows up, you can have it. If he gets here before you finish it, you may have a fight on your hands. It is one of his favorites."

"It looks and smells delightful. It may be tough, but I guess I can share." She smiles as Martha slices the pumpkin roll. As the women sip their cider, the conversation is light.

Father, I can already tell Martha is a very special kind of woman.

"Well, hello," Stan says, walking into the kitchen.

"Hi, stranger." Martha jokes.

"I'm sorry love. I knew you were resting before our guest got here. The mountain looked so beautiful and was calling out to me, so I went up to spend time with the Lord. I guess time got away from me." He smiles lovingly at her.

"Oh, Stan," she blushes as she turns to Evie, "Another favorite place of his. Stan, this is Evie."

"It's a pleasure to meet you, Stan. Thank you so much for allowing me to stay here while I work."

Stan shakes her hand warmly. "We are so honored you are here."

Evie smiles. "That's exactly what your wife said. Did you rehearse that?"

He laughs. "Ooooh! For me? I knew it smelled pumpkiny in here." He grabs the pumpkin roll.

"Evie said you can have some, but just a bite." Martha playfully chides him.

When they finish, Martha stands and motions for Evie. "Would you like to move to the living room where it is more comfortable?" As Martha sits on the sofa, Evie chooses the oversized chair with large fluffy pillows which almost swallow her as she sits down.

"Oh, my. This chair is comfortable."

"That is the usual response we get. If they visit more than once, they choose it every time they come back."

Evie looks out the window. The sun, finishing its descent, hides behind covers of clouds, painting the sky with shades of pink, purple, and gray which only Father God has access to. Within minutes, darkness swallows the sky with a glimpse of a star here and there peeking through the clouds.

Stan comes in with more wood and kindling for the fire just as a slight chill begins to creep in. As Stan works to make a fire, light fills the living room and continues getting brighter.

"It is probably Stan's friend Karl," Martha tells Evie.

As the lights pass, Stan jumps up and goes to the door. Before Karl has a chance to knock, Stan opens it.

"Hey man." Stan greets him. Karl tips his head back in greeting.

"Hi, Karl. Come in. How are Renee and the girls?" Martha asks as they approach.

"They're fine. Oh man, I'm sorry. I didn't know you have company."

"No, Karl, come on in and meet Evie." Stan says as Karl starts back toward the door.

"It's a pleasure to meet you, Karl." Evie smiles as she stands and offers her hand. Karl's hand engulfs hers. Brief eye contact allows Evie to see the anguish in his dark brown eyes as he hides behind a forced smile.

"Come on Karl," Stan prods, "Let me show you my latest project." Evie watches as Karl slowly shuffles his feet like they are just too heavy, and his shoulders are bent forward. He follows Stan through the kitchen and out to the shop. Without saying a single word, his actions announce he is a defeated man, but Evie knows better. Whether he knows it or not, he had been created with a purpose and to know Jesus means to know hope.

Martha cuts in the silence, as if she read Evie's thoughts. "Karl shows up unexpectedly lately, acting as if he has been defeated. His beautiful wife, Renee, says he refuses to talk to her about it and has been distant for a few months. The youngest of their four daughters is graduating from college in the spring. Although she does not know what is wrong, she prays for him."

"I imagine it's difficult, but Renee is doing the best thing by praying."

Thank You Father for sending me in response to her prayers.

"Stan and Karl met at the hardware store in town close to a year ago," Martha says. "Plumbing not being Stan's area of expertise, he asked an employee for help. The plumbing expert was out that day but as Karl walked by, he overheard the conversation and stopped. As the employee left, Karl told Stan he made the same repair the week before and would be glad to help. They have been friends ever since."

"It sounds like Karl needs a good friend right now and God may have set him up."

"Yes. It seems so. He is not usually here very long, so maybe after he leaves you can tell us what you can about why you are here."

"Sounds good."

Silently, they watch the mesmerizing fire. The warmth makes Evie's eyelids heavy. As she looks over, she sees Martha staring into the fire. When the men come back inside, Martha looks at them and smiles.

"Bye ladies. Nice to meet you." Karl says, not even looking at Evie as he walks to the door.

She smiles and replies, "I'll be here, awhile. I'm sure I'll see you again."

At the door, Stan speaks quietly to Karl. After closing the door behind him, Stan runs his hand through his blonde curls, then joins the ladies.

"Sorry about that." He sits by Martha and takes her hand in his. "My friend is having a tough time right now. I noticed small changes in him, but he seems to be more despondent lately. I hoped he would share what's going on, but he hasn't opened up much. It's difficult sharing our deepest, darkest hurts. It's a process to truly trust someone, to believe they care and don't want to harm us. We get hurt. Then we feel like we need to protect ourselves."

"True." Evie sighs. "Which is where the enemy wants us. He wants us to isolate. To feel like we are alone, and no one understands or cares."

"That's a fact," Stan agrees.

As the fire crackles, Martha asks, "Evie what can you tell us about your coming here?"

"As you know, God has a purpose and plan for everyone. Some people have never been told this; others stray from the path God has set them on. On this assignment, I am part of God's plan in the life of four people. As Stan said, it's a process getting someone to trust us and for them to realize we only want good things for them."

"I understand the confidentiality of your assignment, but may I ask a question?" Martha asks.

"Of course."

"How do you know who they are?"

Evie smiles, "I know very little about the people or their lives except they are from this town or close by. Holy Spirit lets me know when someone is part of my assignment when I first meet them. It's a "wow" moment every time it happens. It reminds me of how amazing God is and how much He truly loves us. Getting to know them and hearing their story helps me to love and understand them. It encourages me to help them."

It is quiet for a moment. Then Stan asks if he can pray for her before bed.

"Yes please, but one more thing. Thank you for your obedience and commitment to our Father. I know when I meet my host family, they are special people handpicked by God."

"Yup handpicked." Stan laughs. "I had a dream some guy in a gray three-piece suit handed me an envelope. He said a letter would come in the mail in a few days and I needed to honor the request. Then he told me the Lord sees my faithfulness and loves me. I never had a dream like it before but was humbled to think it was a message for me. When I thought about it, I realized it may have been the slice of pepperoni pizza I had before bed, but then your letter came two days later."

"Evie, how did you know to send us the letter?" Martha asks.

"Your names were placed on my heart. I found your address and sent the letter. To an unbeliever, it may sound unbelievable, but it's how He works."

"It sure is. Well, I have a few things to do before bed so let's pray. Lord, we humbly come before You. Thank You for choosing us as a part of Your plan. We ask You to protect Evie and give her wisdom so she will know 'This is the way; walk in it.' Show her favor with the people. With the authority given by Jesus Christ, Amen." Before he leaves the room, Stan caresses Martha's face tenderly, then lovingly kisses her on her forehead.

"Stan and I read a devotion and pray together before bed. I will join him in a minute but before I go, I want to let you know about our Fall Festival. Tomorrow starts the festival activities and they go day and night, Friday through Sunday, and ends with a community service on Sunday evening. Around here it is a big deal. People from the surrounding towns come. Who knows, this may be where you find your people. You are more than welcome to join us."

"I haven't been to a Fall Festival since I was a child. I'm looking forward to it."

"Good. Well, make yourself at home. If you need anything let me know."

"You have been so kind. Good night."

"Sleep well." Martha softly replies.

Two

Sitting on her bed reading in the book of Psalms, Evie catches herself rereading the same line twice. Distracted by a familiar smell she closes her Bible, refreshed, encouraged, and ready for the day. She pokes her head out the door and hears sizzling come from the kitchen as she sniffs the air. Quickly, she dresses, makes her bed, and looks around to be sure all is in order.

Thank You for waking me today and for the opportunity to begin my assignment. Search my heart, Heavenly Father, for anything offensive and forgive me. I know You will guide me through the day and prepare the way. Please bless Martha and Stan.

Following the enticing aroma to the kitchen, she finds bacon, but no Martha. No Stan either. She jumps as the clatter of metal from the pantry startles her.

"Martha?"

"Good morning, Evie. I am clumsy this morning and dropped a couple of metal bowls. I will be out in just a minute."

"Oh, okay." Looking out the window, she catches a glimpse of Stan coming out of his shop. With pursed lips and a little dance to his step, he carries a large brown basket covered with tan cloth.

Martha, coming from the pantry, sees Evie looking outside. "He works all year long to sell his product specifically at the festival. One of his many projects. People look forward to seeing the twist he puts on them each year."

"Morning ladies," Stan greets them as he strolls in the door. "Great day for a Fall Festival. It's a chilly, great day. Mmmm, it smells wonderful in here. How much longer?"

"Oh Stan," Martha laughs. "Be patient. All good things are worth the wait."

"Oh, how I know. I had to wait nineteen long years for you."

Blushing, she finishes making breakfast and explains how Stan was nineteen when they met, and he knew immediately Martha was the one for him. She was sixteen and her parents were not as sure, but in time it became evident. They married the summer after she graduated.

"As a little girl, I found my mom's wedding gown in her closet," Martha explains, her face flushed from the heat of the open oven as she places the biscuit tray on the rack. "The lace and bead bodice and the flowing, beaded gown looked like something a princess would wear. At least in my mind, but I fell in love and decided I would wear it on my wedding day."

"The best day of my life." Stan chimes in.

Martha's eyes shimmer. "My grandparents had acres of land with a large pond not far from the house. We married on the entrance of the dock under a barely visible trellis full of violet clematis. God showed favor as it was a beautiful summer day with white, fluffy clouds shading us during the ceremony. A few friends and all our family were there. We had a reception in the old barn which had been converted years before the wedding. It was simple, but it was my fairy tale wedding. That was seven years ago."

"With a hundred more to go," Stan announces proudly as he helps set the meal on the table.

"Sounds good to me." Martha smiles, pulling the biscuits out of the oven and transferring them to a plate before sitting down.

Such a sweet love they have for one another. I don't know much about them and their story Father, but You do. I pray Your favor on them and that You provide all the desires of their heart.

After a wonderful, thoroughly satisfying breakfast, as Stan put it, he leaves for town to set up. While he is gone, they clean up the kitchen. Afterward, Evie helps Martha gather the mini cheesecake bites, cheesecake pies, and brownies which she made early this morning.

"Are we going to your church for the festival?" Evie asks as she helps pack the basket.

"No, ours is a little further out in the country. Although the town puts on the festival, the pastor of the only church on the square opens his church for everyone to use. Our booth is on the southwest corner of the square, but people eagerly seek out the good stuff." Martha winks as she looks out the window for Stan.

Evie hears the crunch of gravel on the long driveway get louder, as the older model green truck creeps to a stop. Stan bounds in the door, kisses Martha tenderly on her cheek, picks up the basket of sweets, and goes back out.

Returning from the truck Stan announces, "Ladies, your chariot, or should I say, Chevrolet, awaits. God has blessed us with a wonderful first day of the festival and the temperature is rising. People are already wandering around."

When they get to town, they park in the lot reserved for vendors at the church. Pastor Evans, blowing on his cup of hot chocolate, watches them pull in and strolls over to greet them.

"Stan." He nods. "Martha, you are looking as radiant as usual."

"Thank you, pastor," Martha replies, cheeks rosy.

"Pastor Evans, this is our guest, Evie." Stan turns toward her. "She will be staying with us for a while."

"Evie. What a beautiful name. Is it short for something or is it just Evie?"

"My full name is Evangeline, but my brother couldn't pronounce it when he was younger, so they called me Evie and it stuck."

"Evangeline," Pastor Evans muses, "I believe that means good news, doesn't it?"

"Yes. It sure does."

"Well Evie, it is a pleasure to meet you. You're staying with one of the finest couples I know. Welcome to our humble little town."

"Thank you. Yes, they are very kind."

Tables dot the churchyard. Evie is surprised by the variety of vendors. She passes a table with an arrangement of the length of the table. On a golden runner, which hangs off the table and comes to a point on each end with a single tassel, sits a large pumpkin surrounded by faux fruit, pinecones, small white pumpkins, festive flowers, and burnt orange and yellow leaves.

Another vendor has Christmas arrangements of green and red and silver and gold. Strands of white lights, colored lights, ornaments, and Christmas balls add to the arrangements of garland, flowers, and bows. A table loaded with brilliant-colored booties, scarves, hats, and an array of other knitted items catches Evie's eye. She scans the tables and sees door hangers, yard signs, ceramic doodads, and every imaginable craft available. Her interest piques at the table of crosses of various sizes and colors.

As she makes a mental note to return to the cross table, the smell of fresh baked goodness brings her attention to another area of the churchyard. Homemade food items as plentiful as crafts. Sweets, fresh canned goods, bread, and more. Stan carries the basket of goodies Martha prepared to the tables reserved for Grace Church.

As she walks by one of the vendors, a familiar scent of molasses and ginger, returns Evie to her grandma's house again. The blast of gingery goodness could mean only one thing, grandma's gingersnap cookies! She laughs as she recalls her younger brother sneaking extra cookies and getting a belly ache.

There are jars of relish, black bean salsa, pickled okra, jams, and jellies. Every canned or baked good is here. She understands why people come from all around for the festival.

"Martha, may I help you set up?"

"You are kind, but I have plenty of help around here. Walk around. Enjoy yourself." Looking at Martha's church family, Evie nods.

Evie's first stop is the table of beautiful crosses. She has never seen such an assortment. Reaching over to pick up a baby blue wooden cross embellished with vibrant colored jewels, Evie notices a young girl with dirty purple hair walk up to the end of the table. Watching the vendor's expression change, Evie looks over at the young girl. A customer, making a purchase, distracts the vendor.

Evie watches as the teen, who is keeping an eye on the vendor, picks up one of the smaller crosses made of olive wood and the homemade velvet pouch, and places it in her pocket. Evie watches as she repeats it twice. As she is putting the third in her pocket the vendor sees her and confronts her. The young girl loudly and angrily denies her, and says the woman is judging her because of her purple hair and tattoos. Evie, with money in her hand, states she is paying for the crosses. She pays, then runs to catch up with the girl.

"Hey, hey. Are you hungry?"

"What, you think 'cause I stole something I don't have money?" The girl snaps.

"I just thought maybe you might like to get one of those freshly baked goodies." Evie points to the table where Martha is sitting. "My friend baked this morning and had the whole house smelling like a midtown bakery. I don't know too many women who would turn down Double Chocolate Gooey Fudgy Brownies." Evie turns and slowly walks toward the goodies table and waves for her to come on. Hesitantly she follows her.

Martha smiles as they approach.

"Did you make a friend, Evie?"

Evie, cheeks red replies, "I guess I did, but I'm not much of a friend, I don't even know your name." She says as she turns toward the girl.

"My name is Sassy." She announces, bracing herself for the comments on her name.

"Is that with an *ie* or a *y*?" Martha asks.

"A *y*." Sassy waits. No judgment, no comments.

"Well, it is a pleasure to meet you Sassy. Would you care for one of my fresh-baked, Double Chocolate Gooey Fudgy Brownies?"

"Mm-hm." Sassy stares eyes wide, at the brownie.

"Evie?"

"Thank you, Martha, but I'll pass. We are going to get some hot chocolate and sit inside the church hall for a little bit if that sounds good to you Sassy."

Evie pays for the brownie and walks toward the hot chocolate booth with Sassy shuffling slowly behind her.

"Two hot chocolates please." Evie asks if Sassy likes whipped cream to which she nods emphatically. "With extra whipped cream." Silently, they walk towards the church hall.

Evie knew the minute Sassy put the first cross in her pocket she was assignment number two. *Prayer and love. Lots of prayer and love.* Evie wonders how she will see Sassy again but knows God will work it out. He always does. As they approach the building, a tall, attractive, dark-haired young man holds the door for the ladies.

"It's good to see you, Anastasia," the young man says. Evie thanks him, but Sassy brushes by indifferently, saying nothing.

"Do you know him?" Evie asks.

"Eh," Sassy replies indifferently as she picks a table as far away from others as possible.

"You don't have to tell me. How's the brownie? You should feel highly energetic between the brownie and hot chocolate...with extra whipped cream."

Sassy has some walls; some very tall, thick walls. Not unyielding though.

Not wanting to scare her off, Evie quietly sips her hot chocolate. Suddenly, Sassy's body stiffens, her face changes from soft pink to crimson red, and alarm fills her eyes.

"Look," Sassy spat, as anger replaces alarm, "I don't know what you're trying to do. You've been nice and all, but I don't need one more person trying to control or change me. I'm out."

"But Sassy,"

"Bye and here are the crosses you paid for." Evie watches as she stomps out of the hall.

Wow. She is going to be a tough one. Evie finishes her hot chocolate and picks up the crosses, realizing she only left two of the three. Thinking there may be hope for Sassy after all, Evie stands and pulls on her hood.

Back outside, she walks around the town square. As she turns the corner, she sees Martha standing at the back of a thick crowd of people. All eyes are on a raised stage where four people, each with a stack of pies to the right of them, sat looking back at the crowd.

"What's going on?" Evie asks.

"The annual pumpkin pie eating contest. You are just in time."

"Oh wow. Wait, is that Stan?" Evie giggles. "And who is the young, dark-haired man next to him?"

"Oh yes, Stan participates every year. Bless his heart. He tries. The man next to him is Eli Watson. He is the youth minister at Pastor Evans' church. He is the reigning champion and Stan wants to beat him so badly, all in fun of course. Sassy is up there. Not too many women participate in this event."

"I don't know how she could eat another thing after the brownie and hot chocolate. Is there a prize for the winner?"

"Yes. A twenty-five-dollar voucher for free groceries each month for a year from Mr. Washburn's store, a coupon for two large pizzas with unlimited toppings from Tony's Pizzeria, a trophy, and bragging rights until the next festival. Oh yeah, and they get their picture in the local bi-weekly paper. Here they go."

Joining the whistling, hooting, and cheering all around, Martha cheers for Stan. Sassy holds her own. Stan picks up another slice and hesitates. A little green, he drops the slice back on the plate. He shakes his head. Eli waits only long enough to be sure Stan is out before pushing the pie plate away. The other guy looks like he has no intention of stopping, until he starts coughing and pie comes out of his nose. Sassy keeps eating until the guy pushes back from the table. Instead of staying to claim her prize, she runs behind the booth. Evie follows.

"Sassy, are you okay?"

"I'm fine." She growls as she stands from her bent position and wipes her mouth with the back of her hand. "Too many sweets but I won the groceries and pizza so it should help."

"Should help?"

"Nothing. Never mind. I need my prizes and get my stupid picture. I bet these people are gonna love my picture in the paper. Just something else for them to talk about." She walks around to the front of the booth followed by Evie, to claim her prizes. The area is clear except for Stan, Martha, and Eli.

"Congratulations Anastasia. You did it!" Eli exclaims.

"Why do you insist on calling me that?" She hisses. "It's Sassy!"

She snatches her trophy, coupon, and voucher for Washburn's Grocery, glares for the photographer, and leaves.

"My goodness," Martha gasps. "What happened to the girl you introduced me to earlier?"

"I'm not sure. While we were talking, something came over her and she left abruptly."

"Wow." Eli whistles. "She hasn't let anyone around here even get that close to her."

"That was close?" Evie sighs. "She's harder than I thought. Do you know her?"

"Not really, but I invited her to visit our student's ministry, which hasn't happened. One of our students talks to her on occasion at school, that is, when Anastasia will talk. The student knows she lives with her grandmother and three siblings, and she knows very little about Jesus."

"Why do you call her Anastasia if it seems to bother her so much?" Evie asks.

"I don't know, maybe I shouldn't. It's a beautiful name and although Sassy fits her now, it won't always. She'll eventually come to class and learn God created her with so much love and a plan for her life. I believe in this girl and would like to see her believe in herself. She has some issues going on."

Since Martha is finished for the day, she and Evie walk and look around. Evie meets so many people she knows she will never remember everyone. As the sun slowly sets, they sit on a bench in the petting zoo watching young children delightedly squeal as they feed the animals. Martha looks up and sees Stan watching them. She smiles as he approaches.

"My love, are you ready to go? You look tired." He says concerned.

"I am. Evie, you are more than welcome to stay longer if you would like. Stan will come back after he takes me home."

"Oh no, I'm ready. It has been a lovely time. Since it runs all weekend, I'll come back again, but for now, I'm good."

As they walk to the car, Stan stops by his table.

Approaching his table Evie gasps, "This is what you brought to sell?" He chuckles.

"Yep. What did you think was in the basket?"

"I didn't know, but it makes sense. They are so beautiful."

"Thank," Before he could finish his sentence, the woman behind the table jumps up and says, "That's her. The woman I told you about earlier today."

Surprised, he asks, "Evie stole the crosses?"

"Goodness no! She paid for the crosses the girl with the purple hair tried to steal."

"Anastasia. Her name is Anastasia." Evie smiles and says kindly.

Stan leaves a key with his helper and tells her he will be back shortly.

"Sorry, Evie. People here are not unkind they just don't know what to make of people like Anastasia who do their own thing. Purple hair is new to people in this town."

"I understand. I don't think she is unkind, but I want to give the purple-haired girl a name. Maybe they will begin to see her differently."

"With your help, I'm sure they will."

Back at the house Stan walks the ladies in and asks Martha if she needs anything before he goes back to the festival. She assures him she is fine and is going to take a nap.

He sure does dote on her and it's sweet. Is she okay? Evie wonders.

"Help yourself to anything you want Evie. I am going to rest for a bit."

In the quiet house, Evie wanders into the office and looks at Stan's selection of books. Pulling one she has not yet read; she returns to the living room and her favorite chair. Martha wakes from her nap and finds Evie, book open on her lap, looking out the window.

"I borrowed a book from the office. I hope it's okay."

"Of course. We want you to feel at home."

As they talk the phone rings. Martha answers the phone, listens for a moment, then asks the caller to hang on.

"There is a free concert tonight at the festival. Pastor Evans has offered the church because it will be too cold to have outside. Would you like to go with me?"

Evie nods.

Ms. Alice, Pastor Evans' wife, picks them up for the concert. Sitting the third row in, toward the front, Evie looks around and observes there are only a few empty seats as the little-known group, Baby Wren, brings people to their feet. The group is made of three females, two playing guitars and one on drums, and one male on the keyboard.

Still talking about Baby Wren when they pull up back at the house, Martha asks, "Stan, what do you think? You have not said a word."

"Well sweetheart, if I could have gotten a word in while you two were gushing over them," he laughs, "I would have said I think they are good. I heard someone say they are being looked at for a record deal."

"As they should be. They are better than most bands we have heard lately. I hope they do well."

Inside the house, Evie asks, "What can I do to help before bed Martha? It's been a long day and I'm sure tomorrow will be too."

After telling her that she only needs her help in the morning, they exchange goodnights and Evie goes to her room.

Father, Your Son took the beatings, ridicule, and the cross for our sins as well as our healing and victory. Martha is not well. I ask You to heal her, strengthen her body, and provide the desires of her heart. Bless Stan and remind him of Your strength and provide favor. He is a good husband and loves her, as she loves him. Thank you for Sassy. I trust You will help me help her. Please protect her and begin to soften her heart so I can reach her. I love You and am humbled You call me Your child.

In the small office, Stan and Martha read their devotion, *Miscarriage: Going Forward.* A friend gave them the book as a gift, after she suffered her loss. The note inside reads, "In some of my darkest days this book brought me the most light. Praying it blesses you as well."

Stan prays, "Lord, thank You for Jesus who died for our sins. We never want to take it for granted. You know the desire we hold to start our family. We know Your plan and timing are perfect, and we wait on You. Prepare and strengthen Martha's body. Our hope is in You Lord, and we know You will renew our strength. Thank You for Evie and for allowing us to be a part of Your plan. We pray for her protection, guidance, and wisdom. Prepare her people. Your people. You are faithful to keep Your promises. In Jesus' Name, Amen." Stan cups Martha's face in his hands.

"Martha, we continue to trust Him. We know every good and perfect gift comes from Him and He will not forget us. It will happen. You do what the doctors suggest, and God will do the rest." As Stan kisses Martha, he encourages himself as well by remembering the Lord's faithfulness in the past.

"I know. I will not lose heart. It tears me up and makes me wonder if it will ever happen each time…" Sobbing, she could barely finish her sentence. "We lose our baby." He takes her in his arms until he feels her shaking body relax.

Three

Evie and Martha are in the kitchen finishing the potatoes as Stan comes in from town.

"People are buying up my crosses. They make nice Christmas gifts and stocking stuffers. Smells great in here." Stan says as he takes a fork from the drawer for a sample.

"Today is my favorite day of the festival," Martha shakes more salt and another dash of pepper in the mashed potatoes. "I look forward to fixing a big meal that everyone can enjoy without charge. There are pots and bowls and platters of food everywhere and so many people."

"Food sure does bring people together, doesn't it?" Evie says.

"Especially free food." Stan laughs as they gather the containers.

Once the containers are secure in the back of the truck, Stan opens the door for Martha, then Evie hops in. Stan stops at the door to unload the ladies and potatoes. Tables are already full, and the line of people is snaking around the walls and down the hall. Evie marvels at the number of volunteers to serve as well.

Looking at the enormous crowd, Evie notices an attractive elderly woman with silver hair wearing a lilac satin dress, accented with a floppy gray hat, and tasteful gray jewelry, sitting at a far back table. She looks ready for a ball more than a street festival. Martha looks busy, so Evie does not bother her with questions.

As she walks over to introduce herself, Holy Spirit speaks to her heart, *This one Evie.*

"Hello. I'm Evie. I'm new to Banderidge and I am staying a while for work." The woman looks at her with pain and sadness in her eyes.

"I can't pass by without telling you how absolutely beautiful you look. Your necklace is stunning. I've never seen anything like it."

The woman has a faint twinkle in her eye, "Thank you. I had never seen gray diamonds or heard of them until my loving husband bought me this set on our fiftieth anniversary. He died almost a year ago. I am sorry for being rude. My name is Pearl Daniel."

"Pearl, a beautiful name for a beautiful lady."

"My mother enjoyed reading. *The Good Earth,* by Pearl S. Buck, was one of her favorites. My parents were missionaries in China in the early '30s and Ms. Buck's parents were missionaries in China as well, so mom named me after Pearl. Both sets of parents came back to the states to give birth. The only difference was that my parents never went back. Her parents did. Pearl went on to win the Nobel Prize in Literature when I was a small child. Needless to say, mom was very pleased with my name." Pearl smiles slightly for the first time.

"What an interesting story. I imagine you are proud of your name too. I need to see what I can do to help with lunch. It's a pleasure meeting you." Ms. Pearl nods and Evie leaves to find Stan and Martha.

Martha is setting out plates and silverware when Evie finds her. As she helps stack the paper plates, she tells Martha about meeting Ms. Pearl.

"Ms. Pearl is an interesting person," Martha says as she places the forks in a container.

"Yes, she is. She told me about being named after Pearl S. Buck, the Nobel Prize winner."

"Oh yes, she is very proud of the story. Did she tell you anything else?"

"No. Should she have?"

Before Martha has a chance to respond, Pastor Evans tells them it is about serving time. He asks the volunteers to gather in the kitchen for prayer before they start serving.

"Lord, just as You came to serve us, help us to be like You as we serve our community. Help us show love like You show love. Let them see You through our service to them. Amen. Thank you for being here today and to all who prepared food as well. I will bless the meal then let everyone go through the line, table by table. We feed until the food runs out."

As he walks out of the kitchen, he waits as the room quiets then announces, "Welcome everyone! We are so glad you are here! Squeeze in and make room for others. Let's bless the food."

"Word must have gotten around how good the food was last year," Martha whispers. "There are many more people this year."

"Let's bow our heads and give thanks. God, we thank You for this day and the blessings You have given us. We thank You for this food and ask You to bless it and bless the hands which prepared it. May each person here today leave with a full belly and a happy heart. Amen."

Tapping the spoon of green beans on the side of the pot, Evie greets people with a smile. Martha is beside her doling out mashed potatoes and a kind word. Karl and Renee make their way through the line and Martha introduces Evie to Renee. Martha tells them when the festival is over, they need to come to the house for dinner. Renee agrees. Most of the people are in good spirits as the line shuffles along. Evie sees Anastasia slowly progressing towards her.

"Hi Sassy!" Evie says with too much enthusiasm.

"Hey." She replies and keeps on through the line.

An hour later, Evie sees Ms. Pearl making her way down the line. Martha had been replaced by Alice, Pastor Evans' wife, to take a quick break. Ms. Pearl finally makes her way to the green beans.

"Hello, again Ms. Pearl. I knew we would see each other again soon." Evie smiles as she spoons green beans on her plate.

With a half-smile, she replies, "You are a pleasant person. Won't you come to my house for tea one day this week?"

"Of course! I look forward to it."

"Well, Martha knows where I live. You can ask her."

"Ok Ms. Pearl, but what day and time would you like me to be there?" Evie asks.

"Oh, it doesn't matter, I will just be waiting anyway."

"Okay," is all Evie says before she hears a long, exaggerated, sigh from the dramatic man behind Ms. Pearl.

Evie wonders if she will meet her final person during the festival. As Martha comes back to serve, a young man comes through the line. He looks about seventeen or eighteen years old. He is polite but uncomfortable. As he approaches, Evie knows he is her fourth person. She smiles as she spoons out his green beans and he thanks her.

"Did you say thank you?" Asks the gentleman behind him.

"Oh yes, he said thank you. He is very polite." Evie reassures the man. Martha introduces the family as part of their church family.

So, she met all her "people". Four completely different people with completely different lives. Eager to get started, she forces her attention back to serving.

The last of the food runs out around three o'clock. Clean-up is quick and easy because volunteers cleaned as the meal progressed. Assured there was nothing else, Stan grabs the plates prepared earlier for each volunteer to take home.

Evie remembers seeing the entertainment scheduled for the evening as an illusionist. But Martha looked tired. Since it is still hours until the show, they decide to go home, rest, and enjoy their dinner and see how Martha feels later.

As Stan clears the table and takes Martha's plate, he asks, "Are you not going to finish those amazing potatoes?" She shakes her head, so flashing his winning smile, he finishes the potatoes and discards the plates.

"I am sorry, but I do not feel up to going tonight," Martha says as she gets up from the table.

"I don't think I'll go either. I'll stay home with you," Stan caresses her cheek, then kisses her forehead.

"Renee plans to go tonight. Let me see if she'll come to get you. I'm not sure if Karl is going, but either way, they wouldn't mind. Would that be something you'd like to do?" Stan asks as he picks up the phone.

"I don't want to inconvenience anyone. If it's not out of their way, although...," Evie trails off as she hears Renee's voice through the phone.

"It's all set. Renee will be here at 6:30 to get you."

"Thank you. I look forward to it."

"Now, my love, what can I do for you? Would you like to sit and read in the living room? Take a nap? Start a garden?"

"Oh Stan." Martha laughs as she leans into him.

"Let's skip the garden for now, but I will get into my comfy clothes and try to finish my book. Would you start a fire?"

"Done." Opening the door, a burst of frigid air hits Evie's back. "Brrr." Stan shivers when he comes in to put the logs on the fire.

Oh Father, such a sweet, loving couple. Martha is young and seems healthy. I don't understand why she's so tired. Bless this couple. Supply their needs and remind them of the strength they already have within. Continue to grow their union and love for one another.

Once Martha is situated on the sofa, book in hand, and a fire started, Stan decides to go to the shop. He tells Martha he won't be long.

"Martha, would you like me to fix us some hot tea?" Evie asks.

"Please. Hot tea and a little snow falling would make this perfect. I might be jumping the gun this early in the season though." She laughs.

"Well, I don't know if I can do much about the snow, but I can make us some tea." They laugh as she goes to the kitchen.

Loving Father would a few flurries be doable?

As Evie prepares the tea, she looks out towards the shop and sees faint white flakes falling from the sky.

"Oh Martha, look outside."

"What is it?"

"Look out the window."

She is quiet a minute, "It has not snowed this early in the season in years. Are you sure you did not have anything to do with this?" Evie smiles as she enters with the steaming tea.

"Our Father knows the desires of our heart and does what He can when He can." Evie is unaware of exactly how much Martha needs the reminder.

Thank you, Gracious Father.

My sweet Evie, you know it is my greatest pleasure to show you My favor and be gracious to you and Martha.

They sit in silence for a few minutes, enjoying the fire and the flurries.

"May I ask you a personal question?"

Martha nods.

"Are you okay? I know I've only been here a couple of days, but I noticed you tire easily, and Stan checks on you quite often. You don't have to share if you'd rather not."

Martha smiles as she tries to hold back the tears. "Stan and I love children and have looked forward to having a large family since before our wedding day. We did not want to wait. We were ready the day we said, 'I do'. You saw the custom-made table in the oversized kitchen, and the large house and all the acreage. We have everything ready for a large family except the children." Evie sits quietly, her heart heavy for her new friend.

"For many years I did not get pregnant then when I finally became pregnant, I lost the baby. I had three miscarriages; the last one a few months ago. Not only were we heartbroken about losing another baby, but we were also devastated because I was further along. We assumed I would go to term and that made it even more difficult."

She wipes her eyes with a tissue. Evie watches sympathetically and waits. Most of the time, in her line of work, listening is so much more powerful than words.

"We know God's timing is perfect and He knows what He is doing, but sometimes I struggle, and lose hope. That is when Stan is his strongest. He prays with me and for me, encourages me, and does not allow me to fall into depression. He is a wonderful man, and I am blessed. It has been a test, so I know a miraculous testimony is coming. I honestly do not know what I would do without his love and understanding."

Evie smiles. "I've seen the beautiful love between you. Two things are for sure, you two truly love each other and God loves both of you very much. We know when we submit ourselves to God, which is obvious you two do, He gives us the desires of our hearts. I will keep you in prayer and believe with you."

Stan busts through the door, calling for Martha as he kicks off his boots. "Martha, Martha, did you see? It's snowing! It's only light, but it is snowing." As Stan rushes to the living room, the ladies stifle their giggles.

"I see. Is it not beautiful and very unexpected?" Martha glances at Evie with a raised eyebrow.

"It's been snowing for a while, hasn't it?" He says dryly as he realizes they are giggling.

"Yes," Evie responds. "It started shortly after you went outside."

"That's it. I'm putting more windows in the shop." They laugh as he sits on the arm of the sofa next to Martha.

"Have you finished your book?"

"Um…no." She looks up at him, "I do not think I even opened it. We have been talking."

"And crying?" He looks tenderly at his wife.

"Yes. I told her about the miscarriages. I know she will pray for us."

"Definitely," Evie assures them.

"I better freshen up before Renee comes to get me. If you'll excuse me."

In her room, her heart breaks for her friends, Evie sits in the chair by the window watching the falling flakes as she prays.

Father. You are the giver of life and good and perfect gifts. I thank You for who You are and what You can do in all situations. You know the heartbreak in this home, the home of Your faithful servants. We don't know Your ways or understand why things happen, but we know You are aware of everything we endure. Your Word tells us we will face trials and tough times and You will never leave us and never forget us. For whatever reason my friends must go through this tough time, I trust You. I pray they reach for Your strength in their weak times, healing for their hearts, and for Martha's body to line up with Your Word. Thank You, loving Father. You hear our prayers and collect our tears. Continue to bless and let Your peace fill this home.

Evie hurries to get ready and goes back to the living room.

"Oh Renee, I didn't know you were here. I am sorry to keep you waiting." When Renee looks up, compassion floods Evie as she watches her wipe under her bloodshot eyes.

"Oh, excuse me. I'm sorry. I'll go back to my room until"

"No," Renee interrupts, "it's okay."

As Evie sits, Renee turns back to Stan and Martha and continues, "He isn't the same man I've lived with for the past 30 years. Tonight, after dinner, he stormed off angry. I don't even know what caused it or where he went. I try to hold tight to God but sometimes I feel so, so helpless. Please pray for our marriage." Evie hands her another tissue.

"When we feel helpless is when we take our hands off the situation and allow God to work," Martha says softly. Renee nods as she regains her composure.

"Well enough of that," Renee wipes her eyes and puts on a smile. "Are you ready to go?"

"Yes ma'am! I am!" Evie jumps up and starts toward the door. Not another word is said about their marriage problems as they drive to the show.

"It's nice that Pastor Evans allows the use of his church for festival activities."

"Yes, he is a good man. We have been going to this church for years. I grew up in a church like this and when we moved to town we started attending. Karl had gone occasionally with his grandma when he was growing up, so it didn't matter to him. We shared the belief the girls needed to be raised in a church, so we've gone as a family ever since. I like the church and adore Pastor Evans and Ms. Alice, but I feel like something is missing. I look at Martha and Stan and see something different in them. I know they have gone through some tough times, and I am amazed at how they keep going. They claim their faith in God is what gets them through. I don't know if we have that kind of faith."

Pulling into a parking space, Renee thanks Evie for listening to her ramble. Evie tells her she will be praying for them as they get out of the car and enter the church. Finding seats two rows back and to the left gives them a good view. As Evie looks around, she sees Anastasia sitting front and center. Evie overhears the woman sitting behind her fussing to the lady next to her.

"Did you see the snow today? I can't believe it. It's too early for snow. I hope this isn't any indication of an early and rough winter. Usually, they give us warning, but it came out of nowhere." She said loudly.

The woman to her right repeats, "Out of nowhere." She shakes her head slowly in disbelief, arms crossed against her chest, chin up.

Evie smiles. She knows where the flurries came from, and they were a gift for someone who needs it. As Evie sits waiting for the show to begin, she takes a minute to pray.

Father, thank You for the snow today. It was a blessing for Martha. She needed a little love. Strengthen Renee and encourage her everything will work out according to Your perfect plan. Karl is in a bad way and needs You. I trust whatever evil the enemy is stirring up, You will turn it around for good and Your glory.

The lights go out in the room and the spotlight on the stage illuminates a man who introduces Marvin the Illusionist. Marvin entertains the crowd for an hour and a half. As he bows lights flood the room and Marvin receives a standing ovation. As the man who introduced Marvin returns to the front, Marvin makes his way to the foyer to speak to people as they leave.

Evie smiles as she puts out her hand, "If you ever get bored creating illusions, you will make a good comedian. You are very entertaining."

He looks at her with a hopeful grin, "Thank you. I saw you from the stage and hoped I had the chance to speak to you. Would you like to get something to eat?"

"You are very kind, but I am not able." She replies as she and Renee move toward the door.

"Are you in a relationship?" Renee asks as they walk to the car.

"Oh no. I prefer not to be in a relationship in my line of work." She stops and looks at Evie.

"What is your line of work?"

"I help people who are having trouble."

"Oh. Are you a counselor?"

"Something like that. Plus, I travel frequently. That's tough on relationships."

On the drive back they laugh about their favorite parts. Evie knows Renee needs a good laugh right now.

Evie enters the mostly dark house. One soft light on in the kitchen guides her to her room. As she opens the door, she shivers prompting her to get another blanket for the bed. Sitting on the edge of the bed, she notices a note on the table. It simply says, "Thank you."

As she gets into bed, she remembers Martha saying that tomorrow there will be a pumpkin pancake breakfast hosted by the Girl Scouts and 4H. Hot pumpkin pancakes with warm maple syrup are her last thought before falling asleep.

Four

Warming rays shining in her window wake Evie. Excited for the day, she hops up and starts getting ready. Brushing her teeth, she stops and hears the soft sound of crying. Evie can feel Martha's despair in her voice as she tells Stan she does not feel like leaving the house. She hears Stan encouraging her to dress, and that she will feel better once she gets those hot pumpkin pancakes in her belly.

Father, You are always faithful! Bless this couple. Your gracious favor is all they need. It is in their weakness they are strengthened by Your power. Jesus carried our weakness and bore the stripes so Martha would be healed physically and emotionally. This part of their journey is painful for them both, so place Your comforting, loving arms around them and wipe away their tears. Her body is healed and prepared, in the Name of Jesus, to carry their baby to full term and may their quiver be full.

As she finishes, she hears the shuffle of Martha getting ready for the day.

The pumpkin pancakes with a pat of butter and a drizzle of warm maple syrup are better than Evie imagined. Pumpkin, cinnamon, nutmeg, and the sweet smell of maple syrup mix with the smell of hot coffee. Chattering and laughter fill the hall in anticipation of the holiday season.

Enthralled, Evie looks around the hall, glad to see all four of her people. Jedidiah slouches down in his chair mutely. Pearl, beautiful and dressed like she is eating with the president, is sitting with others, but obviously very alone. Evie watches as, face downcast, a tear falls into Pearl's pancakes. Karl is present physically and although he laughs and speaks to others, he seems disconnected. Renee stays close to his side, smiling and talking to those around her. Evie almost misses Anastasia because she is sitting with an older woman and three younger children. Her hair is up inside a dirty ball cap, and her tattoos are not visible. Between bites, Anastasia is helping the two younger children, while the woman helps the child closest in age to Anastasia.

What an interesting group You have given me, Lord. Each one fearfully and wonderfully made in Your image. Help me to see them and love them the way You do.

As Stan drives to church, Martha tells him, "I am glad I went today. Thank you, Stan, for your encouragement. I would have been sad later if I missed all the yumminess."

He smiles, caresses her cheek, "Of course my love. That's why we have each other. When one falls the other is there to help them up." She returns the smile then asks Evie if she enjoyed the breakfast.

"Oh yes! I never had pumpkin pancakes and those were delicious. It was delightful. You have a sweet little town, and the people seem kind. I'm glad you went. Everything was perfect."

Arriving early to the community breakfast ensured they would leave early enough to be first at church. They go in, adjust the heat, turn on the lights, and start the coffee. Evie places the pumpkin and banana nut muffins Martha made in the oven to warm.

"Welcome to Grace Church. Give me just a minute and I will show you around." Martha tells her. "It is not much to look at, but it is filled with lots of love. This old country church has been here many years. The former pastor did the best he could in keeping it up and of course, we too are doing what we can because we love it so much. After Pastor Bill died several years ago, his congregation found other churches. This church sat empty for years, they felt people would not want to drive out here to attend church. When we got married, we prayed and knew one day we would pastor a church. When the opportunity was set before us, we prayed and were led to start a church here. The longer it sat empty, the better the price was. It was like our little church was waiting for us. We know it was God's favor. He has blessed it more than we ever imagined. It began with four people, which included us." Martha laughs as she walks with Evie around the building.

"It has charm."

"Yes, I agree. You can see why we fell in love with it. We added on a couple of rooms and remodeled others, believing the church will continue to grow." In the hall, they are greeted by Jesus, painted on the wall, followed by several children.

"I'm guessing this is the children's ministries hall," Evie says.

"You are correct." Peeking in the first room Evie sees a changing table, crib, and rockers.

Martha continues, "This is the nursery and the next one is for our children up to 5th grade. This was one large room back in the day, which was the community center. The rooms are spacious for the children, but we believe they will be full one day. Back here are the rooms we added on. This one might stump you." Approaching the room, in large, puffy, neon-colored letters the sign above the door warns **Beware! Entering means you will never be the same again.**

Evie laughs. "This must be the student ministries room. It looks fun." Martha nods.

"Stan suggested this room be inviting and a place the students look forward to going. We are believing it too will be filled to overflowing." Walking down the hall they turn into a room almost as big as the rest of the church. "This, of course, is the new community center. We chose to use the kitchen from the original center because it is big and saved us money. We have plenty of acreage here as well so we can grow out in any direction when needed. Of course, this is all secondary to the most important part of this church, the people. We have wonderful and loving people. That is what makes Grace Church great."

As they leave the community center, a couple comes in toting an infant carrier and large, pink diaper bag. Martha hugs them and introduces Evie. They apologize for being late and explain they are still trying to get into a routine since the baby arrived. Smiling, Martha assures them it is fine. Setting the baby away from the draft, they position themselves by the door.

Walking back to the kitchen to pull the muffins out of the oven Martha explains to Evie, "Steve and Amy are the welcoming team. It is an idea they suggested to make people feel more, well, welcome." She laughs as she puts the muffins on the table next to the coffee, "They were in the process of scheduling a meeting with others who might be interested, but little Abi Grace decided to make her appearance two weeks early. I think the timing is perfect for others to get on board so maybe Steve and Amy could lead the group while adjusting to their new way of life."

"That is fantastic. Between the four of you, Grace has a good core group." Looking around, Evie observes, "You know, I haven't seen Stan since we got here."

"He is in the back praying. He will be out shortly. It is part of the reason we get here so early and so I can have hot coffee for those in need. If you would like to have a seat you can, or you can stand over here with me to welcome our church family."

In total, twenty-five people are at the church, including the young couple they met at breakfast. Martha leads Evie back to the spot where she sits.

Surprised that Stan welcomes everybody to the service, Evie asks, "Martha, is Stan the pastor?"

"Yes," she laughs, "I guess that never came up. I am sorry I should have told you."

"Oh. Well, I should have put it all together. When you were telling me about starting the church, I thought you had a pastor. When you said four people, you meant four people." Evie laughs. "When you said 'we', I thought you meant the church people collectively and everything you were doing was to assist the pastor. It all makes sense because he is pastoral, and you are an amazing pastor's wife."

Evie sees Jedidiah and his family. Head down, Jedidiah looks sullen. His father whispers something to him, and Jedidiah stands straight and looks forward.

Standing at the door after service, Stan and Martha offer hugs and words of encouragement as their church family leaves. The young couple from breakfast stop to thank Stan for the invitation.

"You know, moving from Tennessee, our biggest concern was searching for a place of worship. It was the most difficult part of our move, but we know God brought us to this town. He led us here, so we're sure it was no coincidence we sat by you at breakfast this morning. We appreciate you reaching out and inviting us today."

Stan shakes his hand, "We're glad you came. Hope to see you again next week." The man nods as he holds the door open for his wife.

"I already know they'll be back next week. I feel a connection with them. They're meant to be here." Martha knows Stan heard from Holy Spirit.

Once everything is clean and put away, they leave. Taking a different route, Evie realizes how close the church is. She knows it's a distance from town but was not aware it was so close to their place. The savory smell of beef greets them as they open the door.

"This is the way a house should smell all the time. Let's eat!" Stan announces hungrily.

"Stan, sweetheart, give me a couple of minutes and we will be ready," Martha says as she takes off her coat and Stan hangs it on the rack. She smiles, "I guess it is obvious by now that food ranks high on his list."

Evie and Stan ask in unison, "Can I help with anything?" They laugh as Martha suggests they set the table and pour the drinks.

"I enjoyed the service today and your message was very passionate. You have a warm and welcoming church with very kind people. You'll continue to prosper and do great things there." Evie gushes as she lays out the silverware. Stan nods as he pulls the glasses from the cabinet and fills them with ice.

"Thank you. I believe the same. The good Lord hasn't brought us this far to leave us now."

Father, bless this man. He is the provider, peacemaker, encourager. When he is discouraged, send encouragement, and when he is weary remind him of Your strength inside of him. They are eager for a family, Father, but You already know.

Evie, My sweet child, every day of Stan's life was recorded, every moment laid out before he was born. Remember, I am not slow in keeping my promises. I work on My time, according to the perfect plan I have for each person's life.

Evie realizes Stan is looking at her, "Martha says it's ready. Are you hungry?"

"Yes! I am! My mouth has been watering since we walked in."

After lunch, Martha naps, Stan goes to the church to meet someone, and Evie spends the afternoon reading and praying about her next steps. It is time to start moving.

Karl and Renee are coming over for dinner on Thursday night so that one takes care of itself. Trying to decide what day to see Ms. Pearl for tea, she realizes she should ask Stan when she can borrow the truck. Anastasia and Jedidiah may be trickier.

Father, prepare a way for me to minister to those two. Only You know what will work best. I trust You and thank You for giving so freely of Your wisdom and leading me.

Distracted by the pans rattling in the kitchen, Evie hears the door close and the swishing sound of wiping feet. Stan has returned from the church. She finishes her notes and goes to the kitchen.

"We will head back to town shortly to close out the festival with the community church service. If you are hungry, I can fix something now. If not, a local deli is providing sandwiches and chips after the service." Martha tells Evie.

"Oh goodness no! Please don't make me eat anything else...ever." They laugh.

"Okay then, we will wait until after service." They talk about the festival over hot cocoa. Placing the empty cups in the sink they go to their rooms to get ready for the service.

Stan calls for the ladies as he goes to warm the truck.

"Brrr. I'm glad we got through the festival before the temperature started dropping. It's not the warmest festival we've had, but not the coldest either." Stan says as they hop in the truck.

Letting the ladies out at the door of the church, he drives off to find a parking spot. Once inside, he sheds his jacket. A Christmas song plays softly from the piano as they find a seat.

Booming with excitement, Pastor Evans opens with prayer. A hymn, a contemporary song, and a Christmas favorite play before Pastor Evans comes back to the front and brings a brief message. When he finishes, he invites other area leaders to speak and says Pastor Stan will close in prayer. A priest from St. Joseph's Church speaks about community and the pastor from First Baptist Church speaks about encouraging one another to keep their eyes on the Prize.

When it is obvious no one else wants to speak, Stan approaches the podium. Before he begins, he scans the crowd. Then his twinkling eyes fall on Martha, and he smiles. He shares the story of when he first met Martha and knew she would be his wife. He reminds everyone without love, they are nothing. He prays for the community and encourages them to remember each other and love one another not only during the holiday season, but throughout the year.

After service, some people stand around talking, while others move on to the community hall. No one is in a hurry to leave. After enjoying sandwiches and friends, Stan brings the truck to the hall door for the ladies.

Back at the house, Evie helps Martha then they go to their rooms. Stan and Martha read their devotion then share their day.

"Steve and Amy are blessed with Abi Grace. I want to rejoice with them and share in their joy and I do, but…" Stan smiles and lifts her chin. He looks into her beautiful, sorrowful blue eyes.

"Martha, my love. You are perfect. Your body is healed and stronger than ever. We will have a child of our own and maybe even two or three or six." Smiling, she leans into him as he kisses her forehead. "When discouraging thoughts enter your mind, see them for what they are. Don't let the enemy in. He is trying to create bitterness. Think about good things, praiseworthy and pure. Think about our future little girl with your beautiful gray eyes and shiny brown hair with my curls. Imagine her in a pretty pink dress with a bow. Or our son, think about our little fellow with a handful of worms in one hand and a pole in the other hollering he's ready to fish. Christ paid it all when He died on the cross. We can't give up hope. Be encouraged love, our time is coming." Wiping her eyes, she smiles and nods. Stan sees the flicker of hope in her eyes. The truth is he too felt a pang in his heart when he saw Abi Grace.

He prays, "Jehovah Rapha, you are the God who heals. We know Your Word and Your promises, and we stand on them. Our flesh struggles to understand, but our spirit knows and pushes us on. We trust You, Lord. Show me how to love my wife and be everything she needs here on earth. Thank You for healing Martha's body and strengthening her. We know Jesus went to the cross for her healing and we don't take it lightly. In Jesus' Name, Amen."

Meanwhile in Evie's room, prayers were also being said.

Gracious Father, I don't have to tell You how wonderful Your faithful servants, Stan and Martha are. You already know. They desire to please You and have devoted their lives to You. Although the burden of not being able to start a family weighs heavy on them, they continue to trust You. I am asking for peace that passes all understanding to well up in them and surround them daily. I pray they choose to embrace abundant joy in their pain and distress. Show me how to encourage them and be a good friend. Father, bless their home with lots of little ones who they will raise to love and honor You. All glory from their testimony will be Yours. Thank You, Father. You work best in our weaknesses. We can't, but You can. Your grace is all we need. I love You, Father.

My sweet child. I give power to those who are tired and worn out. I offer strength to the weak. But those who wait on Me will find new strength. They will run and not grow weary, walk, and not faint. Rest well, My child.

Five

"Will Stan join us for breakfast? I'd like to ask if I can borrow the truck if he doesn't mind."

Martha laughs softly, "He does not miss a meal. I do not know how he does it, but his timing is almost perfect. No matter what time I get up and start breakfast, he comes in as I am putting food on the table. He says Holy Spirit gets hungry and tells him when it is time."

They laugh as Evie fills the third glass of orange juice and Martha places the sausage biscuits and gravy on the table. Stan enters the house and Evie wipes the tears from the corners of her eyes.

"What?" Stan asks innocently. "I told you Holy Spirit gets hungry. Looks and smells great, my love. What are you two having?"

"Oh, Stan." Shaking her head, Martha sits down beside him, "Evie was wondering if you need the truck today or if she can borrow it?"

"Oh, yeah, I'm sorry. We have been so engaged in the festival. I also have an old convertible Volkswagen I take out occasionally or you are welcome to use the truck any time. If you take the car though, I advise you not to put the top down today. It's cold out there."

"Oh, no worries. No convertible for me. The truck is fine."

"Sounds good. Do you need directions or looking for any place in particular?"

"Not really. I want to look around to find the young friend I made at the festival."

"Ok. The truck is all yours."

"Thank you." Evie smiles as she places a sausage biscuit on her plate.

Driving toward town, Evie asks her Father to direct her to Anastasia and guide her in the best way to reach her protected heart. She makes her way to town easily, one turn and a straight shot. The sun's rays warm the truck and relax Evie. It is easy to remember how peaceful it is in the country. She thinks about the festival and how everyone came together. It seems like a nice place to live.

She turns into a parking space in the town square. As she opens the door, she shivers and puts on her hat, wraps her scarf around her neck, and pulls on her gloves. It is cold and supposed to be colder tonight with a chance of snow.

The first shop she enters is a warm, welcoming art and craft shop. To the left of the door, Evie spots multi-colored fabrics. Close to the fabric, is a display of delicate lace of many colors and styles. She notices several finished crafts sitting on a display table. Some were perfect while several look as though a young child made them.

"Good morning," a voice calls from the back of the store. As she approaches, Evie reads her name badge.

"Good morning, Amanda."

"Good morning. Oh. You are staying with Pastor Stan and Martha. I remember you from the festival. You know, small town." She shrugs and rolls her eyes. "If there is someone new, they tend to stand out a little. You, and one other young couple, I remember."

"That makes sense. I'm Evie. It is a pleasure to meet you, Amanda. This is a great shop. Is it yours?"

"Maybe one day. It is my mother's shop. I help her when I am not in class or doing homework. I try to come at least twice a week for a few hours so she can run errands or meet with a friend or whatever."

"That's very helpful. What is your field of study?"

"Education, special education."

"That's great. What made you choose it?"

"I made a special needs friend with Down Syndrome when I was in kindergarten. We had so much in common, but our favorite was dance.

At the time, there was a dance studio where the law office is now. Twice a week we were there practicing our little hearts out. There were several dance recitals and most of the town would come to watch. Truthfully, Sarabeth was a much better dancer than any of us and people would come to watch her dance. We were inseparable until her family moved away after first grade. Her father was transferred for his job. We kept in contact for several years. As we got older and got busy with life the contact just stopped. I truly regret it. About a year ago, I tried to contact her. I looked on social media but haven't found her. I have no idea why I told you all of this. Here you are looking for something and I share my life story with you." She laughs.

"I'm glad you did. I have no plans and I'm in no hurry. What is your friend's name?"

"Sarabeth Ingram."

"Very nice. Do you remember what company her dad worked for or what he did?"

"All I know is they moved often because he was very good at what he did. Her parents are Ralph and May. I asked my mom if she remembered if May worked, but she couldn't recall. The last time we had contact they were in Montana and was about eight years ago."

"Well, my special prayer is that you find Sarabeth and rekindle your friendship."

"Thank you so much."

"I guess I'll wander around."

Wax, wicks, and fragrance oils, soap-making kits, leather and woodcraft items, and doll-making kits looked like they were for more experienced crafters. Then, Evie found the section with basic craft items like glitter, glue, foam sheets, felt, Styrofoam balls, pipe cleaners, and her favorite, the googly eyes. After spending some time exploring, she looks at the crafts on the display table. Amanda finishes ringing up her customer and comes over to where Evie stands.

"What do you think Ms. Evie?"

"These are fantastic."

"Two nights a week we have a craft-making class. Mom teaches a class on Thursday nights from six to eight. On Tuesday nights, I have a class from five to six."

"Okay, so your mom teaches the adult class, and you teach the children's class?"

Amanda picks up a brown felt cut-out of a turkey with lopsided googly eyes and colorful feathers.

"Not just children," she smiles. "My class is for special needs people of any age. There is a support home not far from here and the evening support team member is good to bring them out for class. They enjoy it so much. This turkey was made by Toni. She is hoping someone buys it before she comes back tomorrow. I also have three children that come just about every week. And then there are a few people that come occasionally or when they can. Adults and children can keep their projects or let us try to sell them for them. It's all so fun."

"I'll take it," Evie says as she reaches into her pocket and hands her ten dollars.

"Toni will be so happy, and one hundred percent of the proceeds go to the person. I know you are probably busy, but if you would like to visit one Tuesday night, I'd love for you to come to see for yourself how much fun we have."

"I may just do it. Thank you for your time. It was truly a pleasure."

With pink cheeks, Amanda says softly, "Thank you for listening to me ramble on. You are kind which makes it easy to talk to you."

"Thank you for sharing. I enjoyed hearing your story." Evie smiles, takes her turkey, and leaves.

Gracious Father, Amanda is a sweet girl with an amazing heart. Her love for people with special needs is beautiful. She shared a desire of her heart, and I would like to help her find her childhood friend. Would it be okay? Thank You Father, for caring about even the little things.

As she walks towards the next shop, her stomach growls. It is a clothing store, and she has no interest in buying clothes only to know if Anastasia happens to work there.

Evie pushes open the door and barely hears music over the loud chatter of several women. As she looks for a sales associate to ask about Anastasia, she follows the main aisle. As Evie rounds the aisle, she sees a name tag on one of the ladies in the group. She realizes they are looking in a baby carrier. Amy, from church, is waving her over.

"Hi Evie!" she says as she hugs her.

"Hi Amy."

Looking around Amy asks, "Are you alone?"

"I am. I came to town to look around. I stopped at the craft store for a bit then came here. So far, it's been very nice."

Amy nods, "We love it here. We wouldn't want to raise Abi Grace anywhere else."

She introduces Evie to the ladies and tells them she is here on business. When someone asks how long she will be in town, she tells them she seldom knows for sure how long, because each assignment is different. Before she leaves, she asks the sales associate if Sassy works here. Learning she does not, Evie, not easily disappointed, thanks her and turns to leave.

Amy calls to her, "Evie, I am going to have lunch at The Snackerdoodle across the street. Will you join me?"

"I sure will. Get lunch is next. You helped me make up my mind."

They walk to the corner and across the street quickly. They get in and find a seat before the lunch rush starts.

"It fills up fast in here. Our timing was just right." Amy says as the server walks over to greet them.

"I'll have the chicken salad on wheat, a cup of loaded potato soup, and water."

"So, you want your regular, Ms. Amy," the server and Amy laugh as Evie places her menu on the table.

She asks the server, "What is one of your favorites, Leah?"

"The best thing on the menu, in my opinion, is the club sandwich. They load it with meat and serve it with some of the best honey mustard I have ever tasted."

"Then I'll have the club sandwich and water. Only no tomatoes, please. I'm not a fan." Evie crinkles up her nose. "And Leah, thank you for sharing your beautiful smile."

"You're welcome." She smiles again, pleased with the compliment.

Amy tells Evie that Steve runs the family hardware store, Hanson Hardware, on the west corner of the square across the street from Pastor Evans' church.

"People don't always want to drive nineteen miles to a bigger store, so we stay fairly busy. We keep the prices reasonable too, so people continue to shop with us. When the shop next to the hardware store closed, we bought it so we could expand. It has paid off." Evie listens and asks questions about the store, then the conversation turns to church.

"Evie, it was a blessing when Pastor Stan bought the church and land. The church we attended was nice, but we felt we were being called deeper. If that makes sense. We felt God urging us towards greater things, but we weren't sure how without driving forty minutes to another church in a bigger town. We would have done it, but we hoped it wasn't the answer. God answered our prayers. We have learned and grown so much in the last two years. We were there for the first service with Pastor

Stan and Ms. Martha. They are beautiful people, and we are honored to be a part of Grace Church."

Abi Grace stirs. Amy excuses herself and steps away to feed her. Evie looks around at all the people. There may have been two open seats at the counter.

Interrupting Evie's thoughts, Leah approaches with their meals. Ham, turkey, cheese, bacon, and lettuce was stacked thick along with the three pieces of bread.

"Um, how do I eat this thing?" Leah, still laughing, passes Amy coming back.

"You have her cracking up," Amy says, eyebrows raised and a big smile.

"I was just asking for instructions on how to eat this monstrosity. She wished me luck and said she would bring a box."

For the rest of the meal, they talk about the baby and how she has changed their life. At the end of the meal, Evie assures Amy she will be around for at least a month and will see her at church. She hugs Amy and pulls on her hat as she makes her way to the door.

Evie takes her box to the car and then walks back. Next to the clothing store is the law office and then The What Not Shop. She skips the law office and goes into the shop to see if there is any sign of Anastasia. The only other person she sees is the elderly gentleman behind the counter who looks up briefly.

She looks around. The number of knick-knacks and doodads is overwhelming. Not wanting to buy a broken knick-knack, she is careful not to touch anything. She speaks to the man behind the counter; his only response is "don't break anything." She leaves.

She crosses the street to look in the shop located next to the Snackerdoodle. Black bean salads, corn relish, different flavored oils, salsa, pepper jelly, and so much more overflow the shelves. No

Anastasia, but she does order a fresh-baked strawberry cake to take home with her.

Realizing she spent more time in the food shop than anticipated, she decides on one more shop, and then she will head back to the house. She looks around the square. A clothing and accessory store for young people catches her eye.

Shivering, Evie picks up her pace. From behind the counter, a young lady dressed entirely in black looks up from her magazine.

"Hi. Can I help you?" Her thick, dark black eyeliner, green hair, and matching green lipstick do not hide how beautiful she is.

"Yes, please. I'm looking for someone. Do you by any chance know Sassy?" The girl, who looks a bit older than Anastasia, squints, cautiously looking Evie up and down.

"Why are you looking for her?"

"I met Sassy at the festival and want to talk to her again."

"Sassy talked to you? She doesn't talk to grown-ups unless she has to. She doesn't talk to us either if you want the truth." The girl's green eyes widen as she quickly covers her mouth.

Evie looks at the girl and smiles softly, "So she does work here."

The girl sighs, disappointed in herself.

"It's okay. I'm not here to hurt her or make trouble. As I said, I want a chance to talk to her again. She is not here today then?"

"No. She will be back Wednesday at 2:30, after school. Please don't tell anyone I told you any of this. I could get in big trouble."

"No worries sweetheart, I won't say a thing. Thank you and have a good day."

Heading back to get the strawberry cake Evie is excited but disheartened it will be Friday before she can come back and speak to Anastasia. Wednesday night she will be at church service and Karl and Renee are coming for dinner Thursday night.

Oh well. I trust You Father. I know You have a plan, and, in Your time, I'll see her.

Passing an occasional house, resting fields, and clusters of trees remind Evie how much of a country girl she is at heart. She feels more at home here than her last assignment, which was in a loud, busy city. As she pulls up the driveway, gray smoke from the chimney snakes towards the sky as floating flurries start falling.

The house is quiet. She figures Martha is resting in her room and Stan is busy out of the house. Quietly she puts the cake in the bottom of the refrigerator then steps in front of the of the warm, glowing flames of the fireplace for a minute to warm up. Once the chill is gone, she goes to her room and sits in the chair facing the window. She watches the peaceful flurries for a few minutes lost in thought.

She reaches for the book she borrowed from Stan's office. After reading the same paragraph for the third time, her thoughts continue to drift back to the events of the day. Amanda's heartbreak at losing touch with her childhood friend Sarabeth, lunch with Amy, and then finally finding Anastasia's workplace.

Evie decides after tea with Ms. Pearl tomorrow she will use the library computer to look for information on Mr. Ingram and his family. That should occupy her time until Amanda's class tomorrow night at Crafts-N-More.

She thinks about Amy and how blessed she feels being a part of Grace Church. Her faith and loyalty are going to help Stan grow the church. No doubt about it. Evie remembers the others she met today. She says a quick prayer for each person she had contact with on her travels.

Finally giving in, she puts the book down and leaves her room. She decides to sit in the living room in front of the fire and watch the snowfall.

"We both have the same idea," Evie says as she sits across from Martha.

"It is snowing again. I do not recall a time it snowed so much before Christmas."

"Yes, it started as I pulled onto the driveway. It's so very pretty." Evie watches flake after flake tumble over each other as she asks, "Are you doing okay Martha?"

"Oh yes. I woke and saw the snow and thought I would sit for a minute before Stan comes home. Stan went to check on Mr. Joe, from church. Do you recall the older gentleman who sits at the back of the church by himself?"

"I do remember him. He seems sweet."

"He is. He recently lost his wife of sixty-one years and is lonely. Stan goes to keep him company and play checkers when he is able, and I send a meal. Today he got chicken salad and soup. It should last him a couple of days."

"I'm sure he enjoys the company and the meal," Evie responds sincerely.

"So how about you? Did you find your friend?"

"Yes and no. I didn't get to see her, but I know where she works and so I'll see her soon. I walked around part of the town square today. It's a great little town. I met a wonderful girl at Crafts-N-More."

She smiles, "You met Amanda?"

"Yes. She is pleasant. I may go to her class tomorrow after I visit Ms. Pearl. She invited me to tea. I wouldn't want to turn down the opportunity to make new friends. I will need directions before I go. She didn't give me much more than the invitation to tea."

"Of course. It is not difficult to find."

"Wonderful. Thank you. Can I help you with dinner?"

"Stan should be home shortly. He is going by Mr. Washburn's grocery to see if he has any slow-roasted chicken left and some side items. I have some rolls I will warm, so there is not much to do."

"Oh, and I picked up a strawberry cake from the little food shop in town while I was out. I can't remember the name of the place but it's on the square."

"You mean The Little Food Shop?" Martha asks, giggling. "Their cakes are wonderful. Stan especially loves the strawberry cake. Thank you for thinking of us."

The door opens and Stan goes to Martha and kisses her. "Right on time for the food!"

Martha puts the rolls in to warm as Evie sets the plates, silverware, and drinks on the table. As soon as Stan takes the chicken out of the container, the savory smell of garlic and herbs drift through the kitchen.

"Wow!" Martha exclaims. "I did not realize how hungry I was until just now."

They finish setting the rest of the meal on the table and sit down to eat. Stan shares that Mr. Joe beat him at checkers three times and he was grateful for the chicken salad and soup.

Evie shares about her town adventures and reminds them to save room for the strawberry cake. Stan's eyes light up. Full, they decide to wait on the strawberry cake until later. Working together the kitchen gets clean in no time. The ladies sit in front of the fire, Martha with a magazine and Evie with her borrowed book. Stan excuses himself to go to his shop.

About an hour later he comes in and says he needs to go see a family from church.

"Their son got into some trouble today and is being disrespectful and difficult. I'll see what I can do to help. Don't wait up for me. Save me some strawberry cake." Stan teases as he leans in to give Martha a kiss.

"Oh Stan, do you know what you are asking of us?" She jokes right back. "Be safe sweetheart. I will pray."

Not sure whether it is her business, Evie asks, "Martha, is it Jedidiah who got in trouble today? Is it his family Stan is going to see?"

"Yes, it is. He is a good kid, smart too. He is trying to find his way. Hopefully, whatever he did, was not too damaging. Please keep him in your prayers. He needs it."

"I sure will."

They sit quietly each saying a prayer for Jedidiah and his family as large snowflakes drift aimlessly to the ground.

As they are getting ready to go to their rooms, they hear Stan pull up. When he opens the door, they hear him stomping snow off his boots.

"Goodness, it's cold out there. On the drive home I was concerned the fire might have gone out. It looks like it's still going strong. You put another log on there didn't you, Evie?"

"A woman has to do what a woman has to do."

Martha asks, "How are Jedidiah and his family?"

He pauses before he replies, "He knows what he did today was wrong. He was angry at his parents. I talked to the family, then went to talk to Mr. Washburn. Luckily, he won't press charges. He did say, however, Jedidiah is expected to pay for the repairs. I drove back to the McCollum's and told them of the proposal Mr. Washburn and I discussed. They agreed. Jedidiah will go to Mr. Washburn's grocery every day after school and half-day on Saturday until the price of the broken glass door is paid. Jedidiah looked relieved. I think this may have been a good scare for him, a wake-up call if you will. Thanks for the prayers. Any cake left?"

They laugh as they assure him there is a whole cake in the refrigerator. Deciding it was too late for cake everyone went to their rooms for the night.

Six

The snow stopped overnight. In the morning, the cloudless blue sky and fiery sun reflect off the pristine snow, trying to convince Evie it is seventy degrees outside. However, the outdoor thermometer reads twenty-two degrees.

This is the day You made Father and it's beautiful! Thank You, for the snow and the sunshine. It's a relief knowing You already know what today brings and You go before me. I ask You to prepare Ms. Pearl's heart and mind. Open her eyes, ears, and heart to me. Let her be comfortable with me and feel my love and compassion. Give me Your eyes Lord so I can see what You see and use wisdom. Let me speak in a way that helps her see Your goodness and graciousness, love, and kindness through me. May she be filled with joy and gladness as her heart beats for You. Thank You for rescuing us. You never let Your children down. I love You, faithful Father!

My sweet, devoted child. I know Pearl's heart as I am the One who created her and have been with her through the years. How can she not be comforted by your tender heart? Today, wisdom will accompany you. I love you with an everlasting love.

Putting on layers, Evie is ready for anything.

Stan stares out the window as Evie enters the kitchen to the smell of fresh-brewed coffee.

"Good morning. Everything okay?"

"Yes. It will be. Martha is not feeling well, so she is staying in bed a little longer."

Not wanting to pry, she asks if he will join her for breakfast. She assures him she makes a mean bowl of cereal.

"Sure, show me your cereal-making skills," he teases. They sit quietly and eat. After breakfast, he admits she does have skills when it comes to cereal.

He asks if she will be around the house or if she is leaving anytime soon. He would like to go up the mountain if she is staying. She assures him she will be here until later in the day when she goes to Ms. Pearl's house, she is glad to help. He thanks her and bundles up to go.

"I won't be gone long and won't be too far up the mountain if you need me." She nods as he opens the door, and a startling burst of air comes in.

She gets her Bible from her room and decides to sit in the kitchen. At the table, she is marveling at the see-through fireplace when one of the logs shifts and she jumps.

What is wrong with me? Gracious, loving Father my heart is heavy for my friends. I ask You to touch Martha's body and whatever is making her sick be revealed. Give wisdom to her doctors and let them speak life to her and her situation. All glory be Yours Father. Remind Stan his hope is found in You, and when he cries out, You will help him. Lead him and give him wisdom. Let him not grow weary. Remind them both who they are and whose they are. Comfort them as they lean into You; Your loving arms surrounding them, holding them tight. Show me what I can do for them. Let Your words be mine as I encourage and uplift them. I know Your faithfulness! We stand upon Your promises and wait expectantly on You.

"Those who live in the shelter of the Most High will find rest in the shadow of the Almighty." *Yes, Father!* As she continues to read Psalm 91, she feels peace rise within her. Eyes closed, soaking in what she read, she hears the still, small voice reassure her *"it is well."* She knows God is in control and the outcome will be better than anything she can imagine.

Martha comes out of her room, eyes puffy and nose red.

"Are you okay?" Evie jumps up from the table.

"Oh yes! I am better than okay. You won't believe what happened. I woke up sick to my stomach. This has happened with each of my pregnancies and the outcome led to heartbreak. I will make an appointment today with the doctor, but I already know I am pregnant. Stan knows it too. As my stomach was turning, I took my Bible and asked God to show me. I just let the Bible fall open. It opened to Psalm 91."

Evie's right eyebrow raises.

"I have read Psalm 91 many times before, but after reading and thinking about what it was saying to me today, in the peace and stillness of my room I heard, *"It is well."* Evie, it is well! God is in control, and I stand on His promises!"

As they embrace, Stan comes in, Martha sees his concern and goes to him. He holds her as she retells her story. Evie then shares her experience. Same scripture, same voice, same words of assurance.

Tears stream down Stan's face as he thanks God. Martha calls and sets an appointment for Friday to see her doctor. She tells the receptionist she believes she is pregnant. After the call, Martha goes back to bed and sleeps the most peaceful, restful sleep she has had in a long time.

Evie dusts and cleans the bathrooms, then prepares meatloaf and potatoes for dinner. After she puts the food in the fridge, she tells Stan she will not be home for dinner as she will go from Ms. Pearl's to the craft store for Amanda's class. She gives him instructions on how long to cook the meatloaf and when to put the potatoes on, along with the bag of frozen corn. Even if Martha does not feel like eating, Stan will have dinner and she will not have to fix anything.

Once finished she gets ready to leave for Ms. Pearl's house. Stan gives her directions including landmarks. If she leaves now, he tells her she should arrive at Ms. Pearl's house by 2:30.

As Evie drives the unpaved, back road toward Stan's church the fierce sun leaves gaps in the melting snow, revealing dirt roads and fields. Passing the fields, the towering pines confirm her approach to the church. Once past the church, she turns right, knowing she is close when she passes the house with the large oak tree with a tire swing. Counting the third driveway and the name **Daniel** on the mailbox assures her she found the house. She follows the drive up to a modest cottage, white with black shutters.

The house looks well kept, but tree limbs litter the yard and roof. The walkway is crowded with rocks. She straightens the rocks as she wonders if Ms. Pearl has any children to help her since her husband died.

Evie gently raps on the door. After waiting a few minutes, she knocks a little harder. Still no answer. Thinking she may have gone to town, Evie starts down the steps when she realizes there is a car in the driveway on the side of the house. Determined to have tea with Ms. Pearl, she rings the doorbell.

A few seconds later the door opens. Ms. Pearl is dressed like a movie star. Her shiny silver hair sits in a soft bun just above the nape of her neck. A hint of blush on her cheeks and a soft red color on her lips provide a glimpse of how lovely she must have been in her youth. She wears a flowy, full-length royal blue dress accented with silver heels, a matching silver bracelet, and a necklace, each with a red rose pendant and petite red rose earrings.

"Why Ms. Pearl, you look stunning!" Evie gushes as she enters the house. "How did you know I would come today? I hope you didn't do all this just to have tea with me."

"Oh no sweetie, I dress like this every day whether I leave the house or not. I want to be ready. Come in, let me take your coat. Have a seat and I'll start the water for tea."

She leaves for the kitchen as Evie looks around the small sitting room. The sun pours in the windows. A pastel, flowered loveseat sits across the room with a small homemade, empty table in front of it. Curiously, Evie looks around the undecorated room. Nails left in the wall are the only evidence pictures once hung there. The chair, the loveseat, homemade table, and curtains are the only things in the room.

"I don't have any homemade dessert dear, but I do have some leftover cheesecake pie with cherry topping. I bought it at the festival last weekend and it's very tasty." Ms. Pearl says as she enters the room and places the tray on the table.

"Sounds wonderful. Thank you." Evie replies, scooting to the edge of her chair.

"My pleasure dear."

As Evie takes the pie she asks, "Do you have any children?"

Ms. Pearl responds in a mechanical, practiced voice, "I had a daughter who died when she was 11. While visiting my sister at her farm she was helping in the barn when she tripped and fell out the loft door. She died on impact. That was almost 35 years ago."

Evie hesitates, then says, "I'm so sorry. What is her name?"

"Hazel."

"I can't imagine how heartbreaking the news was to receive. Again, I am sorry."

"Yes, well, thank you." The ladies sit quietly sipping tea.

"This pie is good. One thing I'll miss when my assignment is done is the food. It seems everyone in this town can cook well. Well, the food and the people, of course. You live in a warm and welcoming town."

"Well, I guess so," Ms. Pearl says quietly. "I don't have much contact with the townspeople. They think I am crazy and have gone over the edge since Henry died."

"Well, have you?"

"I don't know. I do know I am very sad without him and miss him so much."

Evie asks softly, "How long were you and Henry married?"

"Fifty-eight years. I was seventeen, he was twenty-one. We were so in love. He was better to me than I deserved."

"I'm sure you were wonderful to him too."

The room is silent. Evie wonders why she is here to help Ms. Pearl.

Father, I know I am here to turn your people back to You. I understand I may not learn everything I want to know in one visit but help her to trust me. I thank You, Father.

As she finishes her silent prayer Ms. Pearl says, "I was just wondering if I was truly good to Henry."

"Oh, I'm sure you were."

"I don't know. I just don't know."

"Would you like to talk about it?"

"No, I don't think so. Maybe next week when you visit."

"Oh, next week when I visit. I guess you would like company again?" She raises her eyebrows at Ms. Pearl.

"I would be honored to share another cup of tea with you dear." Ms. Pearl blushes lightly.

The room is quiet as they finish their tea and pie. Evie looks at her watch and tells Ms. Pearl she needs to go into town to see her friend at Crafts-n-More. As they walk towards the door Evie remembers Amanda's friend, Sarabeth.

Evie stops before opening the door, "You have lived here a long time, haven't you?"

"Yes, I have. All of my married life."

"Do you remember Ralph and May Ingram? They moved away maybe 13 or 14 years ago."

"Of course, I do." She smiles. "I haven't thought of May and sweet little Sarabeth in a long time."

"So, you haven't talked to them or know where they are now?"

"I'm afraid not. I wish I did. I never had to work, but after Hazel died there was no reason to sit at home all day, so I went to work part-time at a sewing shop downtown. I worked there until it closed about 10 years ago. It's where I met May. She worked part-time during the hours Sarabeth was in school. May was sad to leave Banderidge. She was fond of the town, and the school did a great job mainstreaming Sarabeth. She also mentioned Sarabeth had a sweet little friend she hated to leave."

"Oh, Ms. Pearl, is there anything you might remember from the last time you spoke to May?"

"We kept in touch for many years then it stopped. My letters went unanswered and phone calls led to recordings. That was three or four years ago. I figured they moved again. Ralph was in high demand in the computer world. Companies kept offering him more money and he followed the money. Last I knew, he worked for a company called Right Stuff in, no that's not it. Oh goodness. Let me think for a minute. Right, Right Cross, yes Right Cross in Colorado. May said she was tired of moving Sarabeth around the country. She also mentioned she, May I mean, hadn't been feeling very well."

"Thank you for the information. It is most helpful. I'll see you soon."

Backing the car down the driveway, Evie realizes she forgot to ask Ms. Pearl why she dresses so nicely every day. She makes a mental note to ask her next week.

Father, thank You for Ms. Pearl and the information she provided about Sarabeth's family. I feel one step closer in my search. I give You all the glory! Show me how to connect with Ms. Pearl. Guide me in what to say and do to lead her to You.

As she pulls into town, she decides she has time enough for a quick club sandwich at Snackerdoodle. She orders, knowing it will not take long.

The large wall clock with floating numbers says she has 20 minutes until Amanda's class. She finishes her meal, pays the bill, and still has a few minutes. Moving the truck to a spot in front of Crafts-N-More she sees movement at the back of the store.

Stepping into the store, Evie hears, "We are in the workshop area. Come on back." She makes her way to the back. "Evie!" Amanda squeals excitedly, hugging her.

"Okay, everyone. We'll start in a few minutes. Let's see if anyone else comes." Amanda announces, then turns to Evie. "I'm so glad you came. You're in for a real treat. We are going to make Pilgrim hats using felt, only this time we will put magnets on the back. If you are still here for Christmas, you will have to come when we make Christmas trees. They turn out so cute, but what a mess with all the little pom poms scattered across the workshop."

"Oh, here they come. Hi Shelby! Hi Sassy!"

Evie whips around as they approach. Calmly she smiles while her insides do cartwheels.

"Hi Sassy," Evie says as Anastasia passes by.

"Hey," is Sassy's only response. Evie watches as they find a seat at the workbench.

Amanda brings Evie a chair so she can watch. As she hands out the pre-cut pieces of the hat, Amanda explains they have everything they need on the table. Once they are finished, they are to let her know and she will attach the magnet.

Evie watches as one of the people from the support home needs assistance, but the other two do well on their own. She guesses one of the three ladies from the support home is Toni whose turkey she bought yesterday. There is only one other child besides Shelby, and he looks to be about seven years old.

Looking around the workshop table, her heart warms as she watches Anastasia help Shelby. As Shelby is placing the buckle on the hat, Anastasia helps guide her hand a bit. Evie remembers the pancake breakfast when she saw Anastasia and her family. Shelby was the child sitting by the elderly lady at breakfast.

Amanda speaks encouraging words as she passes by to see if anyone needs help.

"Good job! Great choice! I like the red buckle!"

Father, You know how to reach cold, distant, and guarded people. You know what will work with Anastasia. Teach me Your ways, Father. Help me be creative with her. Thank You.

"Okay. Anyone ready for the magnet?" The little boy confidently raises his hand. In addition to the silver glittered belt buckle on the hat, he added a wispy gray feather. She glues on the magnet and gives him a scarecrow color sheet while he waits on the others.

"Anyone else ready?"

"Me! Me! Me! Me!" Amanda moves toward one of the ladies from the support home as she waves her hand in big circles above her head.

"Oh Toni!" Amanda laughs. "Where did you get those googly eyes? They weren't on the table." Evie glances at Toni's felt hat. There, directly above the gold glittered belt are two googly eyes.

"I put some in my pocket last week when we made the turkeys," Toni explains, proudly. "I thought I might need them someday."

Amanda tells her, "And they came in handy, didn't they? It looks great. One of a kind," Toni's head bobs up and down enthusiastically, "but let's leave the supplies here. If you want to add something, tell me and we'll see if we can do it. Okay?"

Still smiling, Toni nods again. Amanda winks as she hands her a color sheet and moves to the next child. As she makes her rounds, she shows attention to each of her students. Amanda has a God-given passion and is doing His will.

At the end of class, Amanda reminds everyone next week is the last class before Thanksgiving and they will finish with cornucopias. As Toni walks by, Amanda calls her name.

"Toni, will your cornucopia have eyes next week?"

Toni turns her head and looks away, "Uh-huh."

"It's okay Toni, but no more in your pockets. I called you over to meet Ms. Evie. She bought your turkey yesterday." She rushes into Evie with such a big hug that Evie stumbles backward and must catch herself.

"Thank you! Thank you! Thank you!" Toni gushes. "Do I get my money now?" She turns and asks Amanda eagerly.

"We give it to you at the beginning of each month, remember? Did you already spend your money?"

"Well yeah, Ms. Amanda. It was festival weekend."

"Let me guess. You bought some home-cooked goodies, didn't you?"

She blushes and giggles, "Yep. I did."

"Well hold tight and you will get your money in December. Maybe someone will buy your Pilgrim's hat."

"Oh, I don't know. I may take this one home, but maybe someone will buy my corny thing next week."

As Evie stands at the door with Amanda, Anastasia walks by. She catches a sly look at Evie. When everyone leaves, Amanda locks the door and she and Evie finish cleaning up.

"You do a fantastic job, Amanda. You are definitely in the right line of work."

"Thank you. I love people and enjoy helping them feel good about themselves. I am especially fond of people with special needs." They finish cleaning and go back toward the door.

Amanda opens it. "Thank you again for coming tonight. It means a lot to me."

"It is my pleasure. I will be back again."

"Great! Come any time."

Evie drives leisurely out of town back to the house. She thinks on the amazing ways God works all things for the good of those who love Him and have been called according to His purpose. Father God loves the people He places in her care. He loves them so much He sent Evie here to help them. It reminds her of Jesus, who was sent to save the world and guide people to His Father.

Caught up in her thoughts, when she draws closer to the house, she sees the familiar soft gray smoke curling from the chimney as a few scattered flurries fall from the sky.

Warm air greets her as she opens the door. She is unaware of how cold it is outside until she feels the warmth. Stan scrapes the bowl of leftover mashed potatoes into a small container. Evie sets her purse on the table and shoos him aside.

"I'll take it from here."

He smiles, "It's all yours."

As Evie takes over, she sees two plates sitting by the sink.

"Did Martha eat too?"

"Yep. She was ravenous, her exact words, and ate quite a bit. She feels a little better. She had morning sickness with each of her pregnancies, but we know this one is different."

"Yes, it is." Martha says as she comes out of her room.

"Hi. I heard you're feeling better."

"Oh yes. Quite a bit better. Your meatloaf was delicious."

"Aww thank you. I'm glad you enjoyed it. Looks like plenty left for another meal too."

"Or a late-night snack," Stan adds.

"Oh, Stan. Yes, Evie. It will be perfect for before church tomorrow night." Martha says.

Evie tells them she will finish cleaning the kitchen, so they go to the living room.

"Would either of you like a hot drink before I join you? Hot apple cider?"

"Yes please!" Martha responds.

"Make that two." Stan chimes in.

A few minutes later she joins them.

"I guess you noticed, but it has been flurrying again. It started as a beautiful day with clear skies." Evie looks out the window.

"Yes, it happens around here but not usually this early in the season or as often." Martha squints and raises an eyebrow at Evie.

Evie chuckles, "What?" Shaking her head, Martha strongly believes Evie has a secret snow connection.

Stan and Martha cuddle up on one end of the sofa. He holds her close and caresses her hair. Every so often, he kisses her on her head. Evie cannot help but think what good, loving, wonderful parents they will be.

"How did your day go? Did your plans to see Ms. Pearl and go to Crafts-N-More work out?" Martha asks.

"It was a good day. I had tea with Ms. Pearl this afternoon. She is quite interesting. She even helped me with something I am working on."

"Anything we can help with?" Stan asks.

"Maybe. Do you recall Ralph and May Ingram? Their daughter, Sarabeth, was good friends with Amanda."

"I recall the Ingram family. I believe they attended Pastor Evans' church. Check with him. He might know something."

"I'll do it. Ms. Pearl kept in touch with them up until about six years ago. It's my understanding they moved often, but maybe, just maybe, they slowed down a little."

"And the craft store. How did it go?"

"It was fun. Amanda is amazing, patient, and kind with her students. They made felt Pilgrim hats with a magnet attached to the back. They were quite creative." Evie shares about Toni and her surprise googly eyes and seeing Anastasia.

"Sounds like you had a nice day," Martha says.

"I did and I'm tired. If you will excuse me, I think I will go get ready for bed. Good night."

"Good night, Evie." They respond as she collects the empty cups and takes them to the dishwasher. As she turns the doorknob to her room, she looks back through the kitchen into the living room and sees Stan helping Martha up from the sofa and pull her close.

Seven

The next morning Evie is up and out of the house early. Stan is scrambling eggs as she leaves for town. Before she leaves, she asks for directions to the library which opens at nine o'clock. He also tells her Pastor Evans' church office opens at nine-thirty. He suggests with it being a church night, Pastor Evans may not be there as early, but someone will be.

Excited that the information she has is more than what she started with makes it a win. Hopefully, she will be able to tell Amanda exactly where Sarabeth is before her assignment is over, otherwise, she will share what she does know.

The library does not open for another fifteen minutes so Evie goes to the square. She did not notice the store to the right of Hanson's Hardware when she was here yesterday. Sweeter Than Your Grandma, one of the smallest buildings on the square, looks like it cannot hold another person, and all parking spots in front are full. She parks two stores down. People are coming and going quicker than Evie has time to think.

As she opens the door three people, and the aroma of fresh-brewed coffee and warm pastries, sweep past her.

"Hello!" A friendly, plump woman says as Evie walks in the door.

"Hello."

"Sweetie, we have been going like this since five-thirty this morning. I know you are new to this area, but surely you have heard about our famous cheese and cherry Danishes. Homemade and delicious!"

As she approaches the counter, overwhelmed, she sees the Danish and thinks if they are half as good as they look, they will be amazing. As she stands there trying to decide between the braided pecan Danish or a couple of the mini pinwheels with apricot filling, several people come and go.

"This is not a decision that should take this long." She laughs to the woman behind the counter.

"I've seen people take longer. Take your time hon. Some things are just that important."

"Well, I've narrowed it down to about twelve items. No, I'm kidding but what would your suggestion be between the cheese or peach Danish?"

"Believe this or not, our absolute best seller is the cheese."

"Then I'll take the cheese Danish, please." She pays for the Danish and cup of coffee and sits at an empty small table.

"Wow!" Evie exclaims.

"I told you so." The woman behind the counter smiles.

"Now I understand why you stay so busy."

Finishing the last of her coffee, she tosses the cup and drives the block over to the library.

Father, as I continue my search for Sarabeth, would you please open doors to make this successful and lead me to those who have answers? Show me favor with everyone I encounter. Thank You.

Finding an open computer, she begins her search with Right Cross. She discovers their headquarters is in Littleton Colorado. The company employs about fifteen hundred people. Evie hopes one of them is Ralph Ingram. She writes down the address and telephone number, then reads more about the company. Next, she researches Ralph and May Ingram but finds nothing.

She stops to gather her thoughts and an idea occurs to her. Maybe Sarabeth is in special needs sports or other activities. She types in variations of special needs dance, Sarabeth Ingram, and Littleton, Colorado. Finally, about three pages in, she finds a brief article about a

Sarabeth Ingram leading a dance class in Littleton, Colorado. The article is dated February 2007 and goes on to say she hopes to one day own a dance studio. There is no photo nor any mention of Down Syndrome.

Thank You, gracious Father, for the article. I am grateful! It will be great if Pastor Evans has more information for me.

Encouraged but not satisfied, she leaves the library and goes to the church. On entering the building, the receptionist is on the phone and mouths. "Sorry" to Evie and silently signals her to have a seat. The nameplate on the desk reads Ella Markum. Ms. Ella looks as though she has worked here a very, very long time.

In the reception area, she is greeted with a soft flowery fragrance and warmth. The lighting is soft and calming and faint piano music is playing. Once the music stops and she hears no commercials, it dawns on her the music is live. She realizes it's coming from down the hall.

"Oh hon, thank you so much for your patience. Sometimes people just need to talk. I feel I should listen and pray with them as needed." Ms. Ella says to her while she gets a cup of coffee from the machine behind her desk.

"Would you like a cup, hon?"

Not one to pass up coffee Evie replies, "Yes, please. That would be nice. Your prayer with the caller was touching."

"Thank you, dear. I am but a mouthpiece for God to work through. What can I do for you today?"

"I'm Evie and I am hoping to speak to Pastor Evans."

"Pastor is here. On Wednesdays, he comes in around seven, before I even get here, and works on his message for the night's service. I try not to bother him unless it is an emergency. Is it an emergency dear?"

"Oh no, not at all Ms. Ella. I wouldn't want you to bother him. Pastor Stan suggested he may have information which can help me."

"He usually breaks for lunch around eleven-thirty if you would like to wait. That's about forty-five minutes, but you are welcome to sit here or look around. It's up to you dear."

"Well, I hear some beautiful music. Is it okay to go back there until Pastor comes out?"

"Of course, dear. Make yourself at home."

Evie follows the soul-soothing sound coming from the sanctuary.

"Eli! I wasn't expecting you to be the one playing the piano."

"What! Do you think my only talent is student ministries?"

Blushing, Evie laughs. "What brings you here?"

"I have a question to ask Pastor Evans, but he is busy until lunch. I followed the beautiful melody and here I am. How about you? Are you practicing for Sunday?"

"Oh no," he laughs heartily, "they don't let me play. That's when I use my youth director superpowers." He winks and continues, "I have something on my mind so I'm spending time in prayer and worship seeking answers."

"Oh. I'm sorry to interrupt you. I'll go and let you continue."

"It's okay. I'm pretty sure I have my answer."

Eli goes to his office to prepare, leaving Evie to sit in the quiet sanctuary.

Gracious Father, You are the answer to all our questions. We plan our course, but You are the one who directs our steps. You know the answer before it became a question. Guide Eli in the way he should go and ease his burden. You are so good and kind, Father. Thank You.

Evie never hears Pastor Evans come into the sanctuary.

"Good morning, Evie. Are you okay?"

Jumping as he speaks, she answers, "Oh. Hello. Yes, Pastor. How are you?"

"I am well. I'm sorry, I didn't mean to scare you, but Ms. Ella tells me you want to speak to me."

"Yes, I won't keep you but a couple of minutes as I know it is lunchtime. Can you give me any information on the whereabouts of the Ingram family? It's my understanding they attended church here while they lived in Banderidge."

"They did, but they were very private people. Not bad people, just very private."

"So, do you know anything about them since they left town?" He does not say anything for a minute but appears to be debating something.

"Evie, why are you asking about the Ingrams?"

"Oh," she giggles, "I'm sorry. I jumped right into it didn't I? Amanda, from the craft shop, told me about her childhood friend Sarabeth. She shared how close they were and what good times they had. Finally sharing with me her desire to know where Sarabeth is now. I think it might be nice to give her the gift of knowing. Did something bad happen?"

"Well," he hesitates, "as their Pastor at one time, I want to respect their confidentiality."

"I understand completely. I'll tell you what I know to this point Pastor. If you feel there is something you can share it will be great and if not, no worries at all. Is that okay?"

He nods.

"I found a 2007 internet article in the Littleton Times about a Sarabeth Ingram. It talked about her desire to have a dance studio of her own one day. Two things I know for sure is Mr. Ingram worked for Right Cross, which is in Littleton, and Amanda and Sarabeth were in dance together and Sarabeth was good at it. Also, Ms. Pearl said her last contact with the family was about six years ago after that the phone was cut off and letters unanswered."

Pastor Evans nods. "I'll tell you what I can. Mr. Ingram was top-notch in his profession and because of that, they moved often. He was here longer than any other job he previously had. He confided in me he liked our church and liked what we did in the community. He asked if he could continue to send his tithe check here until he found another church to attend."

He stops and looks at Evie. Rubbing his chin, he starts then stops again.

"It's okay Pastor. I don't want you to do anything against your judgment."

"Thank you for understanding, but I think this is okay." Then continues, "He sent his check for many years and several job changes. About six months before his last check, he wrote a letter and sent it along with the check. In the letter, he told me May was very sick and asked that I keep them in my prayers. He talked about Sarabeth and was concerned about how she would take May's death. The next time I heard from him, about a month after the letter, he sent a brief note with his check telling me May died. They were still in Colorado. I received maybe three more checks from him, and I believe, if my memory is correct, the last one was postmarked from Virginia in early 2008. I think his family lives in Virginia. That's about all I know."

"Is there any chance, at all, you still have the envelope the check came in?" She asks.

He laughs. "I doubt it but let me check. Be right back." Slowly shaking his head, Pastor Evans returns with an envelope in his hand. "It's a good thing for you Ms. Markham is old school and keeps everything, just in case we need it." He hands her the envelope, and she jots down the return address to her notebook.

"This may be all I need. Maybe Ralph moved closer to his family for Sarabeth's sake. Hopefully, they are still there. Thank you for your time."

Evie goes back to the library. Back at the computer, she types Falls Park, Virginia. It's a little town with a population of 4,400, located close to the mountains. There are not many opportunities for employment in Falls Park, let alone in Ralph's field of expertise. It is possible he drives into a larger city or works from home.

Curious, she checks how far it is from Banderidge to Falls Park. A trip there will take three hours and twenty minutes. Evie mentally makes plans. then realizes she is getting way ahead of herself. Slowing down. she decides her next step will be to send a letter to the last known address and wait for a response.

It is mid-afternoon and she wants time to write the letter and get ready for church service. Before she goes to the house, she stops at Mr. Washburn's store in search of office supplies. Walking toward the cashier, she sees Jedidiah working off his debt.

"Well, hey there."

"Hello, ma'am." He replies as he rings up her purchase.

"Will you be at church tonight, Jedidiah, or will you still be working?"

"Yes ma'am. I will be there."

"Good. I'll see you then."

"Yes ma'am and thank you for shopping at Washburn's today." She smiles as she waves goodbye.

Spending time with Holy Spirit for the words to put in the letter to Ralph gets the letter written quickly. Evie, almost jogging to the mailbox, watches as the mail carrier approaches. Swapping incoming mail for outgoing mail, Evie is relieved she makes it in time.

In the kitchen, tearing apart a head of lettuce Evie tells Martha about the letter to Ralph. As Martha reaches into the refrigerator for salad dressings, shredded cheddar, and the leftover meatloaf and potatoes, she asks how Evie found them. Chopping the carrots, red onion, and hardboiled eggs, Evie tells her about her visit with Pastor Evans. As they eat, Evie shares her hopes and plans if this is Sarabeth.

Shortly after dinner, they leave for church. Pulling onto the church lot, Evie is reminded of Jedidiah and tells Martha and Stan about seeing him at Washburn's earlier in the day.

"Uh-oh. That reminds me," Stan groans as he parks the truck, "I didn't find anyone to teach the class tonight. When Jedidiah and his family joined us, he made three in the class. I have three volunteers who committed to teach once a month, so it only leaves one week for me to beg, plead, and grovel."

"Oh, Stan." Martha looks at Evie, "It is not that bad. Someone always steps up before the groveling begins."

Laughing Stan adds, "Agreed. Beg and plead yes, but I've not yet had to grovel. Needless to say, no one has stepped up permanently. We are growing, and I do understand it's a commitment, but we need someone."

"They will come. Is it okay if I teach tonight?" Evie offers.

"Yes! That will be great! Thank you. Do you have anything prepared?"

"Preach the Word of God, right? Be prepared in season and out of season is what the Word says, and I am ready." Stan chuckles and nods.

There are fewer people tonight than on Sunday, but the young couple who moved from Tennessee return and that pleases Stan.

Father, they may be a small group right now, but they are a good group. Thank You for showing me this church building isn't going to be big enough to hold all the people who will come.

After worship, Stan reminds everyone about the annual Bring-a-Dish Thanksgiving meal right after Sunday service the week of Thanksgiving. He asks them to sign the sheet by the door for what they will bring.

Dismissing the students, two little ones cut off Jedidiah as they run to their class.

"Hello, again Jedidiah."

He responds politely, "Hello ma'am."

"Will you do me a favor? If I am going to be here a while, will you please call me Evie?"

"My parents won't like it if I do."

"Okay then, do you think they will agree to Ms. Evie?"

"I think so."

"Good. Well, come on in. It looks like you and me tonight."

Father, this is perfect. Thank You. Please be my mouthpiece and let what I say tonight make a difference. Help him feel comfortable with me.

Sitting in one of the other two chairs set out for the students, Evie asks, "Are you aware God has a plan and a purpose for your life, and He knew what it was before time began?"

"I heard something like it before, yes."

"Do you believe it?" He sighs and shrugs. "I know you don't know me very well, but if you feel comfortable, I'd love to hear your thoughts. I don't like to do all the talking."

He looks at her as if studying her, "The Bible says God has a plan for my life. Good plans and not a disaster to give me a future and a hope."

She nods, "I see you know your Bible."

"My parents make sure I know it. It's like, my parents think their plans for me override God's plans. I don't think they care what God's plan is."

Evie listens to this young man, arms across his chest and brows furrowed, sharing his heart.

When she is sure he is finished, she asks, "What are your parents' plans for your life?"

"To be a pastor. That's why they named me Jedidiah. Fred would have worked, but no, they wanted something from the Bible. I'm just glad I'm not a Moses."

Trying not to outright laugh, she continues, "What is your plan for your life?"

"To go away to college, far away, and have a career as a writer."

"What is God's plan for your life?"

"I don't know and at this point, I'm not sure I care." She nods gently.

"My parents shove so much "God stuff" on me all the time. I'm over it." Jedidiah looks at the floor, "I'm sorry Ms. Evie. I shouldn't have said that."

"Do you not mean it?" Jedidiah, thinking he may have gone too far, is quiet. Seeing a flash of concern cross his face, Evie wonders if it is the fear of God or his parents.

"Listen Jedidiah. You said it because it's how you feel. First, God is not mad at you for feeling the way you do. He already knows and continues to care about you. Second, I learned long ago we are not able to change people and we can't ask God to change them. However, we can ask God to change us, the way we see others, and change our heart towards those we have an issue with or have an issue with us. Does that make sense?"

"Yes."

"But it doesn't help you feel better, right?"

"No, not at all."

"It sounds like Pastor is finishing up out there. Would you like to pray?" Evie asks.

Jedidiah looks down and shakes his head, and Evie prays, "Loving Father, You have loved us forever and we can't do anything to make You stop loving us. Your Word tells us in so many ways and so many places how You love us, and we thank You. I am asking for Your peace to rise up and overflow within Jedidiah. May Your love encourage him to allow Holy Spirit to comfort him and begin healing his broken places. Guide him and place in him the desire for more of You. As he grows in You, gracious Father, show him Your plan for his life. The plan where he will be a blessing and best used for Your Kingdom. Help him trust me and reassure him what he shared tonight I will keep between us. Protect us as we leave and keep us safe. In Jesus' Name, Amen."

Jedidiah stands and pulls on his jacket. As he turns to leave, Evie calls to him.

"Jedidiah," she looks him in his eyes, "I meant what I said in my prayer. This conversation stays between us. I'll see you Sunday if not before."

"Yes ma'am, I mean Ms. Evie." He nods and half-smiles, "Have a good rest of the week."

"You too."

As they walk out together, Evie is lost in thought.

Father, it's obvious he is a good kid who's lost his way. How many kids would say have a good rest of the week? I know Your Word says to teach your children to choose the right path and when they are older, they will remain on it. Jedidiah has strayed off course and needs guidance to get back on the path. Show me my part in Your plan. Protect him on his journey back to You. Keep him from all harm, trouble, and evil during this time of questioning who he is and who You are to him.

Dearest Evie. Your compassion reaches deep into My heart. Your love for My people is beautiful. Remember, sometimes trouble comes as a result of disobedience and when it does, it is unpleasant but necessary. My promise is I will cause everything to work together for the good of those who love Me and are called according to My purpose. I have a purpose for Jedidiah, just as I do for all My children.

"Evie," Martha says gently, "Are you okay?"

"Oh yes. Is there something I can do to help?"

Martha assures her nothing needs to be done and they are waiting on Stan who is with the couple from Tennessee. Stan has his hand on the man's shoulder and their heads are bowed. Martha sits and Evie joins her.

Stan walks the couple to the door, and they continue talking for another ten minutes. After they leave, Stan sits with the ladies.

"I wish I had a church full of people like that couple."

Evie nods, "Stan, in this season, your concern is not to be the number of people who are coming to Grace Church, but the caliber of people. You will begin seeing more people like Steve and Amy and the couple from Tennessee. God will bring them to you. With the growth coming to Grace Church, God knows you need a good, strong, faithful group. Consider this a time of growing leaders as individuals and as a community. Big things are coming to this little church. You will need to be prepared for it. Just a heads up." She smiles.

"Wow," Stan says. "I'd say I got a prophetic word. Thank you. I'll be ready and so will the people God sends to us." He stands and the ladies lead the way to the door.

"Wait here a minute and I'll warm the truck."

While they wait, they talk about dinner for Karl and Renee. Stan parks the truck at the door and helps the women before turning to lock the church.

As they approach the house, Evie tells Stan she enjoyed her class even though it was only her and Jedidiah. She asks if it will be okay if she leads class while she is in Banderidge. Visibly relieved, he tells her he is more than okay with it.

Eight

Evie sits up on her bed and stretches. A thin blanket of white covers the ground outside. Propping her pillow behind her back she reaches for her Bible and watches the snow dance and swirl in the morning air.

Father, thank You for the pure white snow which reminds me of the precious Lamb, pure and white. The Lamb who was ridiculed, beaten, and died for me, and for mankind that doesn't always accept Him. He took our sins, the sins that separate us from You, upon Himself, so we can freely come to You. Thank You for Your Word, which is full of promises. You know the number of hairs on my head and have a plan for hope and a future for each one of us. I humbly thank You for allowing me to be part of the plan in the people I minister to. I seek You Father and ask Your words be my words when I speak to each of them. Help me to hear Holy Spirit when He prompts me. I pray all I do brings glory to You. I want to be pleasing to You and a blessing to others. Let it be a good evening. One that honors You and blesses Karl and Renee. Father protect the child in Martha's womb and let their long-awaited gift arrive healthy and whole and full of life. If theirs is still a season of trial provide them the strength and faith to make it through the storm. Lift Stan's arms when he feels weary. Encourage him as only You can when his heart is heavy, and the burdens feel like they are multiplying. Please send workers to help him harvest his field. Thank You, gracious Father. All glory and honor and praise be to You.

After about an hour of reading, she places her Bible on the table and gets ready for the day. She is looking forward to dinner because she has spent very little time getting to know Karl. She only knows what others have told her about him. It is time to find out for herself. She finds Martha in the kitchen cleaning the morning dishes.

"Good morning. We had breakfast already, but I saved you some. You know I had to hide it from Stan, or you would have been eating cereal this morning." Evie laughs.

"How that man stays so fit is beyond me. Thank you for saving me some."

"It is my pleasure."

"You must be feeling better today."

"I am. If I had not had the Word from God, I would think I have a virus, but I know what He told me. I already feel different this time."

"That's wonderful!" Evie enthuses. "So, what did you fix? It smells sweet and delicious."

"Pecan twirls and of course sausage for Stan. It should still be warm. Help yourself."

"Mmmmm."

Two pecan swirls and two pieces of sausage sit on her plate. She pours a glass of milk and sits at the table.

"What time is your doctor's appointment tomorrow?"

"Later in the afternoon. Since they have no available appointments for two weeks, they are allowing me to come at four forty-five. Taking into consideration my prior pregnancies, Dr. Rogers wants to see me as quickly as possible."

"Oh okay. I'll be going into town. Anastasia may be at work after school. I'm hoping she gets a break and agrees to eat with me. Or do you prefer me to be here when you get back?"

"Oh no, do what you have to do. We will be fine either way because God told me so."

Evie puts her dishes in the dishwasher and asks what needs to be done before dinner.

"Well," Martha says as she goes to get an onion, "since you did most of the cleaning the other day, we should be okay. If you want to double-check the guest bathroom and make sure the living room is in order, that will be great. I will start here, and you can join me. Stan assures me he will have plenty of wood for the fireplace and other than cooking some sides later, I think we are good."

"Sounds like a plan. I'll get started."

Since everything was still in order. Evie is back in the kitchen in no time. Martha is slicing the onion when Evie comes in.

"What can I do for you?"

"If you want to prepare the pan and pull the roast out of the refrigerator, I will brown it when I am through cutting the onions." Evie gets the pan, the oil, and the roast out, and turns on the stove to heat the oil. As Martha slices the last piece of onion, the oil is ready to brown the meat. Once brown, onions are added, covered, and placed in the oven for a long, slow cook.

"I think that is it until four o'clock. Do you have any other plans today, Evie?"

"Not a thing. Is there something I can do for you?"

"No. I may work on one of my projects and read a little and of course, take a nap."

"In that case, I may go explore the mountain if you think it's okay."

"Of course! There are trails, but with the snow, they may not be visible. Be careful and watch your step."

Entering her room to dress accordingly she looks out the window. Sporadically, large snowflakes gently drift aimlessly to the ground. At the kitchen door, as she pulls on the snow boots Stan bought for her safety, she tells Martha she will see her shortly then leaves for the mountain.

When she watched the snow dance and swirl from her window earlier, it was entertaining, but now, not so much as she begins her ascent, the wind dispatches fitful flurries in her face. As the wind stings,

Evie pulls her scarf up over her nose and mouth. The fireplace will be a warm welcome after this walk.

Father, I feel You closest when I am in nature. Like I imagine it was with Adam and Eve, nothing separating us. With the beauty of Your creation surrounding me and no pollution drowning out my thoughts or Your voice. Peace all around. Your works are amazing, and I am in awe of You. What an everlasting love You have for us. It's almost incomprehensible. Thank You Father for your daily peace, strength, and bread. You are all I need.

My sweet child, I will always love you. Always have, always will. Thank you for your obedience and faithfulness, fulfilling your purpose in this season of your life.

As she trudges up the mountain, she receives ministering from Holy Spirit. Nothing moves, no sound is heard on the mountain. Brimming with His peace, she enjoys the beauty of the last few flurries. Unaware of the time that past and how far she has gone, she decides it is time to go back. As she turns, something catches her eye. It is a tiny refuge of some sort. Amateurishly built, it does not look like it could provide much shelter. She guesses a child built it as a fort years ago and grew up without another thought about it. Not wanting to disturb it she goes back to the house. As she descends the mountain, the soft cascading smoke reaches through her scarf. Despite the hindered trail, she picks up her pace, eager to warm herself in front of the fire.

As she quietly enters the house, she wonders if Martha is resting. Taking off her boots, the only sound in the house is the soft hum of music coming from Martha's project room. Evie quietly goes to the fireplace hoping to warm her cold bones. Thawing, she thinks about Karl and Renee. Her heart is sad for Karl because of the confusion and lies the enemy has him wrapped in. As for Renee, she wants her husband and marriage restored to how it once was. Deep in thought, she hears Martha moving around in the kitchen.

"Cider?" Martha asks, offering her a steaming cup, "It helps warm the body and the soul."

"Thank you. Does it look like my soul needs warming too?" Evie smiles and accepts the cup eagerly.

"It looks like you have something pressing on your mind again. I imagine these assignments weigh heavy on you even with the knowledge God is in control."

Evie nods, reflecting on Martha's words as they sit in the nice warm living room.

Finishing her cider, Martha excuses herself to return to her project. Evie gets her book and goes back to the big, comfy chair. As she is beginning the next chapter, Stan comes in.

"I'm hungry!" He peers into the living room at Evie. "Hey there. Are you hungry?"

"Honestly, are you ever not hungry?" She laughs.

"Sure! Right after I push away from the table, but it doesn't last long. How about I fix some grilled cheese and bacon sandwiches and soup?"

Martha comes up behind him, "That sounds great! May I help?"

"No, my lady, you may not." He bows and kisses her hand in jest. "You may go back to what you were doing."

"Oh Stan. You are so silly. Sweet, but silly." Cheeks pink, Martha leaves the room.

Instead of returning to her project, she gets her book. When she comes back, she sits on the sofa across from Evie. The mouth-watering smell of bacon pours over into the living room causing Evie's stomach to rumble. Stan calls them in for lunch.

"This is wonderful," Evie says as she brings another spoonful of soup up to her mouth. "It seems I can't get warm after my mountain trek, but this sure is helping. Thank you, Stan."

"Oh. You went up the mountain?"

"I did. It was incredibly peaceful."

"That's why I like going up there. Best place to pray. Maybe 'cause I'm closer to heaven when I'm up there." He winks and Evie laughs while Martha smiles and shakes her head. Leaning over, Stan kisses her cheek.

"I'm all yours love."

"And I would not want it any other way. I am blessed!" She clears the dishes away.

"Oh yeah, when I was on the mountain, I found a little shelter. It was crudely built like something a child would make. Have you seen it?"

"I have."

"Was it here when you bought this place?"

"It was."

"Do you know anything about it? Who it belongs to or if it has been used recently?"

"I do, but I've been sworn to secrecy. Top secret information that requires clearance and approval. Sorry."

She squints at him.

"Top secret and clearance. I see."

Martha giggles, "Oh Stan, I am sure she is clear."

He grins, "I don't know, she looks kind of suspicious to me. How can I be sure she can be trusted?"

"Hmph." She replies.

"I'm running to town for a few supplies. Can I get anything else while I am out?"

"No thank you," Martha hugs him, and he kisses her forehead.

"I'll be back shortly then."

The ladies prep the side dishes, set the table, and anything else to be ready for their guests. Evie realizes Stan never told her who built the shelter.

Returning from town, Stan pops his head in the door.

"Need anything from me, my love?"

"No sweetheart. but thank you. We are looking good."

"Yes, you are! I will be in after I put the supplies in the shop." Fifteen minutes later, he is back in and bragging about how good the house smells when the doorbell rings.

"Perfect timing," Stan says as he goes to the door to welcome Karl and Renee. The roaring fire is warm and inviting and Karl went straight for the comfy chair. After she hugs Stan, Renee makes her way to the kitchen to see if she can help.

"Renee! You look lovely!" Martha says. Renee, wearing a navy-blue one-piece flowy pantsuit with glittery silver pumps and large, silver, hoop earrings, smiles weakly.

"Thanks. We don't do much together lately, so I am taking advantage of this 'date.' Although honestly, I doubt he has even noticed."

"But you do look very pretty." Evie agrees as she hugs her.

"Everything is ready. Are things any better?" Martha quietly asks.

"No. He has become protective of his phone and seems more secretive. He won't share his feelings with me or what's going on. We are more like roommates than husband and wife. I'll keep trusting him, for now, but I can't make any promises if I find out he has another woman." Martha looks at her sympathetically.

"I understand, but God is faithful. Have you talked to Pastor Evans?"

"No. I'm, well, you know, I like Pastor and Ms. Alice, but" Renee struggles, "but, I'm not comfortable taking this to them."

"I think they will understand and provide wise counsel. Surely, others have gone to them with the same or worse situations."

"I know, but I don't think Karl will be very happy if I talk to them."

"Oh. I see." Martha nods. Evie's heart breaks for Renee.

"We will keep praying for renewal and restoration of your marriage," Evie assures Renee.

"Smells good in here. Are you holding out on us?" Stan jokes as he and Karl walk into the kitchen.

"Yup," Evie jokes, "it's all gone, and it was delicious!" They laugh, even Karl, as they take a seat around the table.

"This looks fantastic Martha," Renee says.

"Thank you. Evie helped. Having her here is a blessing."

"Let's give thanks." Everyone bows their head as Stan thanks God for the meal, the ladies for preparing it, for friends, and for their time together.

When the meal is over Evie brings out the strawberry cake she bought when she was in town earlier in the week.

"Oh, man!" Stan exclaims. "Strawberry cake. My favorite!"

"No offense," Karl laughs, "but aren't they all your favorite?"

"I bought it the other day when I was in town, remember? It was on the bottom shelf of the fridge and forgotten. I found it when I was looking for something this morning."

A visible crease grows between Stan's brows, as he rubs his chin. "No way," Stan whispers as he shakes his head. "You mean to tell me strawberry cake has been in my refrigerator? All week? And I could have been eating it?"

Karl shakes his head as laughter fills the room.

"You're slipping man. Once upon a time, you could smell strawberry cake through a refrigerator door." Karl teases.

They talk, joke, and drink coffee as they enjoy the strawberry cake. Stan suggests moving to the living room now that everyone is full and lazy.

As they move to the living room Karl says, "Hey man, before we sit down why don't you show me your latest project." They go to the shop with the promise of not being gone long.

By the warmth of the fireplace Renee says, "The man who brought me here tonight and sat at the table enjoying himself is like my Karl. It is almost like old times. He hasn't been like this in quite some time. I miss him so much." A tear streaks her face.

"We know what the power of prayer can do Renee. We stand on God's promises with you. Do not grow weary. God is faithful to His promises." Martha speaks with authority and boldness.

Meanwhile, in the shop, Karl confides to Stan he is considering a divorce.

"Divorce? The past few times we've talked, you never told me of any wrongdoing on Renee's part. She's not been unfaithful, right?"

"Renee appears loving around people, like tonight, but the truth is she is cold towards me. She's not affectionate or happy anymore. I don't believe she loves me and honestly, I don't love her like I once did. We've been together too long and have drifted apart." Karl continues his argument of why he should divorce Renee. After about fifteen minutes Karl stops talking.

They stand there looking at each other for a minute, "Karl, I love you, man. I feel we have mutual respect, and I appreciate your friendship. You come to me because you know I'll be honest and straightforward which is what I am going to do. You didn't say Renee was unfaithful to you, so I'll guess she hasn't been. I'm sure you already know this, but it's not God's will for you to divorce her. Please spend time in prayer and maybe even consider talking to a counselor. Either with Renee or on your own."

"I'm not seeing a counselor," he spats, "there is nothing wrong with me. It's Renee."

Stan nods, "I see."

"I'm sorry man." Karl hangs his head. "I mean no disrespect, I'm just tired of not knowing what to do, whether to stay or go."

"The answer has already been given to you. It's on you whether you do the right thing or not. Renee loves you and wants to continue being your wife."

"Thanks for being honest and upfront. You're right, it's why I come to talk to you and respect you. Whatever I decide, know I've heard you."

When the men come back in the women are talking about recipes. The men join them and the air in the room tenses up. Martha quickly changes the subject.

"Your baby should be home on break soon, is that right? She must be excited to have only one more semester."

Renee beams, "Yes! Nia will come home for Thanksgiving then be home the second week in December for the holidays, and I can't wait! I miss her so when she is gone." As the ladies talk about Nia, Evie watches Karl. Crossing his arms across his chest, he sinks in his chair. Sighing and mumbling under his breath he finally stands and announces it is time to go.

"Already?" Renee asks, confused by his abruptness. He glowers. As she stands, she thanks Martha, hugs them, and says goodbye. As she walks towards the door, she winks at Evie and thanks her for hiding the strawberry cake from Stan. Karl shakes Stan's hand, hugs Martha, and says goodbye to Evie.

The three of them are left standing in the living room.

"Stan," Martha says, "Is everything okay? Did I do something wrong by bringing up Nia?"

"No sweetheart. You did nothing wrong." He hugs her and tells them, "Karl is in trouble and needs our prayers."

"Is he in trouble with the law?" Martha asks as she goes to the kitchen with Evie.

"No. It may be even worse." Stan follows. As he opens the dishwasher, he explains, "Karl is looking for something this world will never satisfy. Continue to pray for him. God will work it out."

After the kitchen is clean, Evie asks if there is anything else she can do before she goes to bed. With nothing more, she goes to her room and prays.

Oh, Father. You are wise like no other! Hear the cries of Your children! Our hearts are heavy for Karl tonight. He is hurting and no doubt confused. What he needs is more of You Lord! Only You know where his brokenness comes from and what is happening. Show him Your Glory. Lead him closer to You. I know You have this, and tonight was a part of Your plan. Strengthen Renee. Let Your peace consume her hurt places and help her remain humble and loving toward him. Renew and restore their marriage to even better than before. Thank You, gracious Father.

Sweet Evie, all is well.

Thank You Father for comforting me.

Taking her Bible from the table, the last thing she reads is in the first chapter of Philippians verse six, *"And I am sure that God, who began the good work within you, will continue his work until it is finally finished on that day when Christ Jesus comes back again."* As her head begins to nod, her last thought is, yes Karl the good work within you.

Meanwhile, Stan and Martha are preparing to do their devotional when he says, "We need to pray for Karl and Renee."

"God, our mighty refuge! Our ever-present help in times of trouble. The Great I Am! He is among my flock because You placed him in my life for this time. Only You can bring him what he needs and provide answers. Lord, help him to find rest in You and not seek it in this world. Let Renee not grow weary during this time of trial. In Jesus' Name, Amen."

Stan hugs Martha close and whispers, "I love you and thank God for you daily."

"I love you too, sweetheart."

Nine

The next morning, the irresistible smell of bacon fills the house, courtesy of Stan. Evie sets the table and scrambles the eggs but neither one dare to make biscuits. They will not even consider it because Martha's biscuits are the best.

After breakfast, Stan has work to do at the church, Martha works on her project, and Evie decides to go up the mountain again.

They gather back at the house for a light lunch in the afternoon.

"Evie, did you enjoy your walk up the mountain?" Stan asks.

"Absolutely! I imagine each season displays its beauty."

"Maybe you should stick around and see for yourself." He smiles and winks.

She smiles, "I may do it, but you know, I don't have much say in the matter. You will have to talk to my Father about it." They know full well if Evie is still here come spring it is God's call, not any of theirs.

Martha is quiet during lunch. Evie asks if she is okay.

"Yes. I have been reassuring myself of God's promises this morning. I keep reminding myself all is well. God said it, so it is."

"God is faithful Martha." Evie comforts her, "He keeps His promises and knows the desires of our heart. He won't fail you."

"I know. I mostly remember but every so often doubts slide in. I know this precious child I am carrying will be born and born healthy."

They sit at the table for a while after lunch. Stan sharing his hopes for Grace Church with Evie. He is aware his vision is big, but so is the Lord.

After they clean up from lunch, Evie decides to go into town early and see if Amanda is at the craft store before she goes to find Anastasia. When she leaves, Stan and Martha cuddle up on the sofa, reading.

She does not see Amanda when she arrives at Crafts-N-More. Guessing the woman at the counter is Amanda's mother, Evie walks over to introduce herself.

"Hello. Is Amanda here today?"

"No. Not today. Evie, isn't it?"

"Small town living," Evie says as she shakes her head and laughs. "You must be Amanda's mom."

"Yes, I am, Brenda. Amanda described you perfectly. I knew it was you by your peaceful nature and gentle voice, and the fact yours is a new face in town, of course. Amanda has a project due before Thanksgiving so she asked to only work on Tuesday for the next couple of weeks so she could finish it up."

"I know she won't give up her Tuesdays. She is very passionate about her class. Would you please let her know I was by to say hi? I'll stop again."

"I sure will. It is a pleasure meeting you."

"Thank you, Brenda. It is nice to meet you as well."

Crossing the street, Evie decides to go to Pastor Evans' church. As she walks in, Ms. Ella smiles and welcomes her. Evie explains she has time before she meets someone. They talk for a minute or two before the phone rings.

While Evie waits, Alice comes in. "Evie! Hi. What a nice surprise. How are you?"

"Hello. I am well and hope the same of you."

"Yes, I am. I am getting ready to decorate for Thanksgiving."

"I have about twenty minutes, would you like some help?"

"That would be nice. I have a few ladies who usually help, but they are so busy with other things I am going to do it myself. Nothing fancy, of course."

All the sweet fragrance built up behind the door of her office spills out into the hall when Alice opens the door. Evie spots the source; beautiful, deep red roses, too many to count, fill a large, delicate vase decorated with fading angels, which sits beside Alice's worn Bible.

"Wow! Those are lovely." Evie gushes at the abundance of roses.

"Oh, yes. Thank you. Rick, Pastor Evans, bought them just because. He placed them in my momma's vase and left them on my desk as a surprise yesterday."

"How thoughtful."

"Oh yes. He is a good one. He's always looking for ways to show his love." Alice explains as they gather the decorations and go to the sanctuary.

Alice glances at the clock and gasps. An hour has passed. "Oh no. It's been longer than twenty minutes. You're late."

"No problem. It isn't a scheduled appointment. I am going to visit someone and I still am. I was enjoying myself and honored to help you."

"Thank you, Evie. You are very kind." The ladies say goodbye and Evie waves to Ms. Ella, who is on the phone again.

She parks to the right of Wild Horses. Considering Anastasia has probably only been working an hour or so, Evie figures it is not long enough for her to have a break.

Father, please make a way. Prepare Anastasia's heart for me. Let her guard be down and for her to accept my visit today. Be my voice, please Father.

Evie enters the store. Anastasia is hanging clothes on a rack.

Without turning to see who walks in Anastasia calls out, "Hello."

"Hello."

Anastasia stops what she is doing but does not turn around. She recognizes the person behind the gentle response.

When Anastasia turns, Evie is smiling at her.

"Can I help you find something?"

As Evie cautiously approaches Anastasia, she says, "I found what I came in for Sassy. I've been looking forward to seeing you all week." Anastasia cocks her head. She stares at Evie.

"What do you want? I mean, like, what?"

"Well, I was concerned last weekend when you left so quickly. I wasn't sure what happened and wanted to check on you. I hope I didn't do anything to upset you because if I did, I want to apologize."

Anastasia looks around. "Is this some kind of joke? No one, ever, cares about my feelings. What do you want from me?"

"I'm sorry no one cares about your feelings. It must hurt. I don't want to be like everyone else."

Brows furrowed, she looks at Evie and shakes her head. She looks away then back at Evie again. "No. You didn't upset me. I have work to do so if you don't need help, I'm gonna finish hanging these clothes."

"Okay then. I need help." Anastasia wheels around, cheeks flushed trying to decide how to respond. "You're messing with me now!" Anastasia growls. "You need to get the…"

Just then another shopper comes in.

"Hello," Anastasia says, without taking her eyes off Evie. "Can I help you?" She turns away from Evie and walks toward the customer.

Oh, Father, this is not going well. She looks like she wants to cause me bodily harm.

Patience Evie. I know what is going on inside and out. Trust me.

I do trust You Father. Thank You.

Evie looks at the shoes and the jewelry, and concludes this store had nothing in her style. Anastasia cashes out the customer and starts back toward Evie. Quickly, Evie grabs two pairs of earrings.

"Okay, I need help. Which pair is me?" She asks, completely serious. Anastasia's mouth drops open, then, covers her mouth. Evie hears a muffled giggle from behind her hands.

"Did you even look at them before you just grabbed two pairs of earrings?"

Evie looks down at the earrings in each hand.

"Hmmm." They both laugh. And as much as Anastasia tries, she cannot be mad at Evie.

"Well?"

"What?" Evie asks when she catches her breath. "Are you saying that skull and crossbones and fire breathing dragons are not my styles?"

"Umm. Not really."

Evie finally stops laughing, "When I met you the other day, you touched my heart. You may not understand exactly what that means, but I work with all kinds of people with all kinds of problems and can tell when someone is hurting. I mean you no harm. I am in town on business, but during this time I would enjoy getting to know you better and your story. Would it be okay?"

Anastasia looks at her. Completely unreadable. Eventually, she nods.

"But why? No one likes me and no one cares."

Surprised by her bluntness, the thought of what Anastasia said breaks Evie's heart. She gently replies, "Well I do. Do you get a break? Or do you get off early enough to get something to eat after work?"

"My grandmother expects me home right after work. I usually catch a ride by 7:30. She won't believe me if I tell her I am with an adult, but I'll call her and try." When she returns, the look of confusion answers Evie's next question.

"Well?" Evie asks, eyebrows raised.

"I can't believe it. She says it's fine. My aunt's in town. She will help her bathe the kids and get them to bed, so I don't have to tonight. As long as I'm with you, it's okay. How does she even know you?"

"Small town?" Evie shrugs. Evie has no doubt how it worked out.

"What are you going to do for three hours? Maybe you won't feel like coming back."

"I have a friend who has a doctor's appointment shortly. I will run by the doctor's office first then maybe to the library. I'll be back at seven-thirty, then we'll go eat. Sound good?"

Wary, she says, "Yup." Evie wonders what it will take for Anastasia to trust her.

Evie finds the doctor's office, but the doors are locked. She knows Stan and Martha are inside because she parks by their car. As she turns to go back to the truck, a woman unlocks the door and tells her they are closed. Evie explains she is here for her friends. Upon hearing she is with Stan and Martha, the woman insists she comes in because it is too cold to sit outside. As Evie waits, she prays for Stan, Martha, and the baby and gives thanks for the change in Anastasia. She also prays dinner goes well tonight.

"Evie! What are you doing here? I thought you had somewhere to be." Martha's eyes are brighter than usual as she hugs Evie.

"I've already been. But how about you? What did the doctor say?" Stan and Martha are smiling. Evie realizes the brightness in her eyes is an overflow of joy.

"Dr. Rogers confirmed that I am pregnant. He believes I am eleven or twelve weeks along. I have never made it to eleven weeks and had no idea I was pregnant. I have been tired and not fully myself for a month or so, but I would not have guessed it until I started having morning sickness this week. I had no other typical signs."

"This is wonderful news. I'm glad I'm here to be a part of it. What is the doctor saying about your health? Is he doing anything different this time?"

Stan pipes in, "He told her to rest, eat well, and no rock climbing until at least the beginning of the third trimester."

"Well, we can help with the first two, but you know how she feels about her rock climbing," Evie replies without missing a beat.

Evie still has time before she picks up Anastasia, so she goes to the library. She spends about twenty minutes looking through books for sale. When she gets to Wild Horses, she runs in to let Anastasia know not to hurry, but she is out front in the green truck waiting for her. Five minutes later, Evie watches as Anastasia shoves the door open, runs down the steps, and flings open the truck door. With a huff, she pulls the door closed and crosses her arms over her chest.

"Hey Sassy."

"Hey."

"Everything okay?"

"Yeah."

"Okay then, where do you want to eat?"

"Tony's?"

"Sure. Remind me which way to go?"

"That way."

Evie, following the direction of Anastasia's finger, wonders what put her in a foul mood.

"Oh wow!" Evie says as they enter the parking lot. "This place is full."

"Yeah." Anastasia slumps down in the seat. "Let's go somewhere else. I don't wanna go in there. They'll stare at us."

"Sweetheart, you want Tony's pizza so let's get pizza."

"You don't care if people see you…with me?"

Heart piercing, Evie shakes her head.

"Come on Sassy, let's get pizza."

They go in and a few people do stare at them.

"How can you stand everyone staring at us?" Evie does not respond as she searches for an open table.

Once seated she says, "Sassy, first, not everyone is staring at us. Second, why do you care?"

"Feels like everyone. I don't care. If they think I'm a freak, then so be it."

"I think you do care, or you wouldn't have said anything. It's best to be who you are and not try to be someone you aren't, just to fit in." Sassy shrugs as the server approaches the table.

"Anything you want Sassy."

She proceeds to order two large pizzas, one cheese only and one fully loaded with pepperoni, ham, both types of sausage, ground beef, and both types of bacon, a large side of cheese fries, and a cola. Evie orders a lemonade and a slice of sausage and mushroom pizza.

They talk casually while waiting for the food to arrive. Initially, any question Evie asks is answered with one word. School is fine. Work is okay. Sports yuck and so on. Once the food arrives, Sassy eats three pieces of pizza and almost all the cheese fries. She finally stops, reaches for her cola, and looks at Evie.

"What?"

"I'm glad you're enjoying it."

Sassy picks up another slice of pizza, "Sorry I was mean to you at the festival and earlier when you came to see me. You were nice to me, and I didn't know why. I still don't understand, but I don't think you want to hurt me."

"You're forgiven. Since I'm new here it probably seemed weird that I was trying to be a friend. I saw you put the crosses in your pocket and when you got caught doing it. I didn't want you to get in trouble, so I paid for them."

"Yeah. So, you know how many I took then?"

"Yes."

Sassy keeps her eyes down and eats her pizza.

"I had a reason for taking the crosses. I wanted to give them as Christmas gifts. We don't get to exchange gifts and Grandmother never gets anything. I wanted her to have something nice this year. We each get one gift from Grandmother. There is no extra money and Grandmother is stuck raising the four of us. She gets a little extra money for Shelby because she has special needs. All my money goes to help her pay bills. I wasn't just stealing." Evie smiles.

"So, when you entered the pie-eating contest, it wasn't because you like pie. You did it so you could help feed your family."

"Yeah. I do what I can. Nobody cares about us. We're on our own. Um," she hesitates, "and I only gave you two of the crosses."

"I know. I knew the other day, but I had paid for three of them, so they were all yours. Your debt was paid."

"Uh, also, since I'm coming clean, I have to tell you something else."

"What is it?"

Chewing her bottom lip, Anastasia continues, "I'm not supposed to be here right now. That's why I was mad when I left work."

"I don't understand."

"Grandmother called. She wanted me to come straight home after work because my aunt wanted to see me. I was scared you wouldn't like me anymore. I was trying to be normal so you would, maybe, be my friend so I didn't tell you."

"Well then we will ask for a takeout box for the rest of the pizza and we will get you home," Evie speaks calmly, realizing how fragile Anastasia is.

"Will you ever talk to me again?" She asks, tears brimming her eyes.

"Of course, I will. I'd like to meet your grandmother, so she knows me."

"Really?" Her eyes widen.

The server approaches with two pizza boxes and the bill.

She smiles, "I had a feeling you might need a couple of boxes. You can pay the cashier on the way out. Have a great night."

Anastasia is quiet as she slides the leftovers in the box and cuts her eyes at Evie.

"I ordered too much pizza, so I would have extra to bring home."

"I know. It's okay. Let's get you home."

Anastasia directs her as they drive. Evie explains if they are going to be friends, she will have to be honest always and try to trust Evie. She reassures her again she cares about her and will not hurt her. Leaving the lights of town behind, Evie wonders exactly how far out Anastasia lives. It is about as far out as Stan and Martha's house only in the opposite direction.

The old shack, wood planks rotting and warping, is weather-worn and run down. As Anastasia reaches for the door handle, Evie gently touches her arm. She reaches into her purse and pulls out the other two crosses. Smiling softly, Evie hands them to her.

"I bought these for you and was hoping I could give them back to you one day."

A tear rolls over her cheek and onto her shirt.

"I, no one," Sassy wipes her eye, where another drop is forming, and whispers, "thanks."

When they get inside the door, she calls to her grandmother. Coming out from the back, even though she sees Evie standing at the door, she continues to scowl.

"Anastasia, put the pizza in the kitchen and help your aunt with the kids. I will talk to you later," her grandmother glares as she speaks. Evie is a little frightened until the woman turns to face her with an entirely different disposition.

"I'm sorry I had to show that side of me, but she must obey and believe I am serious. She has been a handful lately. I am Mary, Anastasia's grandmother."

"Hi, Mary. I'm Evie. Very nice to meet you."

"Ah yes, I think I remember seeing you at the festival. Green beans, right?" Evie laughs.

"Yes. I was there and was spooning out green beans."

"It's funny the things we remember."

She talks briefly with Mary and asks if it would be okay for her to spend time with Anastasia. Mary is grateful someone can show her granddaughter the attention she is not able to provide. Evie says goodbye and asks her to tell Anastasia she said goodbye.

Well, it went better than expected. Thank You, Gracious Father! I am grateful. My heart is heavy for this family though, Father. I am asking and believe they will have a new, safer, and bigger house. I pray they lack for nothing and protection over each one of them. I don't know what it looks like, but You do, and my trust is in You, Lord.

It is late when she returns to the house. The office light is the only light on, so she knows Stan is still awake and possibly preparing for Sunday. Silently, she enters her room and goes to bed.

Ten

The next morning, Evie reads the Bible and prays. Martha fixes sandwiches for lunch and invites Evie to join them. Afterward, Stan and Martha leave to meet someone at church. Evie decides to read for a bit before she tackles some housework. Fireplace roaring, Evie curls up in the comfy chair. She has been reading for about twenty minutes when there is a knock at the door. She sees Karl through the glass.

"Hi Karl."

"Hey. Is Stan here?" Karl responds tersely.

"No, he had business at the church. Anything I can tell him for you?"

"No, it's okay." Distracted, he turns to leave. "Hey Evie, are you a counselor?"

"Not exactly, but I do much of the same thing that a counselor does. It's difficult to explain, but I help people."

Head down, staring at the porch floor, "I don't think you could help me; as a matter of fact, I don't think anyone can help me. Would you let Stan know I may stop by later?"

"I sure will and Karl, no one is helpless if they want to be helped."

Turning to leave, Karl hopes the look he gives her does not give away what he thinks about her comment.

Evie continues reading after Karl's visit but cannot focus.

Oh Father, how do I help Karl? I know it's not wise talking to a married man alone. Being able to help him seems almost impossible, but I know all things are possible with You Father. Please show me how to minister to him. I pray he thinks about what we say. Give us the words he needs to hear and words to help him truly know You and find a new and improved life in You. You are merciful. Thank You!

Feeling better, she goes to the kitchen and unloads the dishwasher.

"Hey Evie," Stan calls as they come in the door. "We went the long way home and picked up a pizza for dinner. Are you hungry?"

"Is it from Tony's?"

"It sure is."

"Count me in." She replies as she gets the paper plates and napkins while Stan pours tea. Martha yawns and rubs her eyes as they sit down.

After Stan prays over the meal, Evie asks, "Martha, are you feeling okay?"

"Oh yes. I am fine, but a little more tired than usual. I will probably do a couple of things to get ready for service tomorrow then go to bed. I want to be well-rested."

As Evie is reaching for a second slice of pizza she says, "Karl stopped by to talk to you. He didn't say much but seemed distracted. He said to let you know he came by."

"Thanks. I'll call him after dinner." When they have their fill of pizza, Stan clears the table.

"That was an easy clean-up." Stan smiles, obviously proud of his pizza idea.

"Yes, it was a good choice dear," Martha giggles. "Thank you for thinking of me."

"Always sweetheart, but I've got to be honest, it wasn't all for your benefit." He winks and pulls Martha close.

He kisses her forehead, "Now will you please go to bed?"

"I will but I have a couple of things to do before I go."

"Okay. I'll call Karl and check back shortly." Martha smiles sweetly at Stan who keeps his eyes on her as he walks backward towards the office.

"Okay, let's divide and conquer so you can rest," Evie says, clapping her hands together. "What can I do for you?"

"You are such a blessing. I thank God for sending you here during this season of our lives. I am going to make some lemon poppy seed and blueberry muffins for church. I also need to iron Stan's shirt for sweet Abi Grace's dedication tomorrow. What a privilege to be able to celebrate with Steve and Amy as they acknowledge Abi Grace is a gift from our Father and dedicate her back to Him."

"And soon they will celebrate with you when you dedicate your precious little one as well." Radiant joy flowed from Martha. "Which do you prefer I do?"

"Do you mind ironing?"

"Not at all! I'm glad to do it. Nothing I can do to help with the muffins? It won't take me long to iron."

"How about gathering the dry ingredients from the pantry? Here is the recipe."

"I'm on it."

Evie wants to do all she can to lessen Martha's burden. Once she gathers the ingredients, she goes to the laundry room to iron. There are a few other clothes in the pile, so she irons those too. When she finishes, she goes back to the kitchen where Martha is sliding the pans in the oven.

"I will check them in 20 minutes."

"Will you let me check them in 20 minutes and you go to bed?"

"Well, I am thinking about unwinding with a cup of hot tea in front of the fire while the muffins bake. Will you join me?" Martha asks.

"Of course, I will."

They sit drinking their tea before the timer goes off. Martha tests them, determines they are perfect, and sets them out to cool. After Evie finally convinces Martha to let her clean the kitchen and put up the muffins, Martha places a container on the counter and goes to bed.

Stan comes into the kitchen and points toward their bedroom. Evie nods and he goes to check on Martha.

Closing the bedroom door behind him Stan says, "She's tired, but doing well. She's not fearful like she was with the last pregnancy."

"God is so good."

"Karl should be over shortly. I hope and pray these talks are helping. Sometimes it takes something more to lead someone back to God."

Once the kitchen is clean, Evie goes to her room. She hears Karl at the door and decides to stay there and read her Bible.

Evie, you will have an opportunity to talk with Karl tonight. Stan will be there too. Karl had a lot on his mind when he left here earlier. Tell him to seek Me for answers to his questions. He is seeking answers from you and Stan when he should be asking Me. Do not be surprised because he will tell you he does not know Me. Encourage him to get to know Me. Share some things you have seen Me do for others. I will be with you. Wait for Stan to come to get you. Evie, you are doing an amazing job. Thank you.

Thank You Father for trusting me with Your children. Thank You for speaking to my heart and encouraging me. I know he is Your child, and You will do everything possible for him.

Evie continues reading the Word until there is a knock on her door.

"Evie," Stan sighs, "I have tried and failed to change Karl's mind. He is determined to see a divorce attorney Monday if I can't convince him otherwise. Honestly, I don't think he wants to be convinced. I did however get him to agree to talk with you. He isn't thrilled, but he agreed. Will you come to talk to him?"

"I sure will. Don't be discouraged, we know God is always working." She reassures him as they walk through the kitchen to Karl in the living room.

"Hi Karl." She says cheerfully as she sits down. Arms folded across his chest, he replies with a simple, grunted, "Hey."

Evie, undeterred begins gently, "So what's going on?"

"You mean he hasn't told you?" He growls.

"Not much. When he came to my door just now, he said you are planning to see an attorney Monday about divorce."

"That's exactly what's going on."

"I see. I've never been married, but I know lots of married people and have seen too many heartbreaks due to divorce." She pauses briefly, "When you left here earlier, you walked away asking yourself several questions. You need to know God wants you to seek Him for those answers. He is the only One who has the best answer. You're seeking something from Stan only God can give you."

"It's true Karl," Stan adds. "You want me to say the right thing to change your mind about seeing an attorney. I don't know what, if anything, would change your mind. I don't have those answers, but God does."

Karl sits there for a long moment. Looking first at Stan, then Evie, then the floor.

"I don't know God and have never known Him. I've sat on the same pew at the same church for however many years and I don't even know Him. Honestly, I've done fine without Him."

Evie knows this is not the time to pull out Scripture. She wonders how long this pain and anger have been building in this confused man.

"Karl," Evie looks into his eyes with compassion and love, "I encourage you to get to know God. Put aside things you think you know about Him or what others say about Him and seek Him for yourself. Any reason you don't want to know Him?"

"Look, He is fine for other people, not for me. I went to church for Renee and the girls. The girls needed to be rooted in something good and have some kind of faith. I went so it would be a family thing. It works for all of them, which is what matters. Besides, He never answers my prayers, so I figure I'm not good enough for Him. Renee has faith and she will be fine."

Stan wipes at a tear on his cheek. "I didn't know all this. Why didn't you talk to me before it came to this? I would have told you then no one is good enough for God. It's not what we do which causes Him to love us, but who He is. He created us and wants us to be His children. The only reason we are good enough is because Jesus died on the cross to take on our sins. God loves you. God wants you. I'm sorry you've felt this way."

Silence. Karl's arms slide off his chest and rest by his legs. Evie is gently reminded of the last thing God told her.

Encourage him to get to know Me. Tell him what you have seen Me do for others.

"I can tell you many stories, true stories, of what God has done for people and in people," Evie says. "I have met mean and nasty people, dangerous and scary people, who God made miraculous changes in. I have also seen God do the impossible for many people. As they gave up, God stepped in."

Evie looks at Stan as she continues, "I met a man who was thrown out of a bar and landed directly in front of me. In my line of work, that's called opportunity. Although he towered over me and was very muscular, I was able to help him to his feet. We went to the closest place I found to get him a cup of coffee and I sat with him until he sobered up. When I thought he was coherent enough, I explained I was in town for a few months on assignment and happened to be standing there. He was very, uh, let's say, rough around the edges. Initially, he was extremely gruff but as the greasy bacon cheeseburger, fries, and coffee replaced the alcohol, he became receptive. We met a couple of times for coffee, and I invited him to church. It wasn't long before he traded the bar for the church and a bottle for a Bible. The kindness and prayers of his church family helped bring him from addiction to redemption."

Stan says nothing so Evie continues.

"I've witnessed God bring a group of people together to build a new house for someone who lost everything in a house fire. She was elderly and forgot to pay her homeowners insurance which caused the policy to lapse. I can tell you story after story like it. Did all the people who came together to help build the house know God in a personal way? Maybe, maybe not. The woman that lost her house knew God and was praying for an answer."

Evie cannot see the expression on Karl's downturned face, but continues anyway, "Karl, I don't want to mislead you. Life isn't perfect when we have a relationship with God, but it sure is sweeter. Can we help you with the first step to knowing God? It's not difficult at all."

His hesitation gave hope something was stirring in Karl's heart, but his stubborn pride won out. "No. Not today. Maybe another time."

She nods and from the corner of her eye, she watches Stan's shoulders slump as he wipes a single tear from his cheek.

"Thanks for talking with me. I'll think about what you said, but I'm still going to an attorney Monday."

Evie wants to say something profound but all she can say is, "Speaking for Stan, Martha, and myself, we love you. Renee loves you. Most important though, please know God loves you even more. We'll be praying for you and your beautiful family."

Karl gets up from the chair and rubs his eyes before they can see the tears.

"Thanks again." With that, he is out the door.

Stan, his face in his hands, just sits there.

"We did what we could tonight. As you said earlier, sometimes it takes more than just us to help people. Keep praying."

"I know, but shouldn't I have realized he didn't know God? I ministered to him like he knew God, when in actuality he never cared for what pleases God."

"It's late. You have people counting on you tomorrow. Leave your concerns with God and rest."

"You're right. Sleep well."

"Thanks. You too."

Eleven

Muffins in hand, they are up and out the door to prepare the church for service and Abi's dedication.

Steve and Amy's parents are there, as well as Abi Grace's great grandparents on both sides. The couple from Tennessee are back again and a new couple with two young children visit. Stan preaches a powerful message then he has Steve and Amy bring Abi Grace to the front of the church. He invites their families to join them.

"What a beautiful day God has given us. We have the honor and the privilege to join with Steve and Amy as they stand before God, and all of you, and promise to raise Abi Grace under His direction. In the Old Testament book of Samuel, Hannah vowed to give her son over to the Lord to serve Him throughout his life. She dedicated Samuel to God. Today, Steve and Amy dedicate Abi Grace. Please respond with 'we do' if you agree." Steve and Amy nod.

"Do you acknowledge before God created this world, He knew Abi Grace and she is a blessing and a gift from God to you?"

"We do."

"Do you promise to keep your heart pure and lead a life worthy of the glory of God as an example for Abi Grace?"

"We do."

"Do you promise to attend and be involved in a church that believes all scripture is inspired by God?"

"We do."

"Do you promise to raise Abi Grace according to the Bible's way of love, teaching, and discipline? That discipline is a tough one, but very important."

"We do."

"And to the congregation, as a church body, do you agree to help Steve and Amy raise Abi Grace in the love of the Lord and instruct her in the Word?"

They reply, "We do."

"Let's pray. Lord, we thank You for Steve and Amy and their love and dedication to You. Thank You Abi Grace is a healthy baby. We thank You we can gather as a body and vow to help raise her, according to Your ways and Your Word. We pray she is blessed and highly favored and walks in obedience to You. Help us to be the example she needs in her life and give us the wisdom to lead and guide her in Your ways. Provide her parents with the wisdom necessary in raising her. In Jesus' Name, Amen.

Thank you all for being with us today. Please help yourselves to lemonade and cake through those doors."

"Jedidiah," Evie calls after him as he follows the others through the doors for refreshments, "I asked Eliza and Justin if they would like to get a burger after church. They weren't in class on Wednesday, and I'd like to get to know them outside of class. Their parents are good with it, and I think it would be good if you come too. That is if you want to."

He looks excited for a moment. "I'll need to ask my parents." He rolls his eyes, "You know how they are."

"Well, I hope it is okay, but I already asked them. I want to be respectful, so I check with the parents first." He lights up.

"Really? So, they said it's okay?"

"They sure did."

"Then yeah I'd love to go!"

"Okay. We'll leave shortly. I'll let the others know."

Father, thank You for the favor. These parents don't know me very well, yet they trust me with their children. Help me reach them, especially Jedidiah. Show him he can trust me and can talk freely to me.

Evie helps clean up, then leaves with only a few people left at the church. They drive towards town to the Burger Bungalow. Not the most hopping place to go after church, which makes it perfect for talking and getting their food quickly. Eliza and Justin's mom told Evie they will pick them up after they eat at The Mill.

After they order and the server brings their drinks, Evie asks if anyone wants to pray over the meal. Naturally, the kids look at each other to pray. Finally, because Evie was not budging, Jedidiah says he will pray. Surprised, Evie nods.

"God, thanks for the food that's coming."

"Thank you, Jedidiah. Isn't it interesting when it comes time to pray out loud everyone freezes up? You know, sometimes it happens with people who have a regular prayer life too. Why do you think it might be?"

"I think people are afraid it won't come out fancy, like a preacher's prayer might," Eliza responds.

Justin nods and adds, "Yeah, and they might not have the right words."

Jedidiah pipes in, "Yup, no one wants anyone to know how dumb they are." Almost challenging her to disagree, he raises his eyebrows and cocks his head.

Evie smiles graciously, "I believe you are all right. People are intimidated by what others think of their prayer. It's one ugly trick of the enemy though, and once we realize it, we should be empowered to be bolder. Prayer is just conversation with Father God."

"Finally! The food is here." Jedidiah announces overdramatically.

Father, what is wrong with him? He didn't act like this when I talked to him after church service. Is he showing off for Eliza and Justin?

Eliza looks at him and scrunches up her face, "It didn't take that long. They were quick today."

He shrugs, "Whatever."

Evie asks open-ended questions to which Eliza mostly answers. Justin answers, but the food is his top priority. Eliza, the last one to finish her meal, pops the last bite of her sandwich in her mouth as her mom comes in to get them. They thank Evie and leave.

Once they are gone, her full attention is on Jedidiah.

"I told your parents I will drop you off at home after lunch."

He shrugs, "Okay. Better for me that way."

"Is there something bothering you?"

"Nope. Nothing wrong with me."

"Okay, good to hear. I have one other question then." He slumps in a casual bored way. She says a quick prayer then asks, "Why did you pray the way you did? I know better."

He cracks a cocky, half-smile, "What do you mean?"

"I know you know how to pray. You can pray eloquent prayers with all the Bible you say your parents have 'pushed' on you. So why make yourself look, in your own words, dumb."

He stares almost through her, for several minutes. She looks back at him with genuine concern, waiting for his answer.

"Because I'm being real with God. I'm not playing games with Him." Evie's confusion is evident. "I want my own life. I want to live according to what I want. I don't want to be at church all the time. I don't want to go to Bible camps. I don't want to go to college, or wherever, to be a pastor. I've had enough! I can tell you the Bible front to back, inside and out. I can tell you all the right things to say and do in church, and around church people. I have lived the church life since before I was born. From all I've been taught, God already knows all this, so I am not going to aggravate him by being hypocritical. Besides, if everyone knows how well I do pray, they will make me do it all the time and I don't want to grieve God. It's not His fault I don't like Him!"

Silence. There was so much passion behind his voice that it carried to those around him. There is only one other couple, two servers, and the cook close enough, but just the same he looks around and apologizes for being loud.

Jedidiah looks down at the table. Evie believes he does not like having God forced on him, but not that he does not like God.

Father, I need something here. I know this is a turning point. Speak through me, please. I can't do this on my own.

"Oh Jedidiah," a tear rolls gently down her cheek as she comes in closer, "I am sorry you feel this way. It's a difficult way to live your life. I know God appreciates you not wanting to play games with Him and you're correct, He already knows. Do you want to talk about this, or can I share some thoughts with you? It sounds like you've heard enough adult views, so I understand if you prefer not to."

He looks at her with unblinking, glassy eyes.

"Better yet Jedidiah, how about we don't, and let's order a couple of milkshakes instead."

The server comes over when she notices Evie looking at her.

"May I have a vanilla milkshake?"

"Vanilla milkshake?" Jedidiah looks at her in disbelief.

"Yes. I don't like chocolate ice cream."

He laughs, "There are more flavors than just chocolate and vanilla." The server covers her mouth as she tries to hide the smile creeping up on her as he picks at Evie.

Evie smiles, "Okay, what other flavors do you have?"

The server proceeds to mention at least twenty flavors.

"Oh. Okay. I'll take a vanilla milkshake please." Simultaneously, their mouths drop.

"Okay, okay. I'm kidding. I'll have a caramel milkshake, please."

"Well, I guess that's better. I will have a butter pecan toffee with cookies and cream, please." They stare at him.

"What?"

As they wait for their milkshakes, he apologizes for his outburst, but not for what he said. It is the way he feels, and she tells him she understands.

After the server leaves the milkshakes, he says, "I'm willing to listen to what you have to say, but don't expect me to change my mind."

She smiles, "You are knowledgeable in the things of God, which is good, but I guess my main question is, has anyone ever talked to you about your relationship with Him?"

Jedidiah shakes his head and raises an eyebrow, "Relationship?"

"Yes, relationship. How long have you been going to Pastor Stan's church?"

"Not long. Six or seven months. Why?"

"I'm guessing you are not paying much attention at this point huh?"

He looks down, embarrassed, "No. I haven't paid much attention for a couple of years. How did you know?"

"Because Pastor Stan and I believe the same things. I'm sure the people who led your class believe the same as well. If I lived here, I would attend Grace Church. Stan knows the Word and knows God, personally. Do you know what that means?"

"Relationship?"

"Exactly, and it is what Stan teaches and lives. He walks and talks with God. More than that, he listens to God. They spend time together. Not only does he know Father God, but he also knows about Him and who He is. All the things you do in a relationship, say with a friend." She knows using parents as an example would ruin the moment.

Thank You, Father, for Your wisdom.

They talk for two more hours about who God is and what a relationship with Him looks like. The conversation continues as she drives him home and after fifteen minutes of sitting in front of his house talking. By the time he gets out of the truck, she feels the afternoon is a success. She thanks God again for giving her the words and using her to make a difference.

Twelve

When Evie leaves the house after lunch, the sky is gray and heavy, and the air crisp. As she pulls into Ms. Pearl's driveway, she says a quick prayer then runs to the door.

"Come in Evie. I just knew you would be here today." Ms. Pearl dressed, once again, like she is going on a date to a fancy restaurant. Her full-length, pink dress with lace and sequins sparkles subtly as her pink chandelier earrings steal Evie's attention. When she takes Evie's hand to help her quickly out of the cold, Evie notices the beautiful pink ring which covers the bottom half of her first finger.

"Oh, Ms. Pearl!" She exclaims. "You look beautiful!"

"Thank you, sweetie," she says without missing a beat, "now come in, I have something to show you. I found it after you left last week, and I know you would like to see it. Sit down. I'll be right back dear."

"Sure, I would love to see it." As she sits waiting, she looks around the room. Nothing has changed. A couple of pieces of unopen mail on the table, but not much more. She wonders why, if she loves her husband so much, there are no pictures of him or them together. There are no pictures of Hazel either. Maybe it just hurts too much.

"Here it is dear. It's Henry's Bible."

"Wow. I can tell he used it."

"Yes, and it showed. Henry was everything a good God-fearing man should be. He was humble, kind, patient, and loving to everyone he met."

"He sounds like a wonderful man."

"He was." She replies as she leaves the room to get the tea. Evie flips through the pages of Henry's Bible. It is underlined, circled, notes written out to the side, and full of loose pieces of sermon notes and other interesting articles.

Well, Father, I know beyond a shadow of a doubt You and Mr. Henry were well acquainted before he came to see You. I'm going to help ensure they have a beautiful reunion one day.

"Here's the tea. Hot off the stove and some fresh banana pudding. Do you like banana pudding, dear?"

"Oh yes. It's one of my favorites." Evie replies as she reaches for the tea. "I was looking through Henry's Bible. Is your Bible as "well-loved" as Henry's is?"

"Oh no, sweetie. I put my Bible away after Hazel died, and I haven't touched it or been back to church since the day of her funeral. Henry has been taken from me too. God doesn't much care for me."

"So, you know God?"

"Oh yes. My parents were missionaries. They would not be pleased with me, but I just can't help it. I didn't ask for this pain."

"No one ever does Ms. Pearl. I'm sorry your heart hurts so much."

Father help me! What do I need to say?

They chat about the cold, snowy weather for November. Ms. Pearl catches her up on town gossip she heard about herself. As Evie reassures her what God has to say about her should be her only concern, Ms. Pearl's face went from rosy pink to a pale gray color.

"Ms. Pearl, are you okay?" Evie asks as she gets the phone to call an ambulance.

"Something's not right Evie. Pain in my, my jaw, my arm." Ms. Pearl gasps as Evie calls 911. The dispatcher assures Evie the ambulance is nearby.

Ms. Pearl moans in pain.

"Ms. Pearl, can you hear me?"

As she nods slightly, she whispers, "Yes dear, I can hear you." Evie bends closer to hear her. "Will I see Henry and Hazel today?"

"Oh Ms. Pearl, I'm not ready to lose my friend. I know that's selfish, but won't you fight and stay with me a little longer?"

"Pray for me, Evie. I don't know if He will let me into heaven. Pray for God's will. Let Him decide."

Evie places her hands over Ms. Pearl's hands and begins to pray over her. She continues until the EMTs arrive.

Father, I feel sure this is not the end of Ms. Pearl's life but Your will, not what I want, be done.

Evie steps out of the way, so the EMTs can assess Ms. Pearl. Watching as they place the oxygen mask over her nose and mouth, Evie hears them ask about medication and allergies. Moaning, Ms. Pearl answers their questions as best as she can. Within minutes, they determine Ms. Pearl is stable and load her into the ambulance.

"May I ride with her?" Evie asks the EMT.

"Are you related?"

She shakes her head, "But I am all she has."

The EMT, not usually one to break rules, tells her, "Come on then." He has no idea why he allows her.

She thanks him and God and hops into the ambulance. Staying out of the way, she speaks gently to Ms. Pearl and tells her God is with her. He always has been. He has never left her.

She is weak but nods and whispers, "I know." Hearing this, the EMT introduces himself.

"Nice to meet you, Lou. I'm Evie. Do you have any idea what happened to Ms. Pearl?"

"I'm not allowed to share," Ms. Pearl nods her head, "but we believe it is a heart attack. They will know for sure once we get her to the hospital."

"I understand."

"Evie, I wish you could ride with us all the time," Lou says. "The atmosphere here is amazing. Even in non-life-threatening situations, I have never felt peace and calm as I feel in here right now. What are you, an angel?"

"You are very kind." Evie laughs, "Did you hear that Ms. Pearl? He asked if I was an angel."

Ms. Pearl whispers, "You are dear, you are."

At the Banderidge Medical Center, she is given medicine for the pain and taken directly back. Evie calls Martha to ask her to pray for answers, and tells her she will be here for a while. She asks if Stan can pick her up later and take her to Ms. Pearl's house to get the truck. Martha tells Evie Stan is on the mountain, but she will ask him when he returns.

A nurse calls for Evie and says Ms. Pearl is adamant Evie be with her. As Evie walks into the room, Ms. Pearl cries and Evie goes to her side. She places her hands on her and prays.

"Good, gracious, and loving Father, Your child is in pain. We are aware this causes You pain as well. We have been given the authority to command the pain and what is causing it to go because of the stripes Your Son, Jesus Christ, took for us. Isaiah 53 tells us He was wounded, crushed, and whipped for us, so we would be healed. We don't want His pain and suffering to be in vain. So, with the authority given to me in the Name of Jesus, I speak to the pain and whatever's causing it and tell it to go. Leave! Body, you must line up with the Word of God! You are healed. We claim victory because of Jesus' death on the cross. Thank You Father for healing, strength, and renewal of the mind. When the doctors find nothing Father, I pray Ms. Pearl's eyes are open to her miracle and her heart be softened. May it remind her of Your goodness and love for her. Her testimony will give You all the glory Father. Amen."

Eyes wide, Ms. Pearl speaks steadily, "Why honey, I haven't heard anyone pray with so much fervency in years. I do not doubt in my mind you touched God with your prayer. I feel better than I have in a long time."

As an employee comes to get her, she tells him she feels fine and will be leaving now. He smiles and nods.

"Yes ma'am, I understand, but I got orders to follow. Let's just get these tests done and get you back here. Then you can talk to the doctor about how well you are doing. Okay?"

Ms. Pearl's gently wrinkled, beautiful face no longer pale reddens, "I said..."

"Now Ms. Pearl," Evie says as she glances at the name badge, "Ray is only doing what he's told to do. Why don't you go on and let them run the tests? We know what they'll find, but we don't want Ray getting in any trouble."

Ms. Pearl looks at her, smiling sheepishly. She says to Ray, "Okay, let's do this."

When they are gone, Evie closes the door behind them. She begins to pray and thank God for the miracle. As she is praising, Holy Spirit prompts her to go to the lobby. She quickly leaves the room. As she enters the lobby, she sees Stan and wonders if a member of his church is here. As she gets closer, Martha is sitting in the chair closest to the admissions desk.

"Martha," Evie calmly starts, "What's going on?" Tears stream down Martha's face, as she rubs her bumpless belly.

"I am further than I have ever been. I thought I made it, but now I am hurting. I know this feeling. It has happened too many times before when I, I," She cannot finish her sentence.

As they talk, transport personnel comes to get her. Concerned, the medical team gets Martha in a room quickly.

"You're all over this place, aren't you?" Ray says to Evie.

"None of it by choice Ray. Can I go with her?"

"You can. You will have to stay in the waiting room but come on."

When they get to the labor and delivery wing, Ray directs her toward the waiting room and continues down the hall with Martha, Stan is close beside her.

Evie sits when Ray stops at the door. "Ma'am," He starts.

"Please, call me Evie." She smiles.

"Ms. Evie, thank you for your help getting Ms. Pearl to go for her tests. I remember the last time she was here she gave me a fit, but she seems different today."

"Do you know why?" Evie asks, already knowing the answer.

"Well on the way down for her test, she told me what happened. She said you prayed, and she is healed. Of course, that's the shortened version of what she said. She was still talking when I left the room." Evie laughs.

"Well, you may want to keep up with her story and see the results for yourself. Also, the couple you just brought in, watch their story too." She tells him.

He nods slightly, like he wants to believe what she is saying, "Sure. I will."

Alone in the waiting room, she prays.

Father, I admit I am shaken by this situation with Martha. She is my friend, and I don't want any more pain for her or Stan. A tear runs down her face.

My child, have I not already assured both you and Martha as you read My promise? Do they not live in the shelter of the Most High? In Me? Remember they will find rest in My shadow. I am their refuge, their place of safety. Sweet child, My faithful promises are their armor and protection. Do I not rescue those who love Me? Do I not protect those who trust in My Name? Have you forgotten? Trust and believe what I tell you. My child, do not cry. What happens does so for a purpose.

Evie understands. *I do trust You, but sometimes I falter. I'm sorry. I know what You told us, and I stand firm on Your Word. Thank You for loving me and gently correcting me when I need it. Thank You for loving Martha, Stan, and the baby. Thank You for seeing them safely through. Please give me words to encourage them and help me be a blessing to them.*

With that, Evie goes to the nurse's station and asks if she can go to Martha's room. She is told it will probably be about an hour or so. She asks if they can tell Stan she went to check on Ms. Pearl and will return shortly. The nurse agrees and Evie leaves to find Ms. Pearl.

As she approaches the room, she hears Ms. Pearl talking loudly. Concerned, she cautiously walks into the room. When she realizes Ms. Pearl is not fussing, but rather sharing her story with them, Evie relaxes. There are several people in the room, including her doctor. Of course, he has yet to tell her the results, because he cannot get a word in. Evie, smiling, stands quietly at the back of the room, shaking her head. This is not the same lady she met at the festival.

Thank You, gracious Father.

When Ms. Pearl finally pauses to take a breather, the doctor asks everyone to leave so he can share her results, but she insists everyone stay so they can hear what God has done for her.

"Well okay then, as long as you give me permission to disclose your medical information in front of others." She nods so rapidly Evie thinks her head might bobble off.

"I'm not sure what happened here, but all tests, the blood that was drawn, everything we ran, shows there is not a thing wrong with you. Your vitals, tests ran when you came in, and the excruciating pain you were in told an entirely different story. You are one of the healthiest women of your age, I have seen. You are not one bit surprised though, are you?"

"Nope. Not one bit. Thank you, Jesus!" The doctor smiles and shakes his head.

Ms. Pearl continues telling of the goodness of God and all she is planning to do when she gets out, "Doctor, am I free to go? I've got so much to do. I've wasted so much time already. I've got to hang pictures, invite friends over, well, make friends and invite them over, oh and find a new church to attend."

The doctor tilts his head and looks her over, "I don't see why not. We'll have them start on your discharge. Take care of yourself, Ms. Pearl."

Evie tells Ms. Pearl about Martha, then goes to check on her. As she is going out the door, Evie hears Ms. Pearl talking. She pauses and turns to see Ms. Pearl's eyes closed and head bowed. Evie hurries down the hall to the labor and delivery wing. As she approaches the nurse's station, Evie hears laughter and sees three nurses looking and pointing at something on the computer. As she waits to be acknowledged another round of laughter erupts.

Once the laughter stops, Evie asks, "Excuse me, may I go see the patient in room 315?" One of the ladies looks up and apologizes. She tells Evie yes but not long. Even though she knows what God reminded her, she detects something off in the nurse's voice.

The door is partially open, so she peers in. Stan, elbows propped on his knees, head down, palms of his hands cupping his forehead, looks up. She waves and he motions her in. Seeing Martha sleep peacefully Evie guesses they gave her something to calm her.

"We won't wake her if we whisper," Stan tells Evie.

"What's happened so far? Do you know anything?"

He smiles weakly, "God is still in control. Martha is hooked to monitors to keep a close check on both of them. When we got here, she kept saying 'Not again, not again. My baby'. That's why she is medicated."

She asks if she can pray for them before she takes Ms. Pearl home. Stan is surprised so Evie shares the short version of the story. Stan, amazed, tells her he welcomes that kind of miracle for them as well.

She smiles and begins to pray, "Father, You reminded me earlier about the Word You gave to both Martha and me. You told us "it is well." I now ask You to share the reminder with both of my sweet friends. Help them remember they will find rest in the shadow of the Almighty; You are their refuge, their place of safety. We know Your faithful promises are their armor and protection and You rescue those who love You. I pray the peace Your Word says passes all understanding rise within them both. Minister to Martha's spirit as she sleeps. We know You are in control, and You love your children. We thank You for what You are doing presently and for what is to come. In all things, we give You the glory. In Jesus' Name, Amen."

Stan is overcome with emotions by Evie's prayer. He asks God to forgive him for the doubt which seeps into his mind. He thanks God for His Word and His promises, and for sending Evie for such a time as this. He asks for strength to rise within so he can run with endurance. When he finishes, he stands.

He looks at Evie sorrowfully, "God hasn't given us a spirit of fear and timidity. I am ashamed I have not taken the power He has given us and use it as I should. I have forgotten the only power the enemy has over me is the power I allow him to have. No more."

Stan knows this is not a battle against flesh and blood but the wickedness in the spiritual realm. He speaks into the room with dominating authority. Taking control, he speaks the Word of God, covering his wife and unborn child, and declaring this battle is over because the victory was won by Christ. When he finishes declaring victory and life over his family, he slumps into the chair. Tears splash onto the floor.

Martha woke when she heard him praying. Too groggy to speak, she listened and agreed.

Barely audible, she whispers, "Stan, thank you. It is well." He goes to her, and they embrace.

"Yes. It is my love. It is well."

Doctor Rogers comes back in to check Martha. He sits on the side of the bed and tells her everything looks good, but he wants her to stay a day or two for observation.

Doctor Rogers takes Martha's hand, "You have been through so much and I've been with you through your pain and heartache. I am going to do everything in my power to keep you and the baby healthy so I can share in your happiness."

"Thank you, Dr. Rogers." Stan shakes his hand as he leaves, "We know we are in great hands."

Evie asks Stan if she can borrow the car to take Ms. Pearl home. After, she will come back to sit with Martha, so he can get some things from the house. As she is leaving, a nurse comes in to offer Martha more medicine. Completely at peace, she declines.

Approaching Ms. Pearl's room, it is quiet. Concerned, she gets closer and hears whispering. She finds Ms. Pearl's room empty. She knows she hears a voice that sounds like Ms. Pearl's, so she checks the next room. Sure enough there she sits, chair pulled close to the bed, praying, and holding the hand of the woman in the bed. Evie waits until she finishes. She hears Ms. Pearl encourage the woman and tell her bye. Ms. Pearl finds Evie in the hall.

"That poor dear, I could hear her crying and moaning from my room. I couldn't help myself. I went and offered to pray with her. Oh, Evie, I feel like I have been given another chance and I don't want to waste any more time. Does that make sense, hon?"

Evie smiles and puts her arm around Ms. Pearl's shoulder, "It sure does. Let's get you home." As Evie drives her home, they discuss the different church options. It has been years since she has been to church so Ms. Pearl wonders if it is time for a change. She decides she will try them all. Evie tells her about Grace Church and what time it starts on Sunday.

Evie walks Ms. Pearl to the door and asks if she needs anything. She shakes her head. Evie hugs her tight and promises to be back soon. Ms. Pearl thanks her again and tells her she will pray for Martha.

Back at the hospital, Evie swaps places with Stan as Martha sleeps. Stan feels blessed for the help. Evie prays and reads the Bible while Martha sleeps. As Evie is praying, Karl is brought to her heart. Concern catches her by surprise.

Oh no. Father, something is wrong. It's Karl. I know something is happening. Please Father, help him. Protect him. Give him a way out. He is in Your hands. I know he is playing on his terms and whatever he does, the consequences are on him. My concern is he will make a regrettable decision that will affect Renee and the girls. Protect them as well Father.

Evie reads scripture, then prays for Renee and the girls.

"Where is Stan?" Martha asks faintly.

"He went home to take care of a few things and get a change of clothes, so he won't have to leave you again."

"I am blessed with an amazingly kind-hearted man. Oh, the gifts our Father lavishes on us." A tear rolls down Martha's cheek.

Evie nods, "How do you feel?"

"I feel amazing. I could go home right now, and everything would be fine, but I will not go against the doctor's orders."

"Wise decision."

Evie bought a book and a couple of magazines for Martha. Scooting up in the bed and settling in, Martha is especially excited about the magazine for new parents. As she is reading an article on how to help your baby grow into a child who loves to read, the phone rings.

Evie places the phone within reach so Martha can answer it.

"Hello. Oh no! Okay. Yes. Evie is here with me so I will be fine. Take your time and be there for them. I love you too."

Evie's stomach sickens at the words 'oh no'.

"Jedidiah got in more trouble at Mr. Washburn's today and Stan is going to see him. Officers took him to juvenile holding and are not releasing him." Evie's heart drops.

"That's sad to hear. He's a really good kid."

"Please do not feel like you need to stay with me. I feel great. I will be fine."

"I know you will, but I don't have anywhere to be but here with you until Stan comes back anyway because we only have one vehicle right now."

"Thank you." Martha's eyes convey more than her words ever can.

Eyes closed, praying for Jedidiah, Evie jumps when Martha cries out. Martha, arms crossed against her belly, bends forward, terror in her eyes.

"No! No! This isn't happening again." Martha cries through gritted teeth. Evie goes for the nurse, praying all the way.

Father, I know the outcome. I know she has a healthy baby this time, but why does she have to go through this? I can't stand to see her hurting like this. Can You please bring them through this valley already?

When Evie and the nurse enter the room, Martha is still feeling some pain, but is calm.

"Martha." Evie is not sure what happened, but the atmosphere in the room changed.

"When I am afraid, I put my trust in You. But I trust in You, Lord; I say, You are my God."

Evie knows, Martha is fighting, armed with the Gospel of peace and the shield of faith against the unseen enemy of darkness.

"He cannot steal my peace or destroy my faith, and he definitely will not kill my child. I know where my help comes from. My help comes from the Lord, the Maker of heaven and earth."

The nurse tells Martha the doctor will be here shortly. By the time he gets there, not a thing is wrong. No pain; and perfect readings on the monitors. Everything is normal.

"You had me concerned when I heard the pain began again," Dr. Rogers says, "but you can't convince me anything happened. I'm not sure what is going on, but I know the One who does, and He is close to you. You have carried this child further along and it gives me great hope. Your prayers are working." He winks and tells her if there is no pain for thirty-six hours, they will discharge her. He doubts she will have any more pain until the day she delivers her baby.

When Stan gets back to the hospital with milkshakes it is after nine at night. Martha tells him of the scare and the amazing peace she felt after proclaiming her trust in Father God and in what He is doing in her life.

"Stan, something is different. Peace replaced fear and I feel, I feel free. I am not afraid."

Stan hugs her, "That is awesome, sweetheart! I'm glad you're not in pain anymore and our baby is well too. Our baby has the best mommy ever," He kisses her forehead, caresses her hair, and looks lovingly into her eyes, "and I have one amazing wife."

Evie's heart contains so much happiness. Concerned she will flood the room with tears, she excuses herself and steps out.

What a beautiful love they have for one another. It's a glimpse, however only a sliver, of the love You have for us Father. Adding a baby can only make their love better. Thank You and please forgive my doubting. I know we are each on a journey and You hold the itinerary. You are a good and gracious Father.

When Evie returns, Stan tells them about Jedidiah.

"He and three other boys are accused of stealing. Of course, they all deny it. The officers said they found nothing from the store on Jedidiah but feel he may have thrown it down before they got to him." Stan pauses, shaking his head, "Funny thing though, the other boys were going on and on about their innocence to anyone who would listen. Not Jedidiah. He said one time he was innocent, but because of his recent actions, his parents don't believe him. He has been caught hanging with this troublesome bunch before. He was told to stop, but obviously, he didn't listen. The previous incident at Mr. Washburn's doesn't help either. Breaks my heart."

"What do you believe?" Evie asks.

"After I talked to the officers, I thought it sounded bad for all of them. Then I talked to Jedidiah's parents, and they had me convinced that he was guilty and headed to the electric chair. Once I talked to Jedidiah, I began to doubt his guilt. On the drive here, I was praying for the truth. I don't believe he was involved. I was also reminded that there is nothing hidden that will not be disclosed and nothing concealed that will not be known or brought out into the open. The truth will come out."

"Every time," Evie says.

"When and how long he will stay in juvenile holding is the question. His parents want him to stay there and learn from his mistakes. The Juvenile Court Judge will be in tomorrow at ten to decide."

"Oh Stan," Martha sighs, "you will be there when he goes to court, right? He must be so scared. I do not like this at all."

"None of us do Martha, but God isn't worried. This may be something Jedidiah has to go through for God to get his attention. The beautiful reminder from this is the Lord disciplines those He loves. He loves Jedidiah and we know he has a call on his life, whether he wants to admit it or not."

"True, but you will go, won't you?"

"Of course, I will sweetheart. Evie, Jedidiah wants me to tell you he wasn't involved, and he remembers what you told him about being careful who he calls friends. He said he was bored, and they invited him to hang out."

Evie looks down at the shiny vinyl floor. She knows why this is happening and trusts God.

"Well, I'm glad he at least remembers, but I imagine it was after the fact. I guess I will go to the house if you all are settled in. But the truck is still at Ms. Pearl's house."

"I will be fine. We are not too far from Ms. Pearl's house. The nurses are here if I need anything." Martha assures him.

When Stan lets Evie out at Ms. Pearl's, he says, "Oh yeah, a letter came in the mail for you."

"Great. Thank you."

On the drive home, she thinks about all that occurred today. She decides she will find the courthouse and support Jedidiah in the morning. After court, she will go to Washburn's and get groceries so she can prep meals to last a few days. Realizing she missed her opportunity to see Anastasia at Crafts-N-More, she plans to see her sometime tomorrow.

At the house, she feels the weight of the day on her. She goes directly to her room, sets her alarm, and falls asleep.

Thirteen

The next morning, Evie feels rested. While still in bed she reaches for her Bible. After time spent with her Father, she is ready for the day. She gets dressed and leaves for Juvenile Court. On her way she prays.

Loving Father, I pray Your will be done. You know the truth. I am comforted knowing You love him, and he will surrender and be anchored in You one day. I pray this will be the final challenge to set him exactly where You want him. I pray he knows without a shadow of a doubt, You have called him and created him for such a time as this. I know he is innocent. I ask somehow the other boys come to know You through this time. My trust is in You alone Father.

Inside the courthouse, she looks for Stan. Standing to the right of the doors leading into the courtroom, he is talking with Jedidiah's parents. He waves her over.

"Mr. and Mrs. McCollum." She nods as she greets Jedidiah's parents.

Mr. McCollum thanks them for coming, "We are not doing anything to help him out of this mess. After the incident at Mr. Washburn's, we told him to get it together. Not only that, but those boys are trouble. We told Jedidiah he can't be friends with them. Look where it got him."

Stan nods, "I imagine you have prayed about whether to bring him home or not. If that is what you heard from God, I will stand with you. Please understand though, as his pastor, I will be here every step of the way to support him and do what I can to help him."

Evie nods, "Me too."

They move into the courtroom as they are closing the doors.

As if the weapon holstered to his side is not intimidating enough, the towering bailiff bellows, "All rise. The Juvenile Court of Banks County is now in session, the Honorable Judge Roberts is presiding."

Judge Roberts takes his seat, "Please be seated."

He then reads the docket of cases. Evie is surprised at the long list with this being one of the smaller counties in the state. She wonders if there is anyone available to reach the children in this community. The first three cases are a status offense, truancy, and a runaway. The remaining seven cases are delinquency matters, theft, and drug-related offenses. Stan writes in his notebook.

"Zackary Robbins, Mark Elvoy, Gus Baylor, Jedidiah McCollum, please stand. Boys, have any of you been in trouble with the law before?" asks the judge. All but one boy shakes their head.

"What is your name son?" he asks the boy who has been in prior trouble.

"Zackary Robbins."

"And what happened?"

Zackary boasts, "I pushed a kid off his bike 'cause I wanted it."

"I see and how old were you?"

"Fourteen."

Judge Roberts remains patient and kind. "Did the matter come before the Court?"

"No, but the law came. Threatened next time to take me in."

"And who is here with you today?"

"No one."

"And why is that?" Zackary looks down and kicks at the floor then stares at the Judge, "Son?"

"My mom works two jobs to take care of our family and the man they call my dad hasn't been seen or heard from in years. Probably locked up himself somewhere. Good for nothing piece of..."

"That will be enough Mr. Robbins. I understand. I see the charge against you boys is theft. Were you hungry? In need of food?"

"No." Three out of the four boys reply.

The judge looks at Jedidiah, "Can I assume you were hungry son?"

Jedidiah shakes his head, "No sir. I did not steal anything."

"I see. Okay, you boys who did steal, if you weren't hungry then why did you steal?" No one answers.

"Okay. Here's what we're going to do. We'll meet back here on, let's see, at 8:30 Monday morning and we'll talk again. Until then, you will be housed in the Juvenile Detention Center."

The boys are led back to the unfamiliar, friendless detention center. Jedidiah sees tears welling up in Evie's eyes and mournfully mouths the words, "I'm sorry."

She forces a smile as he goes through the door and wonders why he said sorry. Stan is informed by the officers he is not able to speak to Jedidiah at this time but to contact the detention center to see if they will allow a visit.

Stan and Evie walk out of the courthouse with Jedidiah's parents.

"Whether or not there are visiting hours, we are not going to see him." Mr. McCollum says, "He needs to sit in there and think about what is happening in his life."

Stan asks, "You won't mind if I talk to him, if they allow me, right?"

Mr. McCollum thinks for a minute before answering.

"No. Please go if you can and tell my son that we do love him." Mrs. McCollum sobs. Mr. McCollum comforts his wife as they walk away. Stan watches until they get in the car.

"This is tough on them. They only want the best for their son, which leads them to be so strict. The Lord brought them to Grace Church, hopefully, we can help them before it's too late."

Evie nods, "We need to keep reminding ourselves God can and will use this to accomplish His plans for Jedidiah's life."

"I agree."

As they walk to their cars, Evie tells Stan she is going to the hospital sometime today and asks if he needs her there. He tells her no and hopes if all goes well, Martha will be discharged this evening. Should anything change, he will let her know. She leaves for Washburn's.

Unfamiliar with Washburn's, she is trying to find spaghetti sauce when she hears a man's voice behind her calling her name.

"Ms. Evie, Ms. Evie, I want you to know I don't believe Jedidiah stole anything. I think he was with the wrong crowd when they decided to do something very stupid."

"Thank you, Mr. Washburn. By any chance, did you mention that to the officers?"

"I did, but they need all of the boys for the investigation. He is a good boy. We got to know each other better when he worked to pay for the repairs to the door. I like the young man."

"Don't worry Mr. Washburn, the truth will come out. We need to trust God."

She gathers some food and Mrs. Washburn's freshly made banana pudding for dessert.

Back at the house, she works quickly prepping meatloaf, lasagna, and a chicken, broccoli, and rice casserole. She peels potatoes, cuts them up, and places them in water for mashed potatoes. For lunch, she makes shrimp salad and chicken salad. Once the meatloaf and lasagna cool, she sets half of each in containers in the fridge. The other half she cuts and freezes individually sliced for quick access.

When she finishes, she looks at the clock and realizes Anastasia should be at work by now, if she is working. Evie decides to go to Wild Horses.

Before she leaves, she calls the hospital and optimistically asks Stan if they have an idea of what time they will be home. He tells her the doctor will be making his rounds at four and then discharge will follow if he okays it. She feels confident she has time to go to Wild Horses.

Back to town again, she pulls into a parking spot directly in front of the store. From the sidewalk, she watches Anastasia hand a receipt to a customer. Evie realizes her shoulders are slumped and she does not even look up at the customer when she gives her the receipt. Evie goes into the store to looks at some of the wild and crazy accessories as she waits for Anastasia to finish with another customer. As Anastasia approaches, Evie holds up another funky pair of earrings to her ears.

"What do you think Sassy? Is it me?" Evie asks as she models the green-hatted, purple dolphin earrings.

Anastasia fake smiles and quietly responds, "Nope, not that pair either."

"Well, maybe someday I'll find the perfect pair for here me. So, how's it going, sweet girl?"

"Oh, it's going okay, I guess." She replies, fighting back tears.

"Your eyes tell a different story. Anything I can do for you?" She shakes her head no. "Well then, since you are working, I won't keep you, but I want to know if we can get something to eat Friday night or Saturday."

She perks up, "I'm off Friday. If my grandmother says I can then Friday will work."

"That's fine. Let me know." Evie hugs Anastasia and she feels Anastasia let her. She is not yet at the stage to return the hug, but she has come a long way.

Evie is back at the house when Stan calls.

"We will leave the hospital in about twenty minutes."

"Wonderful. I hope you guys are hungry. Dinner will be ready when you get here."

Evie cooks mashed potatoes, green beans, and corn, warms the meatloaf, and sets the table. Earlier she bought a silver, matte-finished vase and a bouquet called "A Touch of Splash" which she placed in the middle of the table. The overwhelming aroma of meatloaf almost brings Stan to tears as the sight of the beautiful flower arrangement did bring Martha to tears.

As she turns away from the flowers she says, "Oh my. It smells great in here. Doctor Rogers is worried about my appetite, but I doubt it will be a problem."

Stan takes Martha's bag to their room and is back in a flash.

"Well ladies, what are you waiting for? Why haven't you sat yet?" Laughing, they sit, and Stan blesses the food.

The conversation is light and cheery. Stan has seconds and finishes the meatloaf.

"Well, this is a sad moment," he announces, "all the meatloaf is gone, and it was delicious."

Evie shakes her head. "You are a one-man eating machine."

"What?" He laughs.

"I prepared meals for the next few days. There are extra, single servings of meatloaf and lasagna in the freezer for your dining pleasure."

"Yes! Life is getting better all the time."

Martha gets up to clear the table and both Evie and Stan say, "No."

"No ma'am. Take a bath or read a book, but whatever you do, you need to relax." Stan bends to kiss her forehead. Martha, smiling, walks to their room.

Fourteen

At breakfast, Stan asks Evie if the letter she received is good news.

"Oh. I forgot all about it. Where did you say it is?" He pulls it off the counter, where it sits in plain sight, and hands it to her. She giggles.

"I never saw it. Oh! It's from Falls Park, Virginia. That's where Sarabeth lives, I hope."

Sure enough, the letter is from Sarabeth. In the short, but beautifully written letter she tells Evie how excited she is to hear from her, and that she would love to see Amanda again. She put her phone number in the letter and asks Evie to call. Evie nods as Sarabeth finishes with how much fun it would be if they can keep it a surprise for Amanda.

"Yes! Wonderful news." Evie responds after she reads it.

She gets up to clear the table and Martha says, "Let me…" Evie gives her the eye, "just go get my book, put my feet up, and let you take care of clean up."

Evie hangs the towel on the oven door and reaches for the phone.

Oh Father, thank You. You are so good to be concerned with the things which concern us. It is a true testament to Your love for us. I pray continued favor for this reunion and Your will be done in the outcome.

After two rings a sweet voice on the other end answers, "Hello."

"Hello. May I speak to Sarabeth Ingram?"

"Speaking."

"Hi. This is Evie. I wrote to you about your friend Amanda."

"Oh yes! Hello. Thank you for calling. Will I be able to see Amanda?"

They speak briefly about a good halfway place to meet if Sarabeth's father can bring her. Evie tells her she will get with Amanda and talk to Sarabeth again soon.

Although she knows Amanda does not usually work Wednesdays, she is prompted to go. Stan is in his shop, so she checks on Martha and asks if she needs anything while she is in town. Martha asks her to let Stan know when she is leaving and to tell him she is fine alone.

As Evie approaches the shop, she hears Stan crying out, "Abba!" She hears music playing softly in the background. Peering in the window, she sees Stan on his knees with arms held high. She decides not to bother him, she tells Martha Stan is praying and she will wait to go. They talk as the fire dances and wood pops. Within thirty minutes Stan comes in.

"I saw you at the window. I figured everything was okay since you didn't come in."

"I didn't want to bother you. We spent time chatting. I'm going into town and wanted you to know Martha said she is fine in here."

"Oh, okay. I can stay up here."

Martha pipes in, "Stan, sweetheart, I am okay here by myself."

"I know, but maybe I want to spend time with the love of my life."

"How about if the love of your life comes to the shop with you?"

"Deal."

On her way to town, Evie tries to think up a good reason to get Amanda to go on a trip with her. Recalling conversations with Amanda she tries to remember some of her interests. Crafts, people with special needs, and something else. Hiking? Yes, hiking. She stops at the library first, thinking she remembers mountains in the area.

"Yes!" She whispers. Further research proves there is a hiking convention on one of the weekends they are considering. She leaves the library and goes to Crafts-N-More believing, Amanda will be there. Sure enough, she sees her standing at the cash stand, only this time she is on the customer side.

Amanda sees Evie as she approaches the store and meets her as she comes in the door.

"Hi, Evie."

"Hi. Just the person I was hoping to see."

"Your timing is amazing. I dropped by to talk to Mom for a minute. What's up?"

Thank You Father for the delay.

"Well, there's a great opportunity not too far from here, but I don't want to go alone. There is a hiker gathering in Station Place, Virginia, next weekend. Since you mentioned you enjoy hiking, I thought you might like to go too."

"But it's cold."

"The sessions are held indoors but hiking trails are available for any brave souls. I thought we would go early Saturday, stay the night at the lodge, then come back Sunday night. My treat. I would enjoy the company." Evie silently prays Amanda will say yes.

"Well, sure. That would be fun." Relieved, Evie tells her she will catch up with her later in the week with more details.

Since she is close to Ms. Pearl's house, Evie decides to check on her. Pulling up the driveway, she looks twice. On her front lawn sits four pumpkins on two bales of hay. Surrounding the pumpkins are several green gourds that looked dunked halfway up in yellow paint. Dull silver twigs entwine a wreath of thick, brown vines dotted with miniature gold, yellow, and dark red pumpkins, which hangs on the front door. Evie knocks.

Ms. Pearl answers the door wearing a pair of blue jeans and a soft pink sweater. The only accessories she has on are a small pair of diamond stud earrings.

"Ms. Pearl." Evie almost whispers.

"What dear? Come on in out of the cold."

"Uh," Evie looks around the room, slowly taking it all in, "Uh, everything is different."

She laughs, "I am different! And it's wonderful!"

Still talking she goes to the kitchen to make tea. Evie looks around at all the lovely photos she has set out since the last time she was here. If she were to guess, the large photo of Ms. Pearl and Henry in the beautiful gold frame hanging in the sitting room is from their fiftieth wedding anniversary. In many of the photos, she does not appear nearly as happy as she does in the photo of their wedding day. Many of those photos were probably taken after Hazel died.

"Just a couple of young kids." Ms. Pearl smiles as she walks to where Evie stands holding the photo.

They sip tea and talk. Well, Ms. Pearl talks about how much better she feels: physically, spiritually, and mentally. She talks excitedly about the upcoming holidays and a new friend. Evie enjoyed Ms. Pearl's company before, but now she enjoys it even more and does not want to leave.

"I wish I could stay, but I have one more stop to make before I go home."

"Honey you know where I live. Come back anytime. Here is my number. You might want to call first to be sure I am home. I will begin visiting churches this Sunday and I'm going to start with Grace Church."

Evie's heart is full. "Wonderful. I'll be looking for you."

Evie gets in the truck and is backing out of the driveway before she remembers she still does not know why Ms. Pearl always dressed formally before her miracle. She is determined to remember to ask.

Evie drives to Wild Horses, hoping Anastasia will be there. Inside, Evie goes directly to the earrings and holds a tremendously heavy pair to her ears.

"First, no, and second, uh-uh," Sassy says smiling.

"Why not? Am I not cool enough to pull this off?"

"Ha. Seriously, those would pull the lobe of someone your age down to your shoulder," Evie's jaw drops, "and besides when did your interest in spiderwebs with large black widow spiders begin?" They laugh so hard until they hear, "Ahem." They look at the young woman waiting to checkout.

Anastasia apologizes as Evie continues looking at the unique earrings. Most of them are large, dangling, or attention grabbers. There are earrings with spikes, flying bats, a biting dinosaur, and her favorite, grilled cheese. When Anastasia finishes with the customer, she tells Evie she is allowed to get something to eat with her Friday night. They decide on a time as another person needs assistance. Evie leaves as Anastasia goes to help her.

Evie thinks that she had a productive day. Everyone seems to be doing okay, but she needs to find a way to check on Karl. Thinking about how to make it happen keeps her busy as she drives home.

Wow! Thank You, Father. Karl's car is in the driveway.

Evie goes into the house expecting to see Karl, instead, she sees no one. Assuming Martha is resting, and the men are most likely in the shop, Evie goes to her room.

She hears a noise in the kitchen and comes out to find Martha pulling out the lasagna. Evie offers to help but Martha tells her Stan asked for her to come to the shop when she comes home. Evie knocks and says a quick prayer as Stan tells her to come in.

"Hi guys," Evie says as she walks in. The tension thick as pea soup, she says another quick prayer for wisdom.

Call his bluff Evie. It may not feel like the thing to do right now but trust Me. Hear him out then call his bluff. Remind him of what he has.

"Tell her Karl." He just stares as Stan pushes. "Go on."

He grunts, "I waited to go to the lawyer's office, but things aren't any better. I've waited long enough. I have an appointment Monday. I don't love her and don't want to be married to her anymore. She doesn't love me either, so it's not a problem."

"Oh." She is surprised by his nonchalance. "Is that what she told you?"

"She doesn't have to say it. I feel it."

He goes off on a very self-centered, woe-is-me rant. None of it makes a very good argument. He tries to talk bad about Renee, but Evie draws the line.

"Now Karl, I will listen to what you have to say, but I will not listen to you talk bad about the mother of your children; the woman who has stood beside you and shared your bed with you all these years. The woman who isn't here to tell her side of the story. No matter how bad you feel, you know she is a wonderful, loving woman." That stops him, but only for a minute.

"Anyway, I just wanted to tell you I am going Monday."

Father, You know it is not my nature to be unkind, help me to be bold.

"Karl, why do you keep coming here? What do you want from Stan? You keep coming over and he keeps sharing God's truths and doing his best to save you from the biggest mistake you will ever make. I doubt you'll go see the lawyer Monday. You don't want to leave Renee. You have been together for so many years, shared in the birth of four beautiful girls, got them through school together, raised them to be healthy, mature ladies. You know you have a great life, and she loves you. You won't leave her because she is the best thing to happen to you and deep down you don't want to hurt her or the girls. I think you-"

Karl screams, "Enough! You don't know me. You don't know what I think or feel. Good night Stan." The windows rattle on his way out.

Stan, stunned, wide-eyed, and speechless, stares at Evie.

"Stan."

"Evie, what have you done? That was not like you."

"I prayed for wisdom as soon as I walked in here. God told me to hear Karl out then call his bluff. I was to remind him of what he has, his life with Renee. He told me it will not feel like the right thing to do but to trust Him."

Shaken, he nods. "It sure doesn't feel like the right thing."

She leaves the shop. Outside, she hears Stan's tearful prayers for Karl. Evie goes into the house and to her room. A tear slips over her cheek.

Father, what happened didn't feel good. Forgive me if I didn't speak in a way that is pleasing to You or if I did anything offensive. I think I did what You asked, but I am afraid I may have missed it. My heart is heavy, and I am saddened by my actions. Evie weeps.

My precious child, you did not miss it. You did exactly what I asked you to do. You were not harsh at all. You were out of your comfort zone, so it felt harsher than your usual gentle spirit. You spoke the truth. He needed to hear those things. He needed to be reminded of what he has, especially now. Peace child. Well done.

With that assurance, she pulls her covers up to her chin and turns out the light.

Fifteen

Although Stan acts normal the next day, he mentions Karl a few times. Evie tells Stan they have done what they can for him and there comes a time when a person must make their own decision. All they can do now is pray for the family.

Friday morning, Stan receives a call from Jedidiah's father. The judge is allowing pastors to visit the boys, but Jedidiah is the only one with a pastor. The judge suggests Stan come and speak to each of the boys.

"Of course, I will. Thank you for letting me know. What about Evie? Can she come? She has been teaching the youth class."

"He didn't say anything about anyone else going and I didn't think to ask. I'm sorry."

Stan calls for Evie and shares what Mr. McCollum told him.

"I would like you to go with me, but I'm not sure if you will be able to go in and talk to the boys. Especially with you not knowing the other three."

"I'll go and take the chance. If they don't let me visit, I'll wait on you. We might ask if I can visit with Jedidiah, and you meet with the other boys."

"Yeah. Great idea. Let's give it a try." Martha reassures Stan she will be fine. Finally, he concedes, and they leave for the detention center.

Once the officer hears Evie has been teaching Jedidiah's class, he allows her to visit him. Stan goes into one visitors' room and Evie in another. Before they enter, the officer tells them no touching, giving them anything, or receiving anything from them or the visit will end immediately. Both nod and go into the small, bland, white-walled visiting room that has a table, three chairs and a guard in each room.

"Ms. Evie!" Jedidiah cries out. She can tell he wants to hug her but thinks better of it.

"How are you handling things?"

"Eh. I'm okay. I won't make reservations at this hotel again for sure. It's not all it's cracked up to be." Laughing at his attempt to make light of the situation, she explains Stan is with the other boys. He is fine with it because the other boys are in desperate need of a good man to talk to. They talk casually for a few minutes, then it turns serious.

He looks at her, eyes pleading to be believed. In that brief moment, she sees a young man matured by his bad choice.

"I didn't steal anything from Mr. Washburn. He was very good to me after I caused the damage in his store. I would never disrespect him again by stealing or anything else. I know it is my word against theirs, but I am sure the video at the store will prove I'm telling the truth."

"The police are investigating, and they will find proof. We need to trust God. Remember, whatever happens, whether they find proof now, two days, two weeks, or two months from now, His will always trumps wanting our way."

"I know Ms. Evie. I trust Him. I have always trusted Him."

They talk about God and his parents and several other things. When the officer tells them five more minutes, they pray. Jedidiah prays first then Evie.

"I will see you Wednesday night at church," he says confidently.

She laughs, "You better."

As she is standing to leave, he says, "I've been meaning to ask you, have you been up the mountain behind Pastor Stan's house?"

"I have gone up part of the mountain, not to the top though. Why?"

"I was wondering if my fort is still there?"

"Your fort? Is that yours? Why is it on Stan's property?"

"Yes, I built it when I was younger. The church and all the land that Pastor Stan owns were my grandpa's. He was the pastor before Pastor Stan."

"Interesting. I wondered about the shelter."

"If you get the chance before you leave, I don't think you will regret getting to the top of the mountain. It's beautiful."

"Weather permitting, I will take your suggestion. Stay well, and Jedidiah, I believe you." Shoulders relaxing, humbly he responds, "Thank you."

On the way home, Stan shares the details of the visit with the boys. Each of them started the tough guy, especially Zack. He never did make any progress with him. The other two finally opened up but would not talk about what happened. His heart is heavy. Trouble has come to their little town, and something needs to be done to reach the kids heading for a life of trouble.

Evie tells him about Jedidiah. Stan knows how close Evie and Jedidiah have become and he knows she will surely miss him when it is time for her to leave. Stan is pleased things worked out as they did.

Later in the evening, Evie sits outside of Anastasia's grandmother's house, looking for her debit card in her purse. She looks up thinking she hears yelling; she rolls down her window. Nothing. Finding her card, she opens the door to go in when she hears the front door slam and sees Anastasia running down the steps, tear stains on her hoodie.

Evie gets out of the truck.

"Sassy, what's wrong? Are you okay?"

"They can't make me!" She screams between sobs.

Anastasia folds into Evie's loving embrace as though she has been searching for it her entire life. Deep, heart-wrenching sobs, accompany large, rolling tears like a dam giving way. At the window, Anastasia's grandma sorrowfully shakes her head and turns away.

Evie prays for wisdom and words of comfort and encouragement. She holds Anastasia until she pulls away. The whites of her beautiful blue eyes tainted red, expressionless; she looks at Evie.

Evie pulling into a gas station, smiles tenderly, "Where should we go where it won't be too crowded?"

"It's Friday night in a small town. Everything is crowded."

"Give me a minute." Evie steps out to make a call.

"Sassy, do you remember my friend Martha from the festival?"

She thinks for a minute and nods, "Yeah, she made the brownies, right?"

"That's her."

"She was nice, like you."

"Would you feel comfortable going to Stan and Martha's house for dinner? It will be less crowded, and we can talk. I know for a fact there's meatloaf and lasagna there."

Sassy nods.

"Good, because I already told them we would be there shortly."

When they get to the house, the aroma of something far better than meatloaf or lasagna greets them at the door.

"Mmm. It doesn't smell like lasagna in here," Evie says.

"I feel pretty good, so I made dinner. Beef tips with mushroom gravy on egg noodles, green beans, baby carrots with a brown sugar glaze, and cheesy garlic biscuits. It is hot and ready. Hello Sassy. Welcome."

"Thanks."

Stan helps move the food to the table while Anastasia helps Evie pour drinks. Initially, Anastasia is quiet, timid, but she cannot resist Stan's sense of humor and Martha's kindness. They talk and laugh through dinner.

Halfway through dinner, warm chocolate replaces the smell of beef tips. Martha pulls something from the oven.

As Martha sits down, she smiles sheepishly at Anastasia, "If I recall from the festival, you like brownies."

Anastasia's jaw drops as she whispers. "You made your gooey fudgy brownies?"

"When Evie called, I knew it would be a warm brownie with vanilla ice cream kind of night." Anastasia cannot believe someone would go to such trouble for her. Something feels different. Evie's gentle but persistent attempts to befriend her, Martha's kindness, and Stan's warmth and silliness, she feels…loved.

Anastasia begins to cry, which doesn't surprise anyone. Martha hugs Anastasia.

"Sweetheart," Martha says tenderly, "Would you like to tell us what is upsetting you? Or would you like us to leave so you and Evie can talk?"

Wiping her face with the tissues Stan hands her, Anastasia says, "You can stay. My dad has been in prison since I was four. I don't remember him. When my mom lived at Grandma's with us, she told me terrible stories about him and the horrible things he did. Today, they told me he's out and trying to get custody of us. It's not for sure, but they want me to live with him first. Then if things go well, my sister will come live with us. But what's crazy is the two youngest aren't even his, but he wants them too. He doesn't even know them. Why would he want them? Why does any of this have to happen?"

Martha rests her hands on Anastasia's. Evie feels Anastasia's pain in her own heart.

Stan shakes his head, "Sassy, we don't always know why things happen. The Bible tells us God causes everything to work together for the good of those who love Him and are called according to His purpose for them. It also tells us to trust in the Lord with all our heart and not to lean on our understanding. Do you know what that means?"

"No."

"We believe if we love God and are following His plan, whatever He is doing is good. Then, when we don't understand, we know without a doubt we can trust God."

Anastasia sits quietly looking at her hands held in Martha's. When she looks up again, her eyes are brimming with tears.

"This should be good news Sassy. It should give you hope." Martha says softly.

"I haven't been to church very much. I don't know God or anything about the Bible. I don't understand what you said and none of it helps."

"I understand," Stan tells her, "but you know us, right? And it seems you like us and maybe even trust us, right?"

"Yes."

"Well then you can trust what I told you is true because I know God. I know He is real and what He says in the Bible is promised to us. You can get to know Him as we know Him if you want."

"Uh. I don't know."

Stan explains God loves her and wants her to take her problems to Him. If she has any questions, or if she decides she wants to know God in a more personal way, they are here to help her. He excuses himself from the table and returns with a New Believer's book for students for her to take home.

"In case you get curious. It's easy to understand. You are always welcome to come to visit our church."

"Thanks for listening and stuff. So, how about those brownies?" Laughing, Evie jumps up to get the ice cream while Martha gets the warm brownies.

After dessert, Martha excuses herself to go to bed. Stan follows shortly after Martha. Evie and Anastasia move to the living room.

"Sassy I can only imagine how difficult this is for you. People do change though. You might give him a chance."

"My mom told me he is a monster."

They sit quietly for a few minutes then Evie asks, "Where is your mom?"

"I don't know. No one does. She left right after my dad went to prison, promising to come back for us. She would come back for a little while and drop off the new babies, then leave again. She's been gone now for like three years."

"And no one knows where she is?"

"No."

"Are you angry with her?"

"I, well, maybe, but not like I am with my dad."

"Why is that?"

"Because Momma said he was a monster and she told me the stories."

"I see. Well, maybe you should see for yourself. Can you try?"

"I don't know. I guess I could try."

They talk then Evie decides it is time to take her home. On the way, Anastasia talks about how much she likes Stan and Martha. Evie explains Stan is the pastor of Grace Church and both he and Martha truly love people.

At the house, Anastasia quickly hugs Evie, surprising her. She jumps out of the car waving as she goes in.

Sixteen

The weekend goes by quickly. While eating Sunday dinner, they discuss Ms. Pearl's visit to Grace Church this morning, Karl's plans to go to the lawyer's office tomorrow, and Jedidiah and his court appearance tomorrow.

"Both of you are going tomorrow, right?" Martha asks.

They nod and Evie says, "Youth class wasn't the same without him. Feels weird. I have been praying the truth comes out, but ultimately praying for God's will to be done."

Monday morning, they pray for Karl. Only God knows what he will do. If he goes through with it, they know God's grace will take care of Renee and the girls.

Quietly, they drive to the courthouse. Evie watches the mostly bare trees go by and sees a prominent red cardinal sitting on a pine branch.

Lovely! Thank You, Father, for the beauty of Your creation.

Eager to support Jedidiah and be a light in an otherwise dark situation, Evie wonders if she can be called as a character witness. When they arrive, they are told their case is the only one on the docket this morning.

Judge Roberts, determined to let the boys have their say, allows each boy a few minutes at the start. After, he asks them specific questions. Mark and Gus admit they stole from Washburn's and appear genuinely remorseful and apologize for their actions. Zackary boastfully continues to deny his part in any of it. Judge Roberts nods with each lie from Zackary's mouth. Jedidiah goes last. Judge Roberts asks different questions than what he asked the other boys.

"Young man, what were you doing with these boys that day?"

"Your Honor, I was bored. They said they were going to a movie, and I had nothing else to do."

"How did you boys end up at Washburn's?"

"They wanted snacks for the movie. I didn't know then they had no money."

"The officers said they found twenty dollars in your jeans when they took you in."

"Yes sir. I had the money for the movie and concessions."

"It doesn't seem you would have any reason to steal from Washburn's."

"True Your Honor and it's why I didn't. Besides, I wouldn't disrespect Mr. Washburn." Judge Roberts looks at him, not saying anything.

"Are you graduating this year?"

"Yes. Sir."

"What are your plans after graduation?"

"I'm interested in writing."

"College?"

"Maybe. I might commute to the community college in Gent."

"I see. Thank you. You may sit down."

"Thank you, your Honor."

Judge Roberts already knows his ruling but continues with the hearing hoping this might deter them from future trouble. He explains how Juvenile Court differs from the other courts. He reminds them once they turn eighteen, the rules change altogether.

"Do you boys understand?" In unison, the boys say, "Yes." Judge Roberts asks Jedidiah to stand.

"Jedidiah, you are a bright boy. However, I believe you made a bad choice of companions. You may have heard this before, but keep in mind that bad company corrupts good character. You have a good support team with parents who love you and Pastors that do too. The investigation includes a statement from Mr. Washburn, surveillance video, testimony, and the most convincing, a video recording taken off a cell phone. That recording has you telling the boys you aren't going to steal from Mr. Washburn, and they shouldn't either, which proves beyond the shadow of any doubt you are innocent."

Jedidiah's mom weeps.

"Son, what I recommend is you find friends who won't lead you into trouble."

"Yes sir."

"You are free to go. See the bailiff about how to get your things."

"Thank you, sir."

Judge Roberts calls for a short recess. As they gather outside the courtroom, Jedidiah's parents hug him. The McCollum's invite Stan and Evie to a celebration breakfast after they get Jedidiah's things. Stan decides to stay for the hearing, but Evie will join them. As they leave the courtroom, doors begin to close, and the halls are empty once more.

Later as they are finishing dinner, Karl comes to the house. Stan wonders what happened to the man he once knew.

Sneering at Evie, he tells her, "I guess I proved you wrong. I went to the lawyer's office today and hired him. Once I pay them, they'll proceed."

Evie nods. "If it's what you choose to do. Just be sure between now and when you pay them you do some serious thinking about what you are doing. Those papers will devastate Renee and if you change your mind after the papers are served, the damage will be irreparable unless God steps in a mighty way."

Something she says catches him off guard, but he quickly recovers.

"Don't worry about me. I know exactly what I'm doing."

"Come on, let me walk you to your car." Stan offers.

Once he pulls the door closed, Stan stops, "This is a side of you I've never seen. I'm concerned. It's obvious you are angry with Evie, but please consider what she said. Renee will be devastated that the man she knows and loved for thirty years doesn't want her anymore." He looks down and his shoulders slump. When he looks back up, there is darkness in his eyes.

"I don't want to hear any more about Renee's feelings. How about the way I feel?"

"Karl, you've never told me what you are going through. I don't know how you feel. I only know you want to leave Renee."

He starts, but then the anger returns. "Talk to you later Stan." He turns and gets in his car. Walking up the steps as Karl drives away from the house, Stan opens the door and hears the squeal of tires on the pavement as Karl turns onto the main road.

Evie reminds him, "Trust God." Stan nods and goes into his office.

The rest of the week Evie keeps busy. She and Jedidiah have deep, meaningful conversations about God. She has tea with Ms. Pearl and catches up on her new friends. She takes a quick trip to Crafts-N-More to discuss details of the upcoming trip with Amanda. A few days she goes to check on Anastasia at work.

She goes to an ultrasound appointment with Martha and Stan. She chooses to go despite knowing Stan and Martha decided not to find out the sex of their unborn children. On Friday, she cleans the house and packs for the big surprise.

Seventeen

Before the sun is up Evie is in front of Amanda's house. They eat breakfast, talk, and get to know each other better. It is not long before Evie sees the love Amanda has for God.

They arrive earlier than expected. Other than lodge staff and the two officials registering participants, there were only a handful of people wandering around. Deciding to make a full day of it, they register for morning and evening sessions and the two-mile afternoon hike later today. Evie suggests doing only the morning session tomorrow. Evie figures this should get them through until they meet Sarabeth tomorrow at one o'clock.

Excited for the new experience awaiting them, they approach the towering, dark brown wood double doors to the conference room. Evie scans the room.

The dark brown beams and high ceiling makes the room appear larger than it is. She counts ten tables, with ten chairs at each table. Being early has its benefits. After visiting the coffee bar, they find seats close to the front.

At the end of the day, Amanda flops down on one of the two beds in their room. From the inside, it had the rustic appearance and feel of a log cabin.

Exhausted but still smiling, she sighs, "What a fantastic day."

"Yes, it was. What an adventure. The sessions were loaded with great information and oh the hike! Wow. That may have been the most strenuous hike I have been on."

"Thank you for inviting me. It has already been more than I could ever imagine."

"There's still more tomorrow, minus the hike." Evie smiles.

"Yes! Tomorrow will be great too."

The next morning, even though they are sore, it will not stop them as they push through and get ready for their last session. Fun facts, suggestions on where to hike, and lots of noteworthy information fill the final session.

After the session, they check out and load the car. Evie suggests they go to the small outlet mall right outside of town. Sarabeth had suggested meeting at the Japanese restaurant inside the mall.

They walk around and stop in boutiques, accessory stores, candle shops, and almost every other store. The shops are different from anything in Banderidge, so it keeps them occupied until time to meet Sarabeth.

Finally, Evie chuckles, "All this walking has made me hungry. How about we try the Japanese restaurant we passed earlier."

"Sounds good to me."

Sitting at a table close to the hostess stand, Evie spots Sarabeth.

As the hostess approaches, Evie says, "Hi. We are joining a friend and I see her right there. Thank you."

Amanda, following Evie's extended arm, says, "What? Who...?" as she looks past the hostess and sees Sarabeth, she squints. Apologizing to the server she bumps into, without losing steps, she goes to Sarabeth. They hug and cry and talk over each other.

Tearfully, Evie cannot do anything but say *Thank You, Father*. Her heart is full.

After the initial reunion, when the tears and hugs stop, they sit down. Amanda introduces Evie to Sarabeth.

"It's such a pleasure to meet you. Amanda's life was missing an important piece of the puzzle. Thank you for responding to my letter."

"Thank you for reaching out to me. I have thought of Amanda through the years. Wondering how she is and what she is doing. Thank you for making this happen."

"Well ladies, I am going to go wander around and get something to eat. You two have so much to catch up on."

"We do," Sarabeth nods, "You can stay though, Ms. Evie."

"Aw thank you sweetie, but I only intended to meet you and let you girls visit. Enjoy!"

Walking around the mall once more, she imagines the girls talking non-stop, laughing, and crying.

Evie stops at the information desk and asks if there are any restaurants close to the mall. Conveniently, there are several options on the backside of the mall, Evie sets out to find the perfect salad.

Pleased with her find, she finishes her salad and wonders what else she can do to kill time. On the corner, she spots a local bookstore. Walking toward the store, Evie feels a heaviness.

Karl has put himself in a bad situation and will be forced to make a life-altering decision soon. It will be detrimental if he makes the wrong choice.

Evie begins to pray.

Father in Heaven, You are kind and merciful. Your ways are higher than my ways and You know what is happening with Karl. I know You love Karl and Renee more than we do. You don't want anyone to divorce. Right now, in the Precious Name of Jesus, I pray whatever mistake Karl is about to make, he sees Your faithfulness and goodness and is drawn to repentance. I pray he considers Renee and her love for him. Convict his heart, change his mind, oh, I don't know Father, give him a way out. You are faithful. Your Word says no temptation will be too much for us and You will provide a way out so we can endure. Father, please, whatever Karl is doing, I pray he doesn't.

Cheeks wet, Evie dries her face and pulls her scarf up over her nose. As she walks to the bookstore, peace replaces the urgency to pray for Karl. She thanks Father God one last time, knowing by faith everything will work out.

Inside the bookstore, she peruses the magazines, orders a caramel latte, then leaves for the restaurant. Earlier on the news, they were advising people to prepare for heavy snow. She knows she does not want to be here in the mountains when it hits.

When she gets to the restaurant, the girls are in the same spot and still talking. As Evie approaches the table, their smiles vanish.

"Gee, what a warm welcome."

Amanda smiles weakly, "I'm sorry. It's not you."

"I know. How about I go find us some drinks and snacks for the ride home to give you a few minutes longer?"

As if they practiced it, they respond together, "Yes please!"

Evie walks to a convenience store located on the upper level by the entrance to the mall. She gathers a couple of bottles of water and chips and goes back to the restaurant.

"Ready?"

"Yes ma'am," Amanda replies, eyes down.

"Amanda," Sarabeth says, "Remember if everything works out, you'll come to my house over winter break. It's less than a month away."

"I know, but I just got you back. I don't want to leave you now." Amanda giggles. Evie can almost see them as first-grade friends. The girls hug, then Sarabeth gives Evie a big, tight, long hug expressing her gratitude.

On the drive home, Amanda shares what she learned about her friend's life. Sarabeth found her place in life with dance. Tragedy hit her family with her mom's illness and ultimately her death. Although

Sarabeth can probably live on her own, she chooses to live with her dad who is her best friend, cheerleader, and chauffeur.

As Evie drops Amanda off, Amanda thanks her close to the hundredth time. As they hug, Evie tells her it is her pleasure, and she is almost as happy for the reunion as Amanda. Back home, Martha and Stan were already in bed, so she quietly goes to her room and unpacks. Exhaustion hits her all at once.

After sleeping for what felt like only a minute, the doorbell rings. It takes her some time to figure out what the sound is because she was in a deep sleep. She jumps up to answer the door before it wakes Stan or Martha, but she is too late. Stan is opening the door as she approaches.

"Karl? What's up? Everybody okay?"

"Yes," Karl mumbles, "Renee and the girls are fine except they have an idiot for a husband and father."

"Oh, man. Come in." Karl, head down and shoulders slumped forward, comes in

"Evie, I'm glad you're here too." She smiles and nods. As they make their way to the living room Martha comes out.

"Is everybody okay? Renee and the girls?"

"Yes. I'm sorry to wake you, Ms. Martha. I desperately need to talk."

"Oh. No worries Karl. Good night." She says and goes back to her room.

"Come on. Sit down." Stan motions to the sofa. For several minutes no one says a word.

Stan asks, "Karl, what's going on? I know something happened because earlier today Holy Spirit impressed upon me to pray for you immediately."

"He did me as well, Karl."

The tears break loose, and he begins to shake uncontrollably. It is as if the pressure of a wall beaten against over and over had finally broken. It was the cry of defeat and surrender. Neither Stan nor Evie speak. He cries until he is ready to talk. As they wait, they pray silently.

Eventually, he calms enough to talk. He begins with Nia's impending graduation.

"I guess a doctor would call it a midlife crisis, but I would call it almost the worst mistake I could ever make. It is a woman, from work. After the months of talking, which led to flirting, which led to quick hugs and kisses where no one would see us, we finally made plans to be alone this afternoon. To, you know, take this a step further." Saying this brings on the tears again, even worse if it were possible.

"Karl," Stan starts.

"Please Stan, let me get all of this out." He struggles to get himself together to finish his confession. Evie's heart is so heavy, but she sees the hand of God at work. She glances at Stan and sees how heavy the burden is on him as well.

"When I started driving, I was nervous but excited. I had been thinking about this for a couple of months, but as I was driving, I kept hearing things the two of you said to me. I did everything I could do to not think. Then I began to think of Renee at home believing I was going to meet some old college friends. I thought of her faithfulness and love through the years. I felt guilty. Then the girls, the pain was too much, but still, I kept driving." He pauses but then continues.

"I wasn't expecting such an expensive hotel, but it added to the excitement. The doubts and feelings of guilt I had were quickly fading. I found the room and knocked. She opened the door and looked amazing in a form-fitting, scarlet dress, and heels. One look at her made it easy to push other thoughts away. After dinner and a couple of drinks, we went back to the room."

Karl rubs his hand over his chin and down his neck while looking at the ceiling, trying to find the words to not embarrass Evie.

"We sat on the sofa, kissing until she went into the bedroom. When she came back out, she was wearing...uh, less clothing. I stood and embraced her. As I was kissing her neck, I caught a glimpse of us in the mirror, and in my mind something was wrong. The picture looking back at me was not like the picture sitting on the mantle at my house of my beautiful wife and me embracing. Then my mind was flooded with pictures of Renee and me at different times of our life. Pictures of Renee and me together with each of the girls when they were born, pictures in our first house as new parents, family vacations, and more were as clear as if I was standing in my house looking at them." Staring as if he was back in the moment, he stops talking.

"I stepped back, and she tried leading me to the bedroom. I told her I was sorry. I made a mistake by meeting her. She didn't handle it well, which is to be expected after months of flirting and the money she put into it. Angrily, she hissed that everyone at work would know about this. Then she assured me Renee would know too. She's right because I'm telling Renee myself. I've made a big mess. I need to own up to it and pray I am forgiven. I needed to stop here first on my way home."

Stan asks, "How do you feel?"

"Broken, hopeless. Evie, you told me no one is helpless if they want to be helped. I want to be helped."

She nods and tells him, "We can do it."

For over an hour, they talk and pray together. By the time Karl leaves, he has committed his life to Christ.

"Welcome to the family Karl," Stan says as he wipes his cheek.

"Man. No more going through the motions."

"No," Evie tells Karl, "now you're not. Living for Christ doesn't mean all this will go away. There are consequences to our actions. I will continue to pray for you and your family through this time of healing and for your spiritual growth."

"And brother, you know I will be with you every step of the way," Stan assures him. "If you need me tonight, I will be there in a heartbeat."

They pray once more before he leaves. Stan asks the Lord to let Karl feel His presence and to comfort him as only He can do. He prays for Renee. Karl hugs them both and leaves a new man.

Eighteen

At noon the next day, Karl and Renee come to the house. Martha welcomes them with hugs. When Stan hears a vehicle drive up, he comes in from the shop. Evie is folding her clothes in her room. Karl asks Martha to ask Evie to come out. Once they are all in the living room, Karl clears his throat to keep back the tears.

"I can't thank you enough for your time, love, and prayers. I'm sorry for the way I treated both of you. What I was doing was wrong. I didn't want to hear it, but still, I kept coming back." Tears fall down his face. "I thank God that Renee has forgiven me and not thrown me out like she should have done."

"It's called grace," Renee says. "If God is so good to show us grace, shouldn't we do the same? We've decided to see a counselor and find another church so we can continue to grow in our relationship with each other and with God."

Evie grins, "I know a great little church with a fantastic pastor and his beautiful wife who loves people. They are always looking for a few more people to love and help grow."

"We've discussed that specific church. It's the first one we will be visiting." Karl looks at Stan appreciatively.

"We'll be glad to have you visit. We have service on Wednesday night at six."

"That sounds good. Well, we just wanted to stop by and thank you all."

"Why don't you join us for dinner tomorrow night. Martha is making one of my favorite meals and there is always plenty." Stan says.

"Every meal is your favorite meal," Evie pipes in, as everyone laughs.

"Well, that is true."

Renee responds, "Sounds great. We'll see you tomorrow night."

After they leave, Stan tells Evie, "You were right on the mark by telling Karl the things you did. Thank you for being obedient to God. You not only helped save his marriage, but you helped save his life. His eternity is secure."

Later in the day, Evie goes to see Anastasia. Unlike other times, she does not see her when she arrives. Still, something does not feel right. She approaches the counter.

"Hi. Is Sassy here today?"

Evie cannot tell if it is sadness or fear she sees before the young girl looks toward the back office. She swallows hard and tells Evie, "Sassy ran away from home last night and no one knows where she is."

"Oh no!" Evie gasps as she writes down a phone number, "Thank you for telling me. If you hear anything, please call."

"Of course, I will. Oh, and Sassy really likes you. She talks about how kind you are and how good you are to her." Evie smiles weakly and thanks her.

When Evie leaves the store, she sits in the truck to regroup. She decides talking to Anastasia's grandmother might help.

Loving Father. Fierce Protector. You know where Anastasia is. Keep her safe and direct her steps home to us. Oh, Father, this is almost unbearable. Clear my mind to remove thoughts that are not of You. I trust You will keep her safe. Allow no harm to come at her.

When she arrives at Anastasia's grandmother's house there is a Sheriff's deputy standing on the porch. Clinging to the peace already inside her, Evie calmly waits until they finish talking. As the deputy walks to his patrol car, Evie gets out of the truck.

"Ma'am," professional, but polite, the deputy asks, "May I ask who you are and what you are doing out here?"

"I am Evie, a friend of Anastasia's. I went by her job and was told she ran away. I'm here to talk to Mary and find out what's going on."

Relaxing his stance, he says, "I assure you we are doing everything we can to find her. Her grandmother can tell you more information if she chooses. Please don't repeat anything you hear as this is an investigation."

"Yes sir."

Mary, sick with concern, stands inside the door, wrapped in a threadbare blanket, waiting for Evie.

"They told her she will live with her father." Mary sniffles.

"Yes, she told me. We talked about it, and she told me she was going to give him a chance."

Mary continues, "We weren't expecting it so soon. The caseworker said it would take time for him to prove himself fit and complete other measures. Due to circumstances which the caseworker hasn't been told about yet, the Judge not only allowed it but was the one to recommend he get the kids back so soon. Anastasia found out yesterday she has until Friday afternoon to get her things together and then she is leaving my house."

"Where does he live?"

"He decided to move here, to Banderidge. He said he doesn't want to disrupt her life. All he wants is to build a relationship with his children. At least that's what he said to the judge."

"Hmm. It sounds like he wants to be a Dad. Do you have any idea where Anastasia might be? Friend's house? Other family members?"

"She has no friends, and I am her family, well, until her father gets back here tomorrow."

She tells Mary she will pray and look for Anastasia. She gets in the truck and goes back toward town. On the unlit back roads, Evie wonders if Anastasia is brave or determined enough to be out there somewhere.

Back in town, Evie drives up and down almost every street, praying and wondering where Anastasia might be. Doubting she will just happen to see her roaming the streets, Evie goes to the house.

Stan and Martha are already in bed and the only light is the one in the hall leading to Evie's room. In bed, staring at the ceiling, she struggles to sleep.

Gracious Father, thank You for the peace You provided for times like this. I know she is Your child, and You love her more than I do. I trust You, Father, so why can't I sleep? I can't stand to think of her alone out in the cold night. She has no one. Please guide her to shelter, keep her safe, and bring her back to us.

Sweet Evie. Remember, I am not surprised by Anastasia running away.

Yes. Loving Father. I am aware.

Evie, armed with assurance, falls asleep.

Nineteen

The next day Evie tells Stan and Martha about Anastasia running away and asks them to pray and watch for her. They share her concern and promise to pray and be watchful.

Then, she fills them in on the hiking sessions and shares some new information she learned. Describing the reunion between Amanda and Sarabeth, she shares the obvious love they have for one another. Even after so many years the bond between them still exists. To say it was difficult for them to leave each other is putting it mildly.

As she stands to get ready to visit Amanda at work, Stan says, "Oh, I forgot to tell you Ms. Pearl was at church Sunday. She said she enjoyed it and would see us Wednesday night."

"That is wonderful. Thank you for telling me. I look forward to seeing her and Jedidiah tomorrow night."

As Evie drives into town, she reminds herself Anastasia is in God's care, and He is working everything out. She stops at the Burger Bungalow to get lunch. When she arrives at Crafts-N-More, Amanda is handing a bag to a customer and invites her to come back soon. Evie and Amanda enjoy an hour and a half of uninterrupted conversation. Amanda is happier today than when they first met. As Evie stands to leave, Amanda thanks her for lunch and hugs her.

Evie goes by Washburn's, then back to the house. Karl and Renee are coming for dinner, so she wants to fix something special for dessert. The rest of the afternoon, Evie helps cook and clean. She also prepares her dessert and puts it in the fridge to set. Stan sniffs the air as he comes home from the church.

"Ooooh, ladies. Is the president coming for dinner? It looks and smells so good in here. Can I taste test anything for you?"

"Oh Stan." Martha laughs. He goes to her to kiss her forehead and reaches around for a sample of the freshly cooked bacon.

When Karl and Renee arrive, the change in Karl, especially toward Renee, was unreal. He pulls out her chair, makes sure she has everything she needs, speaks tenderly to her, and is attentive. He holds her hand after dinner while they sit in the living room.

"What an amazing meal. I ate way too much." Renee says as she sits on the love seat.

"Ate too much? Is there such a thing?" Stan muses as he puts a couple of logs on the fire.

"Stan, believe it or not, some people do not have a bottomless pit and get full." Karl picks at him.

"Not this guy. Especially when it is my wife's bacon-wrapped tenderloin, sautéed veggies, and yeast rolls."

"You forgot to mention the potatoes."

"Well Karl, it's because they need no explanation." They laugh as Stan walks over to sit by Martha.

Enjoying the warmth of the fire, Karl shares he set an appointment with a Christian counselor on Friday. He tells them the first few visits he will go alone, then Renee will be included too. He pats her hand and says how grateful he is Renee forgave him.

"I'm not going to lie. I was sick, heartbroken, after hearing him tell me about his interest in another woman. I love you, Karl. It's why I am willing to stay together and work through the hurt. Three simple words, 'I forgive you', but not the easiest words to say or do. I said them to you that night but didn't feel like I forgave you when I said it. When we went to bed, I couldn't sleep so I prayed. I knew I had to actually forgive and not just say it, so I asked God to help me. I fell asleep while praying, but when I woke the next morning, I told him I forgave him, and I meant it. It will take some time and work, but you're worth it Karl."

Wiping his face, Karl shakes his head, "I have no idea how I got so lucky for you to love me."

Stan smiles, "Not luck Karl, but by our Lord's grace."

"It sounds a whole lot better said like that. We also talked with Pastor Evans and told him we will be visiting other churches in and around town. He understood when we explained we need a church which would work for both of us."

Evie asks if anyone would like dessert and coffee.

"Dessert?" Stan repeats.

"Yep. I made cheesecake pie." Evie announces as Martha and Renee both start to get up to help. "I've got it, ladies. It won't take but a minute." Evie is already on her way to the kitchen as they sit back down.

The rest of the evening is spent laughing. Evie can hardly believe this new and improved Karl. After Karl and Renee leave, Evie mentions it to Stan and Martha.

"That was not the Karl I met when I first came to town. He is happy, funny, and likable."

Stan replies, "Honestly, he's not the Karl we've ever known. He is free. That's something he never was. One of the perks of living a life for Christ is getting to see a caterpillar turn into a butterfly. So blessed."

Martha adds, "And Renee is reaping the benefit of loving him through it all and keeping her trust in God."

Twenty

Evie leaves for church earlier than usual to go stop by the library. On her way, she looks for Anastasia. Hoping to see her standing at the checkout counter, Evie drives by Wild Horses. Evie sees the girl who slipped and told her Anastasia worked there, but no Anastasia. Pulling into the church parking lot, Stan and Martha are getting out of their car. Following them in, she goes to the youth room, turns on the lights and the heater, and puts her notes down. She prays aloud for class to be a blessing to the students and asks Him to comfort Anastasia wherever she is.

Returning to the sanctuary, Evie realizes how much the little church has grown since she arrived in Banderidge. She sees Ms. Pearl, Karl and Renee, Alesha and Arthur who moved from Tennessee, and Eli. Eli? Evie thinks the man talking to Stan looks a lot like Eli from Pastor Evans' church, although all she can see is the back of him.

She walks over to them.

"Evie, you remember Eli, don't you?" Stan asks.

"Yes. I sure do. Hi Eli. How are you?"

"I'm doing well, thank you."

"That's great. Nice to see you here."

"Thanks. Good to be here."

"Were you aware that Anastasia ran away?"

Frowning he sighs, "No I wasn't. I took some time off and returned just this afternoon. When?"

"Sunday night."

"Thank you for letting me know. I will pray and keep my eyes open for her."

Before service begins, Evie speaks to several people, lingering with Ms. Pearl.

"I didn't need to visit any other church after I came to the first service here, dear. I immediately felt at home and even made a friend." She jerks her head across the aisle at Mr. Joe.

Evie teases, "Behave yourself."

Ms. Pearl laughs, "What fun is that dear?"

When the music starts. Evie goes to her seat. She wants to speak to Jedidiah, but he is busy talking to a young lady that looks familiar, although she has not seen her here.

Worship is beautiful. Arthur, the man from Tennessee, joined the worship team playing guitar and his wife sings as well. What a difference it makes doubling the size of the worship team. Evie knows Grace Church will continue to grow and help change many lives. Stan dismisses the students. Evie stands by the door of the classrooms and marvels to see even the classes are growing. Jedidiah's friend makes a total of four now in her class.

"Jedidiah, would you like to introduce your friend?"

"This is Lily. We met when I went into Wild Horses yesterday."

Evie smiles. "Ah. I knew you looked familiar. I'm sorry I couldn't remember. Wait. You met yesterday?"

She replies, "Yes."

"Really? Jedidiah, you met her and invited her to church?"

"Yes. I've invited every young person I have encountered since, well," he cut his eyes at Lily, "since I was released from juvenile detention." Then he adds, "But so far, she is the only one to come with me."

Lily's cheeks turn pink. "I have been thinking about going to church but wasn't sure where to start. I was lucky someone asked me."

Fighting off tears, Evie realizes Jedidiah now embraces his purpose and has begun to walk it out. "We're glad you're here and hope you come back again," Evie says, reaching for a tissue.

Before she begins, she tells the students about her friend Anastasia running away. She prays for her safe return, that she knows she is loved, and she understands that no matter what happens in life God will see her through. Lily tells the class she works with Sassy, likes her and, wishes she would come back.

Although Evie has a lesson planned, she decides on a group discussion so everyone can participate. Evie talks about how people need people and to know they are loved. Then each student shares some struggles in their life. She is pleasantly surprised by how open and honest they are.

She asks the class if they would like to continue the conversation over food. She hears Stan wrapping up too. Eliza and Justin decline because they need to study, but Jedidiah and Lily want to.

When service is over, Evie asks Jedidiah and Lily to clean the snack area while she picks up around the church. People stop at the door to talk with Stan and Martha. Martha is relieved everything is clean and they can leave.

"Thank you all so very much for helping. Looks like as we grow, we will be needing more and more help around here."

"It's our pleasure, Ms. Martha," Jedidiah replies.

"We are going to Tony's for something to eat. Conversation in class was so good we are going to talk some more."

As Evie and the kids are going to the cars, Martha says, "I have some chips and dip and other snacks if you would like to come to the house. Hearing what is important to you and others your age is important to us. That is if you are comfortable with it."

"Sure," Jedidiah says, "I'm good with it. How about you, Lil? You know not everyone gets invited to the Pastor's house for snacks the first time they come to church."

They laugh and Stan adds, "But we would if they wanted."

Jedidiah follows Evie to the house. They snack and talk about young people. Stan learns so much from listening to them. It feeds his desire to help young people succeed and find a place in this world.

"We should go. I don't want Lily's parents to worry about her."

Lily looks at Jedidiah, "It's okay. I'm one of the kids we have been talking about today."

She shares her story. There were not enough tissues in the house.

Martha hugs her. She looks into her eyes and tells her, "You are loved, Lily, and you matter to me. God has a plan for your life. Do you know before you were even born, before this world was ever created, God knew you and decided a plan for your life? You have a purpose in this world. Jeremiah 29:11 tells us God has a plan for us, a plan for good and not disaster, to give us a future and a hope. We are not only talking about children we don't know. It starts here, in our church, our backyard, our family." Lily weeps.

"I don't remember the last time anyone cared. I work at Wild Horses because we are all the same. Misfits. It makes us like family. No one opens up much or trusts others because of past hurts though. Thank you all for making me feel welcomed, safe, and loved."

Jedidiah asks her, "Do you have a relationship with Jesus?"

Her head drops and she whispers, "I don't know what that means. I know what Sassy told me about Ms. Evie and how she made Sassy feel. I wanted to know what it was like, so when you invited me to church, I said yes. Especially once you mentioned Evie's name."

Jedidiah explains what Jesus did for him and what He means to him. Stan and Martha share the same as well. They talk and share and cry for a couple more hours.

Lily asks many questions. Before she leaves, she not only has a better understanding of what a relationship with Jesus means, but surrenders her old life and gives Jesus, care of her hurts and heart.

"The Bible tells us in Luke 15:10 there is joy in the presence of God's angels when even one sinner repents. The Heavens are rejoicing with us over you Lily! Welcome to the family." Stan hugs her.

Martha encourages her to come back to the church which she tells them she is eager to do. As they are leaving, Lily thanks them for spending so much time with her.

"Sweetheart," Martha smiles, "it is our pleasure. We would sit up all night with you to see you in Heaven one day. We serve God by serving His people. We are here for you."

Martha hugs Lily then goes to Stan who puts his arm around her and holds her close. Evie walks Jedidiah and Lily to the door, hugs them, and tells Lily she will see her Sunday but if she needs anything before then to let her know.

"Amazing. Isn't God good!" Stan says.

"Yes, He is. Who would have thought this morning the night would end like this?" Evie replies.

He nods, "God is full of surprises and good things."

Twenty-One

The next two days, Evie spends a few hours each day away from the house. Some of it at the library, some sitting and praying in the warm truck by a pond she found. She eats in town, walks around then goes back to the library. Saturday, she spends her day fasting, reading the Bible, and praying.

Gracious Father. Thank You for the chance to touch lives above and beyond my assignment. Lives changed, relationships built, and things You have taught me have been amazing. I feel more comfortable each time You send me out and I am grateful. My faith becomes anchored deeper in You and learning Your character is beautiful. It helps me trust You. Father, I know I can't interfere in what You are doing in Anastasia's life. I know what she is going through is forming her. Whatever the outcome, You are working all things together for Your purpose. Please keep her safe until she returns. I trust she will return. She hasn't come to know You and You don't want any to perish. You have told me all is well, and I trust it is. In my selfishness, I am ready for her to be back, but You are God and only You know what she needs at this time. Thank You Loving Father.

Evie reads her Bible, but she catches her mind wandering. She is thinking about Anastasia's father, a man she has never met.

Father, I am moved to pray for Anastasia's father. You know this man, his heart, and his intentions. You know why he was incarcerated, and You know the truth. Mary says he is not the same. I'm sure a thorough check is done before he can get custody of his children, especially the two who are not his. You promote restoration and peace where dissension and chaos are. Please, if there is anything evil that needs to be brought into the light, it is found, and this will end. If he is a good man who truly wants to be the father Anastasia needs, I pray all goes well with the reunion. Help her father to be encouraged and patient as this all plays out. I pray for peace and spiritual growth in him. I know she is Your child before anyone else's, and she is ultimately in Your care.

Evie feels the need to get out and decides a trip up the mountain before the sun goes down might be refreshing. She takes the same trail which leads to Jedidiah's old shelter. She pictures him playing there as a child. She thinks of him pretending he is lost on the mountain and needing shelter all the while knowing his grandpa was just down the trail.

Walking around it, something catches her eye. There is a red blanket full of holes and on it, something shimmers. As she bends down to get a closer look, she realizes it is a silver earring.

"Sassy!" Evie calls. So many thoughts run through her mind as she looks around the mountain "Sassy! Please come out if you are here. I'm worried about you and so are many others. You are loved. Sassy, please!"

Running down the mountain, she stops at the shop, but Stan is not there. Then she goes into the house to call the sheriff's department. Martha comes into the kitchen as Evie is telling dispatch what she found and the address.

After she hangs up, she tells Martha, "They are sending a deputy out as soon as possible. Oh, Martha, I hope she hasn't been up there all week. I thank God for his protection over her."

Deputies collect the red blanket, silver earring, and find the matching earring against the inside wall of the shelter. The deputy thanks Evie for contacting them and leaves.

Evie is thankful to be at church the next morning. It is always good to go to the house of God. When she goes to the church kitchen to help prepare the breakfast tray, Martha comments, "It seems some of the pastries are missing. I hope Stan did not get hungry while he was here yesterday. I only asked him to bring them, not taste them."

"Well, you know him. It'll be fine." Evie assures her.

When they finish setting out the pastries and coffee bar, Evie goes to her classroom to pray. She prays aloud for the students who come today.

Father help me deliver Your message, so the kids receive it. Protect Anastasia and give her wisdom to come home.

She dries her eyes and visits the sanctuary before service. As she enters the sanctuary, she is surprised to see Ms. Pearl sitting beside Mr. Joe. She smiles as she walks over to them.

"Ms. Pearl, Mr. Joe, how are you?"

"Doing well," Mr. Joe nods as he replies.

"Evie, Joe invited me to sit with him today. We are going to lunch again after service too." She says, smiling sheepishly.

"That's fantastic." She hugs Ms. Pearl and goes to Jedidiah and Lily next.

"It's so good to see you again Lily. Oh, and you too Jedidiah." They laugh.

Worship was even better than on Wednesday night.

Sweeter and sweeter. Father, You are so good. Lives touched; hurts healed. Thank You.

After worship, Stan dismisses the students to their classes.

Evie shares what God gave her on Saturday during her time of fasting and prayer. Her message encourages each one to reach a new level in their walk with God. One by one, the children pray for each other then she prays over them. While she is praying over them, she hears a noise from the closet. Semi ignoring it, she continues after prayer by telling them what she found in Jedidiah's old shelter and how her heart breaks for Anastasia, wherever she is.

"It's been so cold this week." Lily starts to cry, "Poor Sassy." Jedidiah put his arm around her.

"Were there any tracks or anything to know where she went from the shelter?" Jedidiah asked.

"No. They couldn't find any."

"I'm sorry about your friend. I hope she comes back so I can meet her and be her friend too." Eliza says, hugging Evie.

"Maybe we could go look for her. I bet we could find her." Justin says, confidently.

"You all are so kind and loving. Anastasia would be overwhelmed by your love and concern. Probably very surprised too since most of you don't even know her."

The class gets in a circle and hold hands as they pray for Anastasia's comfort and safe return. After the prayer, there is definitely movement in the closet. Anastasia bursts through the door sobbing uncontrollably.

Startled, Evie begins, "Wh, what-" as Anastasia throws herself in Evie's arms.

Tears of relief and desperation mix as Evie holds Anastasia. "I'm" sniff, sob "so," struggling between sobs, she says, "sorry." Evie holds her tighter. The other students gather close. When she calms down, she explains, years ago she went up that mountain with an older cousin. While they were exploring, they found a shelter. She did not think about it again until she started running with no idea where to go. The first day she spent in the shelter on the mountain but as it was getting dark, she realized how cold it was getting. Cold and scared, she went down the mountain and found this church. She tried the doors and found one that was unlocked. She slept and stayed here at the church, hiding when anyone came.

What a blessing Stan always leaves one door unlocked in case someone needs a safe, warm place to rest. Anastasia tells Evie she was hiding in the closet the day of her class Wednesday and heard her praying for her. She heard everything today as well and thanks the others for their kindness and concern.

"With everything I heard this week and especially this morning, I want to give life with my dad a chance. Also, I, I heard you using my full name when you prayed. Anastasia sounds beautiful and then I realized you only call me Sassy when you are around me. You were trying to be my friend. It may be difficult for people to adjust to, but I would like to go by Anastasia."

Evie laughs. "Anything you want Anastasia, I'm just glad you are home and safe."

"I bet I'm in trouble for running away. Do you think I'll be sent to the detention center?"

"We're not going to worry about that right now. Let's wait and see what God does."

When they come out of the classroom after service, Martha is at the door as their church family leaves and Stan and Eli are talking near the keyboard. Stan looks toward the group, goes back to talking to Eli, then looks again, his jaw drops. Eli only stares.

Realizing it is her, Stan starts, "Uh. Anastasia, I mean Sassy. Are you okay?"

"Yeah, I am."

Evie shares what Anastasia told them.

Anastasia, with tears in her eyes, looks at Stan, "Thank you for leaving the door open. I'm not sure what I would have done. I felt safe here. I was here when you were praying and working, and I heard you praying for me to come home safely. I didn't know so many people cared." Anastasia cups her hands over her face. Jedidiah hands her a tissue as Lily holds her.

As Lily and Jedidiah leave, they hug Anastasia and tell her they love her. Meanwhile, Stan calls the Sheriff's Department and within minutes the deputies are there. They ask Stan if it is okay to stay at the church and talk. He agrees, so he sits a few rows back with Martha, Eli, and Evie.

When he hears the deputies wrapping up, Stan says quietly, "Let's pray. Lord, Your hand is in all of this, and Anastasia is back safe. Direct us on how to proceed. We pray she and her father get along and have patience, love, and kindness toward one another. Mend their relationship and restore their family. Use us as You see fit. We give You praise for all You have done for Anastasia. In Jesus' Name. Amen."

When the deputies finish, they ask to speak to Stan. When Anastasia sits down, Evie puts her arm around her. Anastasia places her head on Evie's shoulder as more tears fall.

"I don't remember my mom or anyone ever loving me like this," Anastasia tells her. Evie embraces Anastasia a little bit tighter.

Stan and the deputies return.

"Anastasia," the deputy begins, "We talked to Pastor Stan and checked with the Sheriff. The Sheriff approves of you going home instead of the detention center. There is one condition though, you must report to Pastor Stan regularly. Your father is now in town and court orders state you are to live with him. You'll move in tomorrow. Do you understand everything I said?"

"Yes."

"Now, these people love you. If you have any problems with your dad or just life in general, go to one of them, you hear? Don't run away again. Is that clear?"

"Yes. Thank you."

"We'll take you to your Grandma's. Ready?"

"Yes. Can I have one minute?"

"Sure. We'll be in the car."

Shoulders down and chewing her bottom lip, Anastasia looks at them. "I don't know what's going to happen."

Stan assures her they have already prayed, and they are here for her day or night.

"Pastor," Eli raises his eyebrows at Stan, "May I?"

"Sure, but let's keep it between us until I make it official."

"Beginning next Sunday, I will officially be attending Grace Church. I'll work with all the children. When Evie leaves us, I will teach your class. I have been praying for quite some time and know there is something new for me, that starts here, working with Pastor Stan. You know I have been praying for you for a while, so anytime you would like to come to church, I'll gladly pick you up."

"Um, I haven't been to church much. It was a lot for Grandma to take all four of us, but I can try. Yeah, I guess I'd like that."

They write down their phone numbers and tell her to call anytime. She hugs them. Then she leaves the little church. Although the fear of the unknown concerns her, she is happier now than when she came as a runaway.

"Eli, this is wonderful news," Evie gasps. "God has a way of working everything out, doesn't He? Grace Church is growing every service. Stan needs someone, especially since Martha will have her hands full too."

"It's a good thing. I believe God has been working behind the scenes." Eli shares. "A guy who attended Pastor Evans' church as a youth and went away to school is back. He and his wife moved home a couple of months ago. He's interested in ministry and wants to work with young people."

"Wow! Timing is everything." Evie says.

On the drive home, Evie reflects on the morning.

What an amazing day. Father, You are so generous, compassionate, and loving. You are so good to take care of Anastasia and use us to minister to her heart while she was hidden away. More than anything, I am grateful and honored to be chosen by You to do the work on earth for your Kingdom and glory. Thank You for trusting me with Your children.

Her heart is full as they pull up to the house. Stan opens the car door for Martha.

"It never gets old," she tells Evie as Stan holds out his hand and leads her out of the car.

Stan puts several logs on while the ladies warm the stew for lunch. After lunch, they sit around the fire drinking warm cider and talking. Stan shares what God has placed on his heart.

"I don't know exactly what this looks like yet, but I have always loved children. When the incident with Jedidiah happened, I realized how rough life can be for young people and things aren't getting any better. God showed me how desperately young people need us. Now, more than ever. Then as added affirmation, Eli came to me. He told me he wanted to pray and seek God more, but he believed he was called to serve with me at Grace."

"That's fantastic," Evie says in awe at how God brings all things together.

"When he told you that he was out of town it was because he took some time to be alone with God. He came back and the same day spoke to Pastor Evans. Pastor Evans prayed with Eli and released him with his blessings. I will introduce him next Sunday as our student minister to work with you until you leave."

"Oh Stan, that is wonderful. He will be a wonderful addition to the church. I don't mind him beginning now. I was only helping to fill a need. Besides," Evie feels a pang in her heart, "my assignment is complete. My people are on the right course. I could be called to go at almost any time. If there is still more, He may keep me here, but, again, I could leave anytime."

"No," Martha says tearfully. "Please no. Stay with us. Or at least through the holidays. You said you have no one."

"Martha," Stan starts.

"I know Stan. I know." Martha replies. "She must be obedient to our Father, but it doesn't mean I can't pray and ask Him to allow her to stay through the holidays." Smiling weakly as a tear slips from her eye, falling onto her shirt.

Stan holds her close, "I can't argue with anything she said. I'll be praying the same prayer."

They laugh and Evie says, "Well our Father may think there's a coup starting because I'll be praying too." Scooting to the edge of the chair, she adds, "It's been a very, long emotional morning. I think I'll lay down for a bit." Martha goes to her room as well. Stan is on his way out to the shop when he hears Karl pull up.

"Hey man. Where's Renee?"

"Hey Stan, um Pastor. Uh, Pastor Stan."

"Stan is fine. We've been through too much to worry about formalities. Come on in."

"Thanks. After lunch Renee said she was going to curl up on the sofa and watch a movie. Her movies always make her cry. I don't understand why she watches them." He shook his head and Stan laughs.

"Oh, chick flick huh?"

"Yeah. Anyway, I went in to sit with her for a few minutes and she was asleep, so I thought I'd run by here."

"Anytime man."

"Also, I have a couple of questions about your message this morning, if you don't mind?"

"Of course. Fire away."

His questions are good. Pleased that he was listening, Stan answers his questions and explains how they apply to life. Karl is amazed that what was written thousands of years ago teaches others how to live today.

"You know, I've gone to church ever since I married Renee. I'm not saying the pastors weren't doing their jobs, but I never got very much out of going to church."

"It's because you weren't listening with a receiving attitude. You didn't have a humble and surrendered heart and maybe pride and disbelief blocked the Word. When we are full of pride and self, there is no room for God to work."

"Ouch."

"Now you choose to seek Him. You're entering a relationship with Him because you want this, not for anyone else. You're doing great."

"Thanks. I appreciate you guys. Well, I better go. I left Renee a note, but I don't want her to be concerned with the way this snow is coming down."

"No kidding. We may be in for some kind of winter with as much snow as we've had this early on."

"Exactly!" Karl replies, shaking his head. "I'll talk to you soon man."

Twenty-Two

It snows all day and into the next afternoon. It keeps most everyone indoors. Evie and Martha spend part of the day baking and cooking. Knowing their time is short, they talk about everything. When Stan comes out of the office for lunch, he playfully chides them about tormenting him with all the wonderful smells wafting into his office, throwing off his concentration. Evie jokes back it sounds like he needs deliverance.

At lunch, they talk about the Christmas service. Christmas falls on Sunday, so they decide to do a special casserole and pastries. The smaller children will perform a short song and Evie volunteers the older students to help them. Stan will request a couple of Christmas songs by the worship team as well. Martha says she will decorate the church and of course Evie volunteers to help. By the time lunch is over, they have Christmas service decided.

Standing, Stan pushes in his chair. "A good snow day is what we needed."

Anastasia calls and tells Evie her caseworker does not want to get out with all the snow, so her dad is on his way to get her. They will only move some of her things today. Anastasia is not nervous or worried, but she is not sure why. After talking for a couple of minutes, Evie asks her to call later and let her know how it is going.

Evie stands at the window in her room, a bright red cardinal perched on the fence post flies down to the birdseed they set out after lunch.

Gracious Father, thank You for all You are and how You love us. I have accomplished what You assigned me. I hope You are proud of your daughter. You already know Martha and Stan want me to stay and how I feel too. My first and foremost desire is to please You and be obedient to

Your plan. Since You know my heart and if it is Your will and pleasing to You, I would enjoy staying through the holidays. I love these people. I pray for continued growth in each person I met and ministered to. I pray for boldness for each of them so they can tell others about You and the love You have for them. I love You Father.

Her eyes follow the last few flakes falling gently on the beautiful white blanket already covering the field.

Sweet Evie, am I proud? Do you know how precious you are to Me? I love you more than you can understand. I think of you all the time and every chance I get I show you favor. I will always be proud of you. I hear the desire of your heart. You will not be assigned anything else until the holidays are over. Remember, Anastasia has not committed her life to Me yet. She is your main focus. Check on the others but focus on Anastasia. I have important plans for her future and need you to lead her to Me and disciple her until you leave. Thank you, My precious child.

Now she knows what is expected of her and she will stay through the holidays. Her heart is happy and full.

Later that night, Anastasia calls again. She tells Evie the house is nice, and her dad has been okay too. He bought her a bedroom suite, comforter set, and desk.

"I've never had anything as nice as I do now. I think he's trying to buy me. I'm not stupid, but still, it's nice stuff."

"Your father hasn't had the opportunity to be your dad. Maybe he just wants to do nice things dads do for their daughters. Remember, you're going to give him a chance. Giving him a chance means not judging him and picking apart everything he does for you. Everyone deserves a chance. Right?"

"I'll try but it doesn't mean I trust him."

Changing the subject, Evie asks, "When are you off this week? I'd like to get together."

"I'm off Wednesday."

"Good. I'll come to your house, meet your father, then ask him if I can take you to dinner and church. Sound good?"

"Why do you have to ask him? He shouldn't have a say about what…"

Evie interrupts gently, "Anastasia, that's enough. He is your father. You need to show him respect whether you like him or not. That's called trying."

"Eh."

"Anastasia."

"Okay and yes, I want to go to dinner and church."

After the call, Evie is getting a glass of juice when Stan walks into the room. Martha is already in bed. Evie tells him about the call from Anastasia and her plan to pick her up for church Wednesday. He is extremely happy.

"Did I tell you Karl came by Sunday afternoon?"

"No, you didn't. Is he okay?"

"Yeah, yeah. He had a few questions about my message. I'm proud of him. He has taken this experience and made a complete life change from it."

"That's great! I'm sure he'll be fine." Evie says, finishing her juice. She leaves Stan searching for a snack when she goes to bed.

Twenty-Three

As a senior, Jedidiah can leave school for lunch, so the next day Evie meets him at the Burger Bungalow. They talk about school and Jedidiah wanting to start a Bible Study if the school will allow it. He will ask Eli if he is interested in helping him with it. Evie smiles and tells him she is proud of him. In her heart, she believes this is one of the last times they will meet up outside of the church. As they leave, Evie encourages him to continue to seek God and watch what He will do.

"It sounds like you have great ideas. I foresee an amazing future ahead of you. Spend time with Eli and learn from him. Then you lead other youth and hold them accountable."

"Thank you, Ms. Evie. I am excited about the journey."

Evie drives out to Ms. Pearl's house to spend the afternoon. As Evie walks into the house, she gasps. Christmas decorations cover every part of Ms. Pearl's house. In every window, there is a candle with holly and berries. Her Christmas tree, white, lights blinking, stands proud as the angel on top just misses the ceiling. Modern ornaments mingle with older ones collected during Ms. Pearl and Henry's lifetime together. Evie wanders through the house marveling at the unique and antique decorations spread throughout her home.

Ms. Pearl comes through the door with the tea tray, "I remember walking into grandma's house during the Christmas season, and the wonderful smell of cinnamon, cloves, and orange peel filled the air. This Christmas family tradition has been continued throughout the years."

"It smells very festive in here. Thank you for sharing your tradition with me."

She spends the afternoon catching Evie up on reconnected friends. When Evie brings up Mr. Joe, a pinkness spreads across her cheeks.

"We have been spending quite a bit of time together. *Miracle on 34th Street* was playing at the theater, and he took me to see it. I haven't been to the theater in years, so he went all out buying me popcorn, candy, and cola. We've gone to dinner several times and left town to eat at a fancy new restaurant in Gent. I fixed him dinner here the night he helped with the Christmas decorations. I know it may seem silly to be decorating and celebrating so much, but I stopped celebrating Christmas because I had not been happy for years. Joe knows I'm excited and goes along with me. He is a real gentleman. I think Henry would approve."

"I'm happy for you. It seems like you are enjoying life and it makes my heart full. Mr. Joe is a super nice guy too, so hold onto him." Evie teases as she winks at Ms. Pearl.

She blushes. They talk about how much Ms. Pearl enjoys Grace Church and how she feels closer to God than ever.

Knowing Ms. Pearl is happy and doing well makes Evie happy, but it too is bittersweet. She figures this may be her last visit with Ms. Pearl, so she hugs her a little tighter and thanks her for her friendship.

As Evie drives to Crafts-N-More for class, she thinks about Ms. Pearl. She knows Mr. Joe is a strong Christian man and he will lead her well. Although her heart rejoices with each of them, she is sad about leaving her new friends. Then again, she usually is when she leaves an assignment.

Amanda is setting up for class as Evie arrives. Eager to help, Evie places Styrofoam cones and shiny red, green, and silver-colored pom poms at each seat.

"I will be going to Sarabeth's house for most of my winter break and I am beyond excited."

"Oh! That sounds like fun! I wonder if you two will sleep any."

Amanda replies, "Ha-ha. Sarabeth said she is making all kinds of plans for us. She is also going to show me her studio and wants me to sit in her classes. She loves her students, several of them have special needs. I am looking forward to it."

"I have no doubt you and Sarabeth will have an amazing time and you won't lose each other again. As for sleep though, I still doubt you'll get much."

Amanda smiles sheepishly, "Agreed."

Evie wonders if Anastasia's dad will allow her to bring her sister tonight. The first student comes in and others follow. It is a full house despite the snow. Amanda is welcoming everyone when they hear the door open again. It is Anastasia and Shelby, followed by a man who Evie guesses is their father. The girls go straight to the craft table. Anastasia waves and smiles at Evie. The man stands awkwardly off to the side not knowing what to do or where to go.

"Hello. I'm Evie," she says, introducing herself. "You must be Anastasia's dad."

"Yes. Hi. I'm Ian." He puts out his hand. "You're the one who is coming by the house tomorrow to meet me, right?"

She laughs, "Yes it's me, but I think it has already taken care of itself."

He laughs. "Yes, I suppose it has. Anastasia tells me you would like to take her to dinner and church?"

"That's the plan if it's okay with you."

He agrees. They talk for a couple of minutes then it is time for the students to start gluing the pom-poms to the Styrofoam cone. Amanda asks Evie to help a couple of the students.

By the end of class, they created some interesting-looking Christmas trees. There are as many pom poms on the floor as on their trees. Most of the students use all three colors for their trees but Toni uses only the silver pom-poms for her tree and puts a green one on top.

"Great job everyone!" Amanda tells the class, "Now remember, we have one more class before we take a break for the Christmas holiday. I have another fun craft for you and a surprise next week. See you then."

As Toni walks by Amanda asks, "No googly eyes this week?"

"Nah, Ms. Amanda. Christmas trees don't have eyes."

"That's right. Silly me. Have a good week, Toni."

Anastasia hugs Evie and tells her she will see her tomorrow. Evie helps clean up and walks out with Amanda. Evie tells her she will be here to help with the class next week.

"So, you are staying through the holidays?" Amanda squeals as she hugs Evie.

"I am!"

"That is awesome. You are such a blessing."

"As you are to me. Please tell Sarabeth hello for me when you talk again. See you later."

Sweeter Than Your Grandma was still open, so Evie picked up some chess squares. When she gets to the house, it is quiet. She is putting the sweets on the counter when Stan asks her what she bought. She lets out a yelp in surprise.

"I'm so sorry Evie." Stan chuckles.

"I thought you were in bed."

"I guess you didn't see the light on in the nursery or maybe the door was closed. I don't know but anyway, sorry." He says, again trying not to laugh.

Evie squints at him. "Mhmm. Chess squares, but you can't have any because you're laughing about scaring me. Is Martha in the nursery?"

"No. She was helping but got tired, so she went to bed early. Will you forgive me for laughing and share your chess squares?" Stan pleads.

"Of course."

As he eats, Stan shares about the first time Martha became pregnant when they chose the décor for the nursery. After the miscarriage, they could not work on it anymore. When they found out they were pregnant again, they started buying things to finish the nursery. Then the second miscarriage happened.

"We couldn't take the pain again, so we decided to wait and see if things would be different. It doesn't sound like trust, but by that point, we were disheartened. Now, we are sure we will be using the nursery, so we want to get it finished. It's so much fun to be able to prepare for our little man."

"We went to the doctor today for a checkup." Startled again, Evie spins around as Martha continues, "They did another ultrasound and asked if we wanted to know the sex. We wanted you to be the first to know. I heard you and Stan talking so I came out to share the news."

Stan gets up and goes to Martha. "Her timing was perfect."

A tear escapes Evie. "Congratulations! A boy. That's wonderful!"

"We thought so too," Martha says proudly.

Martha sits by Stan and discuss all the things they look forward to doing and their hopes of more children. They have time, but they already started praying about a name, but neither has an answer as of yet. They start tossing out names for fun until Stan took it too far.

"Methuselah." Stan confidently announces. Martha and Evie give him the same look.

"What? It's Biblical." They laugh.

While Evie places the last two chess squares in a container, she tells them she would be honored to help with the nursery if they would like but understands if they want to do it alone. She says goodnight and goes to her room.

Father what a full, wonderful day You gave me. Thank You for the many blessings. Ms. Pearl and Jedidiah are doing well, I spent time with

Amanda, I saw Anastasia and met Ian, and the great news of my precious friends having a baby boy. My heart is full. Thank You for allowing me to stay longer and help Anastasia. Tomorrow I will begin spending as much time as I can with her until I leave. I know Ian is trying to build a relationship with her as well, so Father I pray You make the way possible. Soften Ian's heart if it needs softening and help me guide him to You Father. I trust You and know the way is already prepared.

Twenty-Four

The next day Evie spends the morning working in the nursery with Stan and Martha. Martha goes to her sewing room to work on the curtains when it comes time to paint. Because the nursery is the smallest room in the house, it does not take long to finish. When the first coat is on Evie goes to clean the paint out of her hair and get ready to pick up Anastasia. Stan goes to his study to review his notes for service. Martha stays in her sewing room happily making curtains.

By the time Evie is ready to leave, Martha is in the kitchen preparing dinner.

"See you in a bit," Evie says as she leaves.

"Okay," Martha replies, slicing a carrot.

Evie smiles as she pulls into the driveway of Ian's house.

What a sweet little house. It will be so much better for the children. Thank You, Father.

Opening the door, Ian explains Anastasia is still getting ready and offers Evie a seat on the sofa. He sits on a nearby chair.

Evie senses his uneasiness. "This is a great house. It feels welcoming. You put some thought into making it comfortable for the girls."

He laughs, "Is that a nice way of saying it doesn't look very manly?"

She laughs, tilts her head, and replies, "Well..."

Just being herself helps put Ian at ease.

"So, you are taking Anastasia to dinner then to church?"

"Yes. If it's still okay with you."

"Oh yes, of course. I was just, um, I was wondering, uh, would you come back after dinner and take me to church too? I haven't said anything to Anastasia because I am still new to all of this. I'm afraid I will mess up and she won't believe I'm trying."

Evie thinks she might cry. "Definitely. I will come back and get you for church."

Anastasia comes running down the stairs. "Okay, bye Ian. Evie will bring me back after church." She grabs Evie's hand and runs out the door.

Evie looks back at him, "I'll see you soon." He nods.

As they walk to the car Evie says, "Ian? Did you just call your father Ian?"

"Yes. It's his name."

After Evie starts the truck, she turns sideways in her seat to face Anastasia, "Listen to me, due to the sheer fact he is your father and he took part in creating you, please stop calling him Ian. Father, Dad, Daddy, Papa, it doesn't matter which one you use, choose the one that works and start calling him it."

"But it doesn't feel right," she whines.

Evie raises her eyebrow, "I understand how it could be uncomfortable, and I know you don't understand this right now, but you will. The Bible tells us to honor our Mother and Father. I'm asking you to do this because it is the right thing to do."

She huffs, "Okay. I'm sorry. I do want to start doing the right things."

"I want you to do the right things too. I'm extremely proud of you."

At dinner, when the meal comes, Evie stops Anastasia before she puts the first bite in her mouth and reminds her it is good to thank God for the meal set before them. After Evie prays, Anastasia shares things about her life. Occasionally, Evie would comment or ask a question. As they are waiting for the check, Evie tells her they will be going back to get her father for church.

"What?" Anastasia looks aggravated and confused.

"Your father asked if I could come back for him, and I said yes."

"I, I don't understand."

"Let's just wait and see."

"Uh, okay."

They pick up Ian and without being asked Anastasia gets in the back seat. Once there, Evie introduces Ian to Stan and Martha, and they welcome him with open arms. It is a powerful worship service. Ian has tears streaming down his face. Classes are dismissed for the students. Earlier in the week, Evie asked Jedidiah if he will share his testimony with the class tonight.

The testimony begins with his name. He explains his name means beloved of God and his parents chose it because they wanted him to grow up to be a pastor. They had pushed him from a young age to learn all about the Bible. He tells them when most little kids were learning about Noah and Jonah, he was being taught about Enoch and Elijah.

"About three years ago I became rebellious. I disrespected and lied to my parents and eventually, it led to me hanging around the wrong crowd. A couple of weeks ago, I found myself with the wrong crowd once again. Only this group decided they were going to steal from Mr. Washburn's store. I was arrested with them and taken to juvenile detention. It was a difficult time. Because of the way I was acting before the incident, it was difficult for the people who cared about me to know if I was lying. There were a couple of people who knew in their hearts I didn't do it. Realizing those who knew me doubted me, helped me decide I didn't want anything to do with that life. God used this situation to open my eyes."

"Thank you, Jedidiah. It takes courage to share our stories. The Bible tells us the blood of the Lamb and our testimonies is how we defeat the enemy. Well, I hear the music, so Pastor Stan is finishing up. Jedidiah will close in prayer. I'm sure if anyone has any questions, he will be glad to talk to you. Have a great rest of the week and see you all Sunday."

After service, on the drive home, Anastasia asks Evie, "What does the blood of the Lamb and the word of our testimonies mean and what enemy are we fighting?"

"I see you were listening. I'm proud of you."

"Jedidiah's cute and he talks like you, soft and calm. I couldn't help but listen." Ian clears his throat and Evie laughs.

"The enemy we are fighting is Satan. He is called many things, but what you may have heard him called is the Devil. The Bible tells us he comes to steal, kill, and destroy and he's like a roaring lion looking for someone to devour. He is as real as God, and he causes chaos wherever possible." Anastasia sits quietly so Evie continues. "The way we defeat him is by the blood of the Lamb, which is the blood of Jesus Christ, who died on the cross for us, and when we share our stories and victories."

"Wow. I've never heard that," Ian admits. "The prison preacher never mentioned it. Thank you."

"You're welcome. The Bible is full of great things we need to know."

She drops them off and makes plans with Anastasia. Ian says it is fine for Evie to get her early Saturday so they can spend time before Anastasia has to go to work.

Saturday morning Evie picks Anastasia up at nine-thirty and they go to breakfast. Anastasia brings a backpack. No sooner do they sit at the table when Anastasia digs in her backpack and brings out a Bible.

"I, um, borrowed it from my dad. I have some questions."

"When you say you borrowed it from your dad, is it borrowed with his permission?" Anastasia says nothing. "Anastasia there are things you have to stop doing. Taking things from others without permission is one of them. Do you remember Jedidiah's story?"

"Yes. I do. Sorry, but after what you told me the other day I wanted to know more."

"And that is fantastic, but there are other ways. Let's do this. We'll eat breakfast then go get you a Bible of your own. Once we find you a Bible, we will go to the coffee shop and talk about your questions before you go to work. Sound good?"

"Sure does!"

Driving Anastasia to work after the coffee shop and Bible talk, Evie asks, "Have you given any thought to why your dad has a Bible?"

"No. I guess he was just trying to get out of prison quicker. Maybe to make himself look better."

"What about him coming to church with us Wednesday?"

"Same. Just trying to look good."

"What about him crying during worship service?"

Anastasia hesitates, "Well, anyone can fake tears."

"Your dad wasn't faking tears. He had an encounter with God while in prison. He's a new man. Although he may not do everything right, like you, he is learning. You need to give him a break. He truly loves you."

"My mom told me all about him and what he did to hurt us," she growls in defiance. "I don't like him. I don't want to like him. I sure don't want to forgive him. He broke up our family and ruined our lives."

"I'm sorry you feel this way. You may feel like he ruined your life, but he is here now with a desire to restore your trust and love. I think we need to sit down with your dad and hear his side of the story."

"Whatever. It won't change the way I feel about him."

"Good, tomorrow after church we'll sit down with him."

Unfortunately, Anastasia leaves in a bad mood, but Evie sees Lily is working. Maybe she can help calm her down.

Returning home, Evie tells Stan and Martha her desire to sit down with Ian and Anastasia tomorrow to hear his story.

"You know I adore Anastasia and want to help any way I can. They can come here after church. I will put on a chuck roast and make barbecue for sandwiches. We will have the potato salad you made the other day too and whatever else we find." Martha offers.

"It sounds like a great plan. Thank you." Evie is humbled by their graciousness.

Twenty-Five

The regular crowd is at church, including Anastasia and Ian. Worship service moves Ian to tears. The altar is open for those who want prayer. Ian went. Stan prays with him as several men gather around him. He is overwhelmed by the support and so grateful. Anastasia, scowling, watches her dad at the altar. Before Stan dismisses the students, he calls Eli to the front. Eli stands next to Stan facing the people.

Stan begins, "As you know Evie has been gracious to help with our students since she came here to Banderidge. We knew Evie would leave us when her assignment was over. Of course, God knew we would need someone for the students. Some of you already know Eli, but for those who don't, Eli was the student minister at Pastor Evans' church. After much prayer on Eli's part and blessings from Pastor Evans, Eli will now lead our student ministry. He and Evie will work together until Evie leaves us after Christmas. Help me in welcoming Eli Watson."

After a warm welcome for Eli, Stan dismisses the children to their classes. Eli leaves with them and tells Evie he is going to sit in on the smaller children's class today and hers next week. As the student's minister, he leads nursery through twelfth grade. Since Abi Grace is the only child in the nursery, Amy keeps Abi Grace with her.

When service is over, Evie asks Ian and Anastasia if they would like to come to the house and have lunch with them.

Stan walks up, "The smell in our house had my mouth watering this morning. They had to physically remove me just to come to church today. I guess it's a good thing I'm the pastor."

"Sounds too good to pass up. Count us in." Ian responds as Anastasia gives Evie a disgusted look.

"I'm riding back with Evie," Anastasia announces in Ian's direction. Evie raises her eyebrows and cocks her head.

"Ugh. Ian," Evie's eyes widen, and she stares at her, "Dad, would it be ok if I ride over with Evie?"

"Yeah, of course, that's fine. I'll follow Evie."

On the ride back to the house she told Evie she felt like this would be a waste of time. She said her momma already told her what she needed to know. Once again, Evie reminded her to give him a chance and see what comes of it. She has no intention of letting Anastasia off the hook. This needs to be done.

The smell of savory barbecue fills the house. Martha puts the final touches on the BBQ as Stan and Evie prepare the rest of the meal and set the table.

"I haven't had anything tasting that good in years. Thank you for having us over." Ian gushes.

"It is our pleasure. We would not want Stan to be stuck eating it all." Martha winks.

After lunch, as they move to the living room Stan puts more logs on the fire to keep the room good and warm.

"We'll be asleep in no time after the wonderful meal and fire," Ian says as he sits back in the comfy chair.

Anastasia blurts out, "Why did you hate us so bad you hurt Mom and went to jail?"

"Anastasia," Evie starts when Ian told her it is okay.

"I didn't hate your mom or you and Shelby."

"Then why did you hurt her and get put in jail?" She snaps, years of hatred and hurt in her eyes.

"I always wondered what your mom told you happened."

"Ian, we were going to bring this up today. She is very hurt, and I felt maybe she needed to hear both sides of the story, so she has the facts straight. Are you comfortable with this right now and with all of us here?" Evie asks.

"Of course. I don't want any secrets, but it's not what you think, I'm sure." He talks without interruption. "We were very young when your mom became pregnant. She was sixteen and I had just turned seventeen. Both families wanted her to end the pregnancy, but it didn't seem right to me. I promised to stay with her forever and do whatever it took for our new family if she would keep our baby. On the day I found out I was going to be a dad; I got a job at the lumberyard on the outskirts of town. I finished my senior year taking my classes in the morning and working in the afternoon. I took any side jobs I was offered. In the beginning, our families wouldn't help us, so we rented a cold, tiny, one-room apartment over someone's garage."

Ian pauses, staring at the corner where the wall meets the ceiling.

"It wasn't much, but we did the best we could. Just before you were born your mom started to get mean. I heard somewhere women's hormones go crazy when they are pregnant, so I blamed her hormones, but it only got worse after your birth. There wasn't a thing I could do to please her. Once our families met you, they fell in love. Angie, your mom, started leaving you with her parents and going out while I was at work. Many times, after I had worked all day and did a side job, she would leave you with me and go out with her friends.

I hoped it was a phase and it would pass, I finally said something to her when it didn't. She blew up and told me she didn't want to be with me anymore and she wanted her freedom. Enraged, she left the house. I couldn't find her for a week. You were two years old. I didn't want my family to be torn apart, so when I finally found Angie, I asked her to come home. She agreed and about a month later we found out she was pregnant again. My family doubted the baby was mine. It didn't matter at that point because I was still determined to keep my family together. As far as I was concerned, the baby was mine.

What I didn't know was while she was gone for the week she was on drugs. Over time, she became addicted. Unfortunately, I didn't know it until Shelby was born." Evie looks at Anastasia who shakes her head no and glares at him.

"As soon as Shelby was born, they hurried her out of the room. We had no idea what was happening until someone from protective services came to talk to us. They talked to Angie first while I waited in another room. I was irate with the accusations they were making about my wife, but they brought in a doctor who verified Shelby was born addicted and appeared to have brain damage. I sat there and cried."

As a log cracks, Ian wipes his cheek.

"When I calmed down and was able to comprehend what was happening, the caseworker explained what my options were. They didn't have any reason to believe I was using drugs, or I was aware Angie had been. I was told if I wanted to keep you two, I would have to take a drug test and your mom would have to stay away until she completed rehab. Once she was done with rehab, there were other criteria she had to complete before she was allowed to come home. I promised her I would love her forever, but the woman I promised was not the same woman. Still, I hated to break my promise. I was ashamed I didn't realize she was using drugs. I never knew anyone who was addicted.

It was the longest night of my life. Once I decided, I told Angie she needed to complete rehab and do exactly what protective services said before she could return home. I told her I still loved her and would be there for her, but for now, I needed to focus on taking care of our babies.

When she left the hospital, she partied for a week before she went to rehab. My heart was broken but raising two little ones, one which needed extra attention, left me little time to worry about her. Three months went fast, and Angie was released from rehab. We were glad to see her, and she looked healthy.

She was clean when she went to protective services. They began supervised visits. All she had to do was to follow the steps in the plan for her return and never fail a drug test. If she followed the rules, she would come home. Both families encouraged her. Initially, she went to meetings, went for drug tests, and met with caseworkers. She was doing well. Within three months, she was approved to come back home, and we were finally a family again. Protective services expected her to continue the twice a month drug test and after a couple of months, they dropped it to once a month. Within six months, her case was closed.

Things were fantastic for about three months. Then one day, while I was at work, she asked her mom to watch the girls while she ran some errands. Her mom told me someone she didn't recognize got her. I didn't know any of this because she was home with the girls when I got home."

Ian's voice cracks. "When I look back on it, I realize she was not herself that night. I never gave it any thought though because she was doing so well. I had my family back together. Then it became more frequent and eventually, her mother told me what had been going on and how long. I was sick about it. I still loved her.

I decided I would wait and see if I noticed anything different. When I did, I realized she was more irritable and had little patience with the girls. When I mentioned it to her, she freaked out and denied using drugs. I asked her to take a drug test. She slapped me across my face and called me hateful things. She made a call and left the house. We didn't see her for a week. She came back home apologizing, but still not admitting she was using.

Things were calm and she treated me okay for a couple of weeks. One Friday night I came home, and Shelby was in her crib, face blotchy, nose running, and screaming. Her diaper was sagging. Anastasia was missing and Angie was asleep on the bed. I was concerned because, initially, I couldn't wake Angie. I didn't know she was lying to me. She said she was sleeping in the recliner because her back was hurting, but later I found out she hadn't slept for days. I called for you, Anastasia, and you finally came out of the closet. You told me you were scared because you couldn't wake mommy and she wasn't moving. You didn't know what else to do. Shelby was crying forever and so loud that you didn't want to hear her anymore." Evie looks at Anastasia, but she is unreadable.

"Things got really bad. Once I was sure she was alive and going to be okay, I packed what I could for you girls and took you to my parents' house. I told them what happened, and they agreed to keep you girls, for the weekend.

Then, I went back to the apartment and waited. Finally, Saturday night, Angie woke up confused and irritable. I thought I saw her at her worst, but I was wrong. I stayed at the apartment with her all weekend although she told me she hated me and said the only reason she came back was that she had nowhere else to stay. The hurtful words were difficult to hear but I didn't respond to her onslaught of nastiness. I realized at the time this was going to be an ongoing battle if I chose to stay. I knew I had to think of the safety of our children.

On Sunday night, after I thought she calmed down, I told her I still loved her. I said I would stand by her if she wanted to get help. That ignited her anger to a whole new level. She said she hated me and started throwing things at me. She said she didn't want me in her life anymore. Then," Ian hesitates, broken as he struggles to continue, "she broke a glass bottle and started cutting herself. She pulled out clumps of her hair. At first, I thought maybe this was part of withdrawal, but I was wrong. Shortly after her self-inflicted injuries, she called the police and told them I was abusing her.

I was dazed. When they arrived, there was blood on her, on me, all over. They put her in the ambulance and me in the patrol car and it was the last I saw of her until trial. They questioned me, drug tested me, and eventually let me call my family. They didn't have money, so I stayed in jail until they could get the money together. I could have no contact with my children or Angie. The children were staying with Mary, Angie's mom, by then because she was addicted again. They've been with her ever since. Mary told me Angie would stay with her for a few days, then be gone again. After my conviction, she left town and returned only to bring her other babies. No one has heard from her in years.

At the trial, Angie looked beautiful, clean, and sober. She put on an outstanding show. She told the officers I broke the glass bottle and began cutting her. She did a number on herself, and it looked believable. Even with my character witnesses, it was her word against mine.

I was sentenced to eleven years and released in eight. Initially, I tried to convince people I was innocent. I can't tell you how many times I was told 'everyone in here is innocent,' so I stopped trying. Then one day I was brought to the Warden's office. Two friends of Angie's from her partying days got sober. After the first girl went to the D.A., they pulled my file and looked at it again. Within a week, another girl, who said she didn't know the first girl, went to the public defender who represented me at trial. By then, the D.A. and the public defender had already spoken. A few other things checked out and I was free to go. I spent eight years in jail for something I never did.

The judge not only recommended I get my girls back, but he provided me with compensation. That's how I can rent this house and furnish it. I am forever grateful for the sobriety of those two girls and the tender heart of the judge.

Until I came back for custody, I hadn't seen my girls in about ten years. There it is Anastasia. That's my side of the story."

All is quiet except for the crackling of the logs in the fireplace.

Anastasia stares at him without blinking, "Mom said Shelby was the way she is because you shook her when she was a baby because she wouldn't stop crying. She said you took us from her because you worked and kept all the money and could take us from her. She told me you did other bad things to us too. She said you ruined our lives. You're lying! Why would you lie to me?" She demands fiercely.

He looks at her, tears in his eyes, "Why would I lie to you, Anastasia? What would I have to gain?"

"Because you want to keep on hurting us and the others too."

He shakes his head slowly, tears flowing from his eyes. He excuses himself and goes to the bathroom.

It is quiet again except for Anastasia's sobbing. Evie does not know what to say.

Thankfully, Martha speaks to Anastasia, "Come, sit here by me," she pats the spot next to her. As Anastasia moves to sit by Martha, Stan gets up and goes toward the bathroom to intercept Ian and take him to the office. Martha holds Anastasia close against her. Evie wonders what Anastasia believes. She is smart. All she needs to do is put two and two together.

Father, this is rough. Please comfort Ian and Anastasia. Fill their hurt spots with love. Heal and restore them individually as well as their relationship. Help us help them. Give us the words to say if any words are needed.

Martha is caressing Anastasia's hair and speaking softly which only Anastasia can hear. She nods or cries when Martha speaks. Although Evie's heart hurts for them, the peace of God flows within knowing Anastasia will be fine, her relationship with her dad will be restored, and Martha loves her.

When Anastasia sits up, she reaches for the nearby tissues.

"I don't know how I know," she sniffles and dabs her eyes, "but I think he is telling the truth. I'm not sure how to do it, but I want this to work. I want my daddy back." Stan and Ian, as if perfectly orchestrated by God, walk out in time to hear those words. When Anastasia sees him, she runs, and he opens his arms to receive her.

Thank You, Father. You heal the brokenhearted and bind up their wounds. You are so good.

Ian looks at Evie and mouths "Thank you." He smiles at Martha and nods at Stan. Tears of joy fall freely. They sit down again, but this time Anastasia sits on the sofa by Ian.

Ian says, "I don't know what to do. I intend to get Shelby and the two younger children so I can keep everyone together. I don't know much about raising kids and with Shelby being-" Ian hesitates.

"Special, Dad. It's okay. She has some special needs is all. You will learn how to care for her because I will help you." Anastasia encourages him.

His eyes well up again. Stan suggests he come to church and allow the members to help him. He tells him there are good people at Grace Church and they have become family. Ian is concerned he doesn't know much about God or the Bible, only what he learned when a prison preacher came to speak to them.

Anastasia perks up, "It's okay Dad. I don't know anything about God. We can learn together."

"What can we do to help you?" Stan asks.

"I would love to get the children back together as soon as possible."

"Do you have everything you need to bring them to your home?"

"As far as I know. I have completed the checklist they gave me. They were going to give us three months and see how things are going with Anastasia, then integrate Shelby in. Then eventually the same with the two younger ones."

"Let me talk to someone and get back to you. Anything else we can do?"

"I need something," Anastasia announces, tears rolling down her cheeks. "I, I don't know what to do or say, but I want God."

Stan chokes up. "We can make it happen right now." He leads her in a prayer for salvation and at the end, he tells her the heavens are rejoicing because of the commitment she made. "Welcome to the family."

After hugs and more tears, Stan asks, "Anything else?"

"I don't believe so. What more can we ask for?" Ian shakes his head.

As they leave, Stan prays over them. He tells Ian he will talk to him soon.

Twenty-Six

With two weeks until Christmas, Evie has only two weeks left to instruct Anastasia. How will Ian feel if she spends time with her when they are trying to build their relationship? She explains to Ian she will be leaving after Christmas and wants to spend as much time with Anastasia as possible. He is sad to hear she is leaving, but grateful for all she has done and the time she wants to spend with Anastasia. Anastasia, on the other hand, did not take the conversation of Evie's leaving so well.

"No! Please, no. I want to call your boss and ask for more time. You can't leave! I am finally getting to be a likable person. I need you." She whines.

"Sweetheart, listen to me. God has worked miracle after miracle in your life, just since I've been here. First and foremost, you know more about God than you did and that's the most important thing. Your relationship with your dad, who loves God, is being restored and he loves you very much. You have friends and people who truly care about you. God has set you up perfectly to succeed. I may be leaving but look at all the amazing people in your life now. Your father, your friends from church, and Stan and Martha. Those people and your church family love you just the way you are."

"Evie," She sees abandonment in Anastasia's eyes, "there is so much I don't understand about God and why He or those people would even love me. Please don't leave me."

Evie holds her close, "I am not leaving you. I'm leaving my assignment. We're going to spend so much time together these next two weeks you'll be glad to see me go."

"Not likely. I don't ever want you to go."

"Are you sure? I'm going to be explaining, teaching, and guiding you for two weeks straight. It might get old."

"Again, not likely." She scowls.

"Well, your dad said he is glad for me to do it so let's make the best of this time."

For the next two weeks, they are together almost constantly. Evie picks her up after school and when school is out for Christmas break, they begin the day early with breakfast. Although they spend much time alone, sitting in the truck at the pond, at the coffee shop, or any other quiet place they can find, they spend time with Stan, Martha, and Ian as well. One day they help put the finishing touches on the nursery.

Evie's days are long, and she is grateful all four of her assignments now attend Grace Church. It makes it easier to check on all of them. They all seemed to be growing spiritually.

Twenty-Seven

Finally, it's Christmas morning. Evie up early, packs her bags, and prepares to leave the next day. Her heart is a jumble of emotions, but she knows she is leaving the people of Banderidge better than she found them. It was a successful assignment.

Gracious Father, You provided me with everything I needed. You gave me hope, wisdom, understanding, everything you promise in Your Word, You gave to me right on time. Thank You. I have met wonderful people. I will miss them, Father. Please bless and protect them. Smile upon them and be gracious to them. Show them Your favor and give them peace. I pray on their behalf for prosperity, love, hope, wisdom, guidance, and every day they draw closer to You. Thank You for this opportunity.

Anastasia asks Evie if she will pick her up, since it's their last day. Evie leaves early, but not before swiping two squares of breakfast casserole, which were made, cut, and on platters on the counter ready to take to church, and a couple of small bottles of orange juice as she goes out the door. She and Anastasia sit outside the church in the truck, eating and talking.

"Martha playfully scolded me as I was running out the door with the goods. She says Stan has rubbed off on me and I'm no good around food anymore. She says nothing is safe. Can you believe it?"

"You know that's not good," Anastasia laughs. "I've seen Pastor around food."

They finish their breakfast as Stan and Martha are pulling up. Anastasia jumps out first and goes over to help Martha.

Thank You, Father. She is getting it. Thank You especially for her being a quick learner.

As Evie follows them in, Stan asks if she will prepare communion. Martha and Anastasia set up the breakfast table. There is an atmosphere of peace and joy.

Stan welcomes everyone. "I wanted to ask everyone to wear their ugliest Christmas sweater to service today, but Martha wouldn't let me. Even after I told her the Lord said to." Everyone laughs.

"We'll keep service short so you can enjoy time with your families. We know you will be in a hurry to go after service, but please be sure to say goodbye to Evie. Her assignment is finished, and she will be leaving tomorrow."

The worship team plays several Christmas songs, the children put on their play, and communion is taken. Stan did not lie; it is a short service. Evie goes to the back door, so people can hug her and go. She is surprised at how quickly people leave. Ms. Pearl and Joe, Jedidiah and his family, and Karl and Renee spend a couple of extra minutes, but they too are gone quickly.

Renee and Karl's girls are home, Ms. Pearl and Joe said they have somewhere to be, and Jedidiah and his family said they are meeting someone. Evie loves these people and knows God has great things planned for all of them.

As she is leaving, Evie looks for Martha to tell her goodbye.

"Stan, where is Martha?"

He shrugs with a grin, "Oh she's around somewhere. I'll tell her you'll see her at home."

"Oh. Okay. Thank you."

As she turns to leave, Anastasia asks if Evie will take her home. Evie knows her leaving is difficult for Anastasia and agrees if Ian is okay with it. She tells Evie she asked him earlier and he is fine with it.

When they get to the house Evie asks, "Where's your father?"

"Mmm. Not here but come open your gift. It's from dad and me."

"Shouldn't we wait for your dad since he bought it too?" Anastasia stares blankly at Evie.

"Okay, okay. Goodness." They laugh.

Evie unwraps the gift.

"These came in the last day I was at work. I just knew." Anastasia proudly babbles as Evie holds the dangling, silver, multi-cross earrings up to her ears.

"Are these me?"

Anastasia giggles. "Absolutely!"

"I have a little something for you too."

She hands her a box. Inside is a beautiful soft blue Bible with her name engraved on it to replace the smaller, temporary one Evie previously bought her. On the inside, is a personal note of encouragement for Anastasia to go back and read whenever she needs it. There is a matching journal in which she wrote another note and listed some of her favorite and most used scripture. Evie also bought her a long sleeve, cobalt blue dress, light brown ankle boots, and a silver necklace with a pendant that reads "Child of God."

"I love it all! Thank you so much."

As she hugs Evie, the phone rings, and she goes to answer it.

Evie can hear her saying, "Hello. When did you decide that? Okay. Okay. Sure. I'll ask her if she wouldn't mind. Love you too."

"That's odd." Anastasia mumbles. "Dad went back to the church after we left because he left his hat. Pastor Stan invited us to eat Christmas dinner with them since it was just the two of us and no other family. He went straight there, thinking when we were done exchanging gifts you could bring me back with you."

"Wonderful! Of course. Let's go."

As they approach the house, billows of gray smoke come from the chimney, a welcome sign of warmth on this cold, snowy day.

When they get to the house Anastasia jumps out first and runs for the warmth of the house. As Evie walks through the door a chorus of "Surprise" startles her.

Eyes wide she stammers, "What in the world?"

Someone shouts, "We're going to miss you, Evie."

She is speechless. Every single person from Grace Church, Pastor Evans and Alice, Amanda's mom, and many others from around town are here. Even Sarabeth and her father who brought Amanda back for the gathering.

"We wouldn't have missed this for anything," Sarabeth whispers as the girls hug her. Amanda thanks Evie again and tells her she will never forget her and all she did for her. Mr. Ingram tells her the girls may have never found each other if it was not for Evie taking the time to locate them. He thanks her for caring so much.

Evie cannot believe all these people came out to say goodbye to her on Christmas day. She is blessed. It is a festive time, with good food, good friendships, and love.

Stan calls everyone in to pray over Evie before anyone leaves. They gather around her, and he prays.

"Lord God, You sent us a gift over two thousand years ago in the form of a baby. You sent Your Son to save us from a nasty eternity of death and darkness. We thank You for our gift, our Savior, Jesus Christ. Today, we honor another gift You sent us. Placed in our path for such a time as this. Evie touched each of our lives in some way and we are grateful. We wish she could stay forever, but we know Your will must be done, not ours. As she leaves, we pray You protect her, bless her, and wherever her next assignment might be the people around her are as blessed as we are. In the Blessed Name of Jesus, King of Kings, Amen."

Even on Christmas day when many of them have plans with their families, they hate to leave. Mr. Joe and Ms. Pearl leave to eat Christmas dinner with his children in Gent. Before she leaves, Ms. Pearl hugs Evie tight and thanks her for everything. Encouraging her to get back this way again soon, Ms. Pearl wipes at a tear. As she turns to leave, Evie calls to her.

"Ms. Pearl. There is something I meant to ask you, but I always forgot. When I met you and each time I came to visit, before your hospital stay, you dressed like the president was coming to your house for tea. Why was that?"

"Oh sweetie, it's all so silly. I was very sad without Henry and had no desire to live. I was waiting to die and wanted to look my best when I saw Henry again. I told you I was a little off before God intervened."

"Oh my. I didn't realize how bad things were, I guess." She looks at Mr. Joe and tells him to take good care of this precious lady. He nods.

Karl and Renee are going back to their house, where the girls are fixing Christmas dinner for the parents this year. She hugs Evie, thanks her, and says goodbye. She walks off so Karl can say goodbye. Not knowing where to begin, he tells her he will never forget that no one is helpless if they want to be helped.

"That was a life-changer for me. For the first time in my life, I'm excited to see what's next for us." He wraps her in a big, strong bear hug.

She laughs, "God has big things coming your way. Watch and see."

Jedidiah and his family are meeting his grandparents at their house just outside of town. His parents cannot thank her enough for all she did to help their son and for the faith she had in him.

"Thank you for helping me find my way, purpose, and encouraging me to accept the call on my life." Jedidiah hugs her as his parents go on to the car.

"It is my pleasure. Help Eli get situated and encourage the students to trust him."

"Yes ma'am."

As he is walking out, she says "You know, you may have a secondary call on your life. Many pastors write."

One of the two most difficult good-byes is yet to come. Anastasia has a servant's heart. She and Ian stay until the last crumb is cleaned off the floor. Thinking about the changes in her, Evie can see a little of herself in Anastasia.

After Mary and the children finish their dinner, they will go to Ian's for dessert and presents. Martha gives them the leftover desserts to take too since there is so much.

"Wait, what? Not the desserts." Stan protests.

"Stan, stop it. People will think you have a problem with food." Martha teases him.

"I do have a problem with food. Too much food, never enough time to eat it all. That's a big problem."

Laughing, Ian hugs Evie and tells her she will always be in his prayers. He thanks her for loving his little girl and showing her guidance. Ian and Stan load up the car and Martha goes into her room to rest. Anastasia starts crying when her father tells Evie goodbye.

"Can't you just stay? Please?" Anastasia pleads.

"Sweetheart, we've already discussed this, remember? You know I have a job to do, and it is very important. You will understand someday."

"Will I ever see you again?"

"I sure hope so. You hold a very special place in my heart, Anastasia. Remember, even though I am leaving, God worked everything out, so you have people to love you and guide you when I am gone. Stan and Martha are here for you in the very same way I was." Ian finishes loading the car and tells Anastasia they need to get home.

"Bye Evie."

"Bye Ian."

Ian waits for her in the car.

Anastasia hugs Evie tightly. "I can't. You're my best friend and like a mom too."

She let her hug and cry until she finally stops and releases her on her own. Evie takes Anastasia's hands in hers.

"Father in Heaven bless this sweet girl and keep her in Your tender care. When she needs love, send love to find her. When she needs encouragement, send encouragement to find her. Draw her closer into You and fill her with all of You. Direct her steps. Give her wisdom. Teach her. Help her to understand things easily and help her act as a Child of God. Protect her always and remind her daily You are always nearby. Let Your peace flood her during this time of sadness and comfort her. In Jesus Name, Amen."

"I love you, Evie. Thank you for everything. I know thank you doesn't cover it all."

"I love you too sweetheart. Take care of yourself."

One last hug and Anastasia is out the door.

Once Anastasia is out of sight, the floodgates open, and Evie's emotions spill out. Stan wants to go to Evie, but he knows only God can comfort her the way she needs it. Instead, he goes to the bedroom where Martha is sitting on the bed, crying for her friend. He comforts her with a hug and a kiss on her forehead while holding her silently.

Evie receives comfort from the One True Comforter as she sits in the quiet living room.

Well done my darling Evie. Look at all the people you ministered to. You are growing. Your sweet, gentle spirit has touched the lives of not only the four people on your assignment, but so many more. Your love for people is beautiful. I see you loving as I love. I can't be any prouder of the work you have done. Your people will be fine. Because of you, My people will be fine. You know I have a plan for each one. It is not to harm them but give them hope and a future full of great things. Stan's quiver is getting ready to be full. Not only at home, but in the church as well. Be strong, My sweet child. It is your compassion that makes you love as you do, but it is also your compassion which causes you to hurt as you do. You love so much, and it is a beautiful thing. I love you, Evie. Well done, My precious child.

When Stan and Martha hear Evie getting a drink, they come to the kitchen. She smiles.

"The downfall of these assignments. I love hard. I like to think it will get easier but hasn't happened yet. I will miss you two so much."

"We will miss you more." Martha smiles.

Stan asks, "I know you can't say much, but were we one of your four assignments?"

Evie laughs. "No, you were not."

"Wow. You've helped so many people while you were here, it's difficult to tell who your assignments were."

"I was sent for four people specifically, I guess the others were bonuses."

"Oh goodie! I was a bonus, an afterthought." Stan teases. They laugh.

"It's been a long day and I will need to leave early tomorrow. I think I'll go to bed."

"One more hot apple cider for old times' sake?" Martha asks sweetly.

"Of course. That sounds like a terrific idea."

"Evie, do you know where you are going tomorrow?" Martha asks as they sip their cider.

"I will know before I leave tomorrow where I am to go, but it will only be for a short time of rest. During that time, I will find out more about my next assignment."

"That's good you get to rest and recharge." Stan pipes in.

"Thank you for my wonderful party and all you have done for me here."

"It was our pleasure," Martha replies.

"I guess I will go to my room now. Good night."

Together they both say, "Good night."

The next morning, Martha gets up extra early so she can have breakfast for Evie to take with her. Stan is up too, so he does not miss her when she leaves.

"I will miss the mouth-watering aroma of your cooking. I was hoping you weren't up so I could sneak out without any more tears." She jokes as Stan takes her bags to load in the taxi and Martha finishes packing her a bulging snack goodie bag.

"You're not getting away that easily." He says as he goes out the door.

When they are all back together in the kitchen, tears freely falling, Martha thanks her for all the love, support, friendship, and encouragement as well as help around the house and in the nursery. Stan tells Evie even though they were not one of her original four, they were immensely blessed by her while she was here. Struggling to express how truly grateful he is, he hugs her tightly and chokes out, "Thank you."

She wipes her eyes. "Thank you both for being obedient, faithful, trusting servants of God. He would have made a way because that is what He does if you all would have said no, but then we would have missed out on this amazing friendship. Thank you for having me here and being so accommodating. God is proud of you. He has something big for you and you will be fine. He told me your quiver will be full. Not only at home but the church as well. God bless you, my friends. Take care of each other."

As if she has any left, tears of joy roll softly down Martha's cheeks.

Discussion Questions

1. Because God places such a high value on relationships, He positions people in our lives "for a purpose." We have the opportunity to meet Christ-centered people, people who have not yet decided to follow Him, and people who know little to nothing about Christ and what He has done for us. In *1 Corinthians 3:6-9*, Paul tells us some plant the seed and some water it, but we work as a team with the same purpose, and only God can make it grow. Our mission field is everywhere we are. How would it look if Christ-followers lived believing this? What can you do for those who God places in your path?

2. Evie lives a completely selfless life. She has given up everything to live out her God-given purpose and destiny. Because her focus is not on her wants and needs, but the will of God, she is more attuned to others and what they need. *Philippians 2:3* tells us to think of others as better than ourselves. Being consumed with our own lives leave us unable to spare time for others who are lost or hurting (which is what the enemy is counting on). What can you focus less on in order to reach out to others for God's Kingdom? What can you do to be more aware of other people's needs?

3. Sassy had purple hair, tattoos, and a bad attitude. Ms. Pearl was an elderly woman that dressed in formal wear every day, all day, and appeared unstable. What would you think if you met them in public? Do you tend to pass by people because they are different from the standard of appearance you prefer, the choices they make, or maybe the way they act? *1 Samuel 16:7* should make us rethink the way we look at others. God tells us not to judge by appearance, then tells us He looks at a

person's thoughts and intentions. What do you think God would have to say about our thoughts and actions toward people who appear unusual or are different from us?

4. Think about the four people Evie was assigned. It was a dark time in each of their lives. We may have been there ourselves at one time. Can you share about a time a person or persons reached out to you, your real-life Evie? What was the turning point and what happened to help you change? How do your past experiences help you see other people's pain more clearly? How have you helped them?

5. Several places in the book made mention of *Jeremiah 29:11*, "For I know the plans I have for you," says the Lord. "They are plans for good and not for disaster, to give you a future and a hope." Why was that relevant? What difference would it make? Ms. Pearl had way more past behind her than the future before her. What does it show us? What does it mean to us today?

Salvation is for Everyone

The Bible tells us God does not want anyone to die, but to live forever with Him. It also tells us He is not just taking His time in fulfilling the promise of His return but is patiently giving everyone time to turn from sin and accept Him. Whoever calls on the Name of Jesus will be saved!
John 3:16, 2 Peter 3:9, Romans 10:13

Even though this is the most important decision you will ever make, it is not complicated. We are born into sin and trapped in this condition. With no way out, we need a Savior. If you believe in your heart and confess with your mouth that Jesus Christ is Lord, and He is the only Son of God, who was born, died, and rose again for the forgiveness of our sins and put your full trust in Him, you will be made right with God and be freed from sin. Saved. I promise you will not be disappointed.
Romans 5:12, Romans 10:9-11, Romans 3:22

If you are ready, you can pray the following:
Jesus, I confess that I am a sinner and need You to save me. I am sorry for my sins and I do not want to live in this trapped condition any longer. Forgive me. I believe You are the only way to God, and eternal life and I need You. Thank You for dying on the cross for me. I know God raised You from the dead after three days and for that I am grateful. Thank You for saving my soul and promising to always be with me. Amen

If you prayed the prayer and believe-congratulations! Heaven is celebrating you today! Be sure to share the news with someone! You are now a new person living a new life in Christ; the old you no longer exists and all the things you have done in the past have been permanently erased. You are now a child of God. I encourage you to fully surrender

every area of your life to God and anchor yourself in Him by talking to Him every day about everything and reading the Bible. Begin with the **Gospel of John** in the New Testament. It gives you such a clear picture of who Jesus is. And when you see Jesus, you also see the Father. I also encourage you to connect with others who follow Jesus in a Bible-believing church. They can help you learn more about Jesus and support you as you follow Him.
Luke 15:7, Luke 15:10, 2 Corinthians 5:17, 1 Corinthians 6:19-20, Galatians 2:20, Isaiah 33:6, Psalm 62:5-6

Now that you have believed in Jesus and received His gift of salvation, you are completely free, but this is only the beginning! He has so many good things planned for you. Jesus tells us He came to give us a full life and He wants us to discover all of that now! Even though we will continue to experience trials and sorrow here on Earth, Jesus has promised to stay with us and help us through the rough places by giving us peace, joy and hope, and anything else we may need. He also promised we would overcome the difficulties and live victoriously through Him.
John 10:10, John 16:33, Deuteronomy 31:6-8, 1 Thessalonians 5:11, Ecclesiastes 4:9-12

About The Author

Anne lives in Tennessee with her husband, Wesley, their four dogs, and lots of books. When time allows, they enjoy hiking and wandering around Tennessee, looking for adventures.

Anne jokes she never could figure out what she wanted to be when she grew up until in 2018, when she was introduced NaNoWriMo and began writing a novel. Her sincerest desire is to share her one true love, Jesus, with others.

Follow Anne

https://annelcalvert.com/